AGE OF ANTHEMS

HOWLS OF THE HAUNTED

KRISTIAN BECKER

FOR NATALIA AND MIA

TARIUM

How many years had it been? A thousand? She couldn't remember and had made no real attempt to count the years anyway. There were just those moments when old memories popped into her mind and made her aware of the passage of time.

At first, she would not leave her hiding place deep in the mountains. They were steep and full of boulders that made landing a ship impossible. Real paranoia gripped her in the early years. Surely, they would hunt her down again. She had done terrible things. Her father had done terrible things. Surely a wave of vengeful souls would find her. All was quiet through the years and her name, and her crimes, were forgotten.

Gaining confidence, she began to explore her new world. It was only a moon that orbited a large, green planet. She didn't even know its name, so she called it Tarium. There was a short winter that was bleak and chilling, and she virtually had to hibernate when the storms came. She endured, and over time had walked everywhere on her home.

Even the meagre wildlife had grown accustomed to her. They

shared their lonely world together. The few birds and strange, six-legged, spider-like creatures that lived by the small lakes and ate the red reeds that grew along the shore were the few living things she had encountered. The outside universe was indeed far away.

It must have been near sunset when she noticed the great streak of cloud across the sky. For a moment, she thought it was another comet, but as she watched it fly on in a straight trajectory and make no effort to fall to the ground, she became troubled. To be safe, she turned around and headed back through the skeletal forest to her hideout in the mountains.

The forest seemed be full of evil hands, all reaching up to the sky in a dying curse to the heavens. Great birds of grey, leathery skin, each with two heads, snapped at each other with sharp teeth, screeching and crying out at the three moons that hung in a diagonal line across the sky.

A deep rumble shook the trees, shaking the birds from their perches and sending them in a great mass of cries into the air. Their mass followed a single bird in the sky, blocking the stars as they circled the tall peaks. They waited for the danger to pass before returning to their home.

In that mass of birds, a small starship flew low, scattering them in great cries of protest. Slowly, it passed over the forest, and then the peaks. It flew along the green rivers before settling on a rocky plateau.

She watched it from her hiding place in the outcrops of the hills with mounting dread. There was no point in hiding as there was nowhere to hide. It had been thousands of years and, deep in her heart, she knew time would eventually run out. Someone would come and look for her. The circle would turn and her name would be renewed. Now, they had finally found her.

She hid herself deeper into her mountain dwelling, once a simple cave but now transformed into spaces filled with trees and plant life.

Short beats of time passed before he appeared as a shadow in the light of the entrance.

"I know you're there," he said.

She remained silent for a moment, as she hadn't spoken to anyone in so long. The urge to talk was strong though.

"Leave me alone."

"No, I'm looking for Thara," he said as he stepped further into the cave.

"I haven't heard his voice for a long time. Burned up in a sun. Who knows?"

He breathed deep. The news seemed to disappoint him. In the dark, she couldn't make out his features, but he was tall, and his body was hidden under the bulk of heavy clothes.

"So, now you know. Leave me be."

"No, I need your instruction," he replied forcibly.

She stepped out of her hiding place.

"Who are you?"

"I am Iminus Kaw and I've come with purpose to wage my war on the Sangreal."

She managed a laugh of joy at the recognition of her father's wisdom. He had told her long ago, when she still was able to speak to him, that someone would come.

"Here I am," he said.

It had been so many years and now the day had come. Her eyes burned bright and her heart beat with a mighty fire that this man had erupted. A storm was coming, night was falling over the land, and soon her work would be done.

DARK PLACES

"I will not let this trinity fail," said the Dark Lord with determination. He sat, cloaked in blood red robes, at the top of a dais that had several steps leading up to the throne platform. The throne itself was black and simple. It was at the centre of a turntable that allowed him to turn about and look at the large screens that showed the night sky. They could be transformed into data panels which showed all sorts of information about his dominions. He could even watch the live feeds of battles across all reaches of the known galaxy.

There were no guards but four Sons of Gorgoth slept close by in hidden antechambers on either side of the throne room walls. Only small lights illuminated the throne room, but they could be energised to full, blighting light that made anyone without proper eye protection blind.

To the right of the dais was a large flat wall behind which sat a communication room manned by the strategy droid, Zigma, which controlled all information coming into and out of the fortress of Tere Kaw.

The throne room itself sat at the top of a tower. It contained levels of communication and command rooms used to plan and control military campaigns. Hangers held squadrons of fighters and transports. There was a single lift to the throne room, heavily guarded by specialised Striketroopers and backed by the Gormarr, Kaw's personal guard.

Surrounding Tere Kaw were other fortresses of his Axis. The Wrydluk and Gunadar had their own places close to their Master. Many of the Diamalord traitors had their own little battlements as they competed for status and power.

All these fortresses formed a defensive ring around Tere Kaw making access to the Dark Lord a suicidal gamble. The massive shield complexes made death a certainty.

In orbit were several large battleships and battlestations, adding another ring of protection. Elsewhere, there were the usual shipyards and factories.

Few came here and then only at personal invitation. Axis commanders either returned lauded for their work or never returned at all.

"The Ethereals live?" Cryacur questioned.

"This shouldn't be," the Dark Lord replied, his voice now a deep, computerised growl caused by the grill that covered the lower half of his face. His hands were clasped together but still he twisted his fingers as he contained his rage.

"Only corpses now, their power gone from the universe," replied Cryacur.

"No!" growled Kaw, rising to his full height. He showed his hands, covered with blood.

"This proves otherwise." He clenched his fists.

"They were powerful beings in their time and even in death their magic can curse us. I have seen them. All my years I have been fighting a universe built to deny my will. And now this mystery."

"Your sorcery is stronger, my Lord."

"Indeed, but a wise warrior must be three moves ahead of his enemy."

"You only need to give the command and I will kill everyone and destroy anything that gets in your way."

The Dark Lord laughed behind his mask. "You are the embodiment of fear, the perfect chalice for my malice, Cryacur."

"All in your name, my Master."

"Go now to the hot plains on Kiam and find Gilkasha while I dwell on this."

"As you wish, my Master."

Cryacur turned and left the throne room. Kaw had summoned Zigma to assist him with new strategic visions. He disliked the company of other sentinel beings, preferring the ordered and programmable droids to be in his close personal orbit.

The dais turned as he sat back down, the blank screen now showing images of the universe full of stars, nebulae, and colour.

Everything about his physical being reminded him of his hatred and the pain caused by the Ethereals. The metal grate across his lower face masked the void of his mouth. His voice was now just a computerised replacement of his own once deep and powerful tone. A solid helmet hid the rest of his head with the ruined crown of the Sangreals seared at its top. It was meant to mock them and the Order's failures.

It was long ago, and he had managed to bury the memory of

it deep. There had been work to do and purpose that had reinvigorated him. He had been so close, and those creatures had taken it from him.

Their blue eyes bored into his own murky green as he lay collapsed on the stone floor. Where that was, he never knew; perhaps some place deep in death where those creatures now lauded in their own decay.

They had begged him, and then warned him. Iminus Kaw, was now the greatest of all Dark Lords and he would not stop. He would not fail.

Subconsciously, he was rubbing the blood that he had taken from Cryacur's hands with his fingers. He raised up one hand to look at it. *What did this mean?*

They had warned him. She had begged him. He closed his eyes to concentrate on blocking out her voice. Nothing could sway him from his mission. He would not fail. The Ethereals were dead, the Sangreal had fallen. He would destroy the decayed Bond of Seven Kings.

The throne room was dim but for the lights of the universe. This was the domain of the Dark Lord.

Outside Jasmin, the ruined capital city of Jashir, lies a huge plain, broken by creeks and small woods. In summer, it would fill with bright gold flowers that the southern wind would pick up and shower the city in gold. *Luralie*, the golden days, also became the name of the range of small hills that sat on the plain.

Kaw's offensive out of the dark worlds almost fifteen years ago brought about the last of the golden days. That peaceful plain was now littered with the wreckage of war, bodies of soldiers, and droids, its grass blackened, pot-marked, and burned from the countless campaigns to take or retake the city by Axis and Bond forces.

The last few weeks had seen the Bond brought to its knees with multiple tragedies. The first son of the King of Jashir, Jai Bannade, had betrayed his people by slaying virtually the entire royal family and letting the Axis armies through the system's planetary defences. He had then joined the ranks of the Sons of Gorgoth and watched as Kaw's war pigs began overrunning his homeworld.

In Runamore, Sangreal Gurungu was dead in his apartment, poisoned by deadly ware slugs put into the water supply. The poison had also killed many members of the Order of Light.

Now, on Jashir, a final offensive was underway to win back the planet. A Runamore shuttle, escorted by over a dozen fighters, swooped low through the clouds and headed for the surface, its pilot intent on getting low enough to almost skim across the ground.

On board was Sangreal Laylana, her fingers constantly twisting a wet cloth tucked deep within her palms. The harsh words of Tallen Dore, her chief advisor, still rang in her ears.

"Stop crying. Do you think the soldiers need to see their Sangreal bawling her eyes out?"

She could only glare at him as multiple emotions fought each other deep within her soul.

Stay calm, her inner voice soothed her. It was the voice of her mother.

I'm just a child. After letting herself breathe deeply for a few moments, the anger evaporated and she returned to a state of calm. At least that's the image she wanted to show. Inside, she was just a mess of fear and panic.

Stay calm.

I will mum, for you, I will.

Since she was a small child, she had lived in Runamore with her parents who were members of the Order of Light. Her mother was an aide to the Sangreal Office, her father worked in the library. Laylana had seen four Sangreals killed as Kaw led a systematic campaign to wipe out the Order. The last was Gurungu, a young man not much older than her. Her parents had died with him.

They had been lucky over the years as the fortress of Runamore had withstood multiple attacks by Axis forces. The three assassinated Sangreals were always away from the fortress, but Gurungu had died in his room. Now Kaw had found a way in.

Laylana was gifted with writing and had always been a people person but, as Sangreals and members of the Order had been killed, a crisis had begun. The Order was running out of people and there were few willing to place the crown on their heads. It had become a death sentence.

It had been late afternoon when Dore had come to see her.

"You're now our Sangreal," he said bluntly with a hint of a sly smile he tried to hide.

She had been expecting it. There had been rumours for days. She was pretty, people liked her, and she was smart. In more peaceful times, she might have had the time and tutorage to thrive, but this was war and times were desperate. What would her parents think? They would be mortified.

"So be it," she had whispered. All she could think of was how many days she now had to live.

That was three days ago. Matters were pressing. The Bond was engaged in trying to throw out the Axis from Jashir. They had assembled a huge force to take the capital.

She looked out the viewport and all she could see was sky and puffs of smoke.

Dore left, leaving her with her attendants.

"He shouldn't speak to you like that," her senior aide, Murel Horumm, muttered as she came over to fuss over Laylana's hair. Murel had attended many of the Sangreals over the decades. Her own son, Marlinja, was Sangreal before he was cut down by assassins while visiting Taranova. Now, her eyes always seemed permanently moist with grief.

She shrugged.

"He's right. How can I look into these soldiers' faces?"

Murel took a deep breath. "Wearing this crown is a symbol that has lasted a thousand years. They will need you."

Dore came back in. "We're here."

Murel took her hand and almost pulled Laylana to her feet. They followed Dore out of the shuttle where there was a small group of soldiers waiting to see her. One of them she recognised as Prince Metora. He was just a boy, a few years younger than her.

"Poor child is still in shock over what happened, Dore. Why is he here?" Murel muttered to Dore as they walked down the ramp.

"We need symbols of why we are fighting," he replied without looking at her.

The noises outside of the shuttle made Laylana wince in fright. Fighters flew overhead in great masses.

A short, older man stepped forward and bowed.

"Sangreal, it is a pleasure to see you. I'm Ambassador Adorn, and this is Prince Metora." The young prince bowed stiffly. He looked nervous and out of place. Laylana was aware of what had happened. He and his sister had survived their brother's slaughter. The young boy had even physically fought Jai in the palace grounds. It would have left any young man traumatised and she could see it on his face.

"Hello," Laylana replied.

"Our shuttle will take us to the forward headquarters," Adorn informed Dore.

The Ambassador waved his arm in the direction they were to go.

Further waves of bombers rushed overhead. She tried to walk straight on the uneven ground.

Be poised. Be strong. Stay calm.

The crown on her head made her stand out and the soldiers about her stopped to stare.

As she walked, she stumbled slightly, but Metora grabbed her and she held his arm. She breathed in deeply to steady herself.

"It's okay," Metora whispered.

She caught the sight of Dore. His mouth was clenched in frustration. He wanted to yell but was holding back.

She knew the soldiers had seen her stumble. Murel had told her that many of the younger soldiers liked her. They had giggled over it. The older, wiser ones probably saw her as a lamb going to slaughter.

"Three cheers for the Sangreal!" a voice boomed out and she looked over to see the soldiers cheering her. She was crying now. The Order had always believed in the power of emotions. They shouldn't be hidden as they were powerful, human traits.

Reinvigorated, she straightened up and then blew the soldiers a kiss of thank you as she began to walk with the power and spirit of the Sangreal. The Sangrillion droids, Arundel, Oberon, Kuratah, and Samarah, were waiting for her. The remaining two, Irigur and Janana, were destroyed during past battles. They stood proud with their silver bodies and flowing capes of the brightest blue, each with an individual symbol representing their names.

A battle transport was waiting for them.

"I'm going to join my army," Metora said.

"I wish you could stay with me," she replied.

"You'll be safe here."

She wanted to say she didn't think so but didn't want to be seen as rude.

He smiled. "I'll see you in the city?"

"Yes. I look forward to it."

Metora stepped away and the transport moved off. It didn't take long to reach the Bond's command centre which has been cut into the ground. It was shielded, well-armoured, and held dozens of staff who operated masses of communication equipment. Laylana was amazed at the sight. She wasn't a soldier and all this was new to her. She also didn't want to get in the way.

While the Sangrillions escorted her to a special room where she could see the battle, a massive explosion rocked the city.

"Sins of the fathers!" Dore exclaimed.

Many of the soldiers began running about.

"The battle's started," an officer called to Dore.

Great flashes of light exploded about the plain as fighters fought each other in the low atmosphere. Soldiers and Striketroopers began fighting on the ground.

The command centre rocked with a massive explosion making the lights go out and the air stale.

Dore pressed a communication device.

"What's going on?"

Laylana couldn't quite make out what was being said but it sounded like the command bunker had been targeted and now the power was out.

"Alright," Dore said before turning off the device.

"We're leaving."

"Where to?"

"There'll be no air inside this place soon, so we have to go outside. The Sangrillions will protect you."

Laylana and Murel followed Dore out, but not the way they had come. Soon they were outside. The shield array was gone and she now felt very exposed.

Several soldiers came running up to them. They were unkempt, their uniforms dirty and ripped.

"You need to go! Get her out of here!"

"The Sangreal does not run," Dore replied.

"The Dark Lord has taken the field! The Sons of Gorgoth are looking for her!"

Her blood went cold. She looked to Dore, trying to hide her panic.

"Alright, get us a transport. Sangrillions be on alert!"

A great laugh bellowed out from the darkness around them. The soldiers who had warned them suddenly dropped and their bodies were thrown against the cold steel of the bunker.

More figures appeared. The Sangrillions spurred into action. Their cannons and lances fired at the mass of figures. Kuratah used both hands to fire. Suddenly his arms were shorn from his body, and then his head. His body crashed to the ground. Standing on it was a figure dressed in grey. Two red blood eyes stared at her from its white face.

Samarah's once shiny, silver frame was on fire as the Gorgoth ripped her to pieces. Oberon and Arundel fought hard. Their cannons were destroyed, their bodies thrown kilometres away to land in the dirt among the wreckage of past campaigns.

Dore and Murel were dead, and she was alone. The Gorgoth came for her. One of them approached her. Its face was rotten and its eyes empty, dark holes. It grabbed her and instantly she was flown to the ruins of the Jashir Palace and thrown to the ground. Her crown fell from her head and clanged against the stone floor.

Standing close by was Iminus Kaw. He was dressed in a dark combat suit with a metal chest plate. His face was taut and sickly but his eyes bright and clear.

"Sangreal. A child. Is this all that the Bond have left?" he asked those around him, but the Gorgoth did not answer.

Her body was trembling. What else was she to do? A hand grabbed the back of her cloak and pulled her up, but her feet were hanging a metre from the ground.

"See the destruction of your armies, your hope, and your life," said Kaw.

She was then held from her hair, hanging like a doll. Kaw produced a blade. Laylana closed her eyes and thought of her mother. Then her life went black.

The Son of Gorgoth, called The Right Hand of Kaw, held her head high so all the Bond armies could see it. The image was broadcast to their communication channels. Everyone in the Bond would see that image and never forget it.

Soldiers out on that plain broke down and fell to their knees, their morale instantly crushed. The Gorgoth were now unleashed. They cried out in anger and revulsion.

Little Laylana's body was then thrown to the Wrydluk, who had already started a fire. Their bravest and fiercest warriors would be rewarded with the flesh of the last Sangreal.

Arundel, his body damaged, had made his way back to the armies. He had seen the signal and his body slumped.

Metora had looked away. He couldn't bear to watch.

Iminus Kaw picked up the crown and with relish and placed it on his head. That's when the war changed in a way no one could imagine.

The Black Ash Prince's new command shuttle, *Plexus,* flew low over the plain that had seen the last failure of the Bond to retake Jashir. The shuttle stirred up the dust that had lain over smashed equipment and bodies as it roared towards the large military base outside Jasmin. It was fortuitous for him but unlucky for the people of Jashir, as he arrived back on the planet in the middle of an uprising brought on by the news of the victory on Ophistar.

There was panic on the streets as the Striketroopers blasted their way into buildings and Axis bombers fell from the skies on their bombing runs or chasing insurgents through the streets.

In reality, the uprising was merely a few dozen people with even fewer weapons who had disappeared into the ruined buildings. The response from the Axis was way out of proportion to the threat. A mountain looked down in derision at a rock before crushing it.

Thousands of troops and ships had been marshalled and sent into the city, intent on destroying anything that looked their way.

Cryacur had arrived just in time for the final push. His bloodlust was extreme. He needed to kill things. His sword, already stained with blood, hung by his side.

"Please, my Lord, we are unarmed," an old man sat on his knees pleading.

Cryacur's response was to cut off his head.

People fled from him, desperate to get away. They huddled in corners of the ruins, shielding their children from the horror. Nonetheless, there was one who did not run. Eryan Ammilian was just a boy from an old family who had once served the kings of Jashir. His father had been killed years before, then his brothers and sisters followed. Then his cousins and uncles all disappeared. His mother had raised him virtually alone and now her body was slumped face down at his feet, cut down by Striketrooper fire. His hands were covered in her blood and smeared the pipe that was his only weapon. With one hand he wiped the tears from his eyes so to see the Black Ash Prince clearly.

People continued to flee past him. None pulled him away. He wouldn't go anyway, even if they tried.

Slowly the Black Ash Prince came on and spotted Eryan standing in the road. The Dark Prince merely walked past, having no interest in the boy.

Until a rock hit him in the back. Furious, he spun around to see Eryan lunging at him with his pipe. Cryacur dodged the blow, his robes swirling and ripping up the dust as he took evasive action.

Eryan was quick too and managed to get a good blow with his pipe right across Cryacur's upper arm. Even more furious, Cryacur plunged his sword right through Eryan's middle. The boy fell to his knees, his eyes fixed on the Prince's dark features.

The sword was withdrawn and the boy fell next to his dead mother. Cryacur picked Eryan's body up by the neck and threw it at a huddle of frightened people where it landed and lay like a broken doll. The women turned their heads away, unable to look at the sight anymore.

The Black Ash Prince moved on and was met by General Briar, the commander of the forces on Jashir.

"My Lord, resistance is dying out. It has been several hours since our troops came under fire. I was going to issue orders to the effect that the rebellion has been crushed."

"One last sweep, General," replied Cryacur.

Briar took a deep breath. "My Lord, we're now just killing civilians. These types of atrocities will only add to the people's hatred."

"Defiance must be met with absolute force. I hope your stomach is not turned by our . . . necessary actions."

"No, it is not. I will order the sweep."

Cryacur left him and returned to the ruins of the former palace of Jashir. There he waited for *Plexus* to take him to Kiam. He looked over the old battlefield on which the last Sangreal had fallen, taking with her the hopes of the galaxy. She had been beheaded and her remains eaten by the Wrydluk. He struggled to remember her name.

It didn't matter now. There was work to be done.

AFTER THE BATTLE

Lorian's euphoria at seeing his brother was short-lived. He felt sick, dizzy, and the city whirled about at a high rotation that forced him to shut his eyes. Dez's tired smile gave way to shock as his brother fell to his knees.

"What's wrong with him?" Dez asked.

Kuring-gai kneeled down to console Lorian and saw the skin on his face was raw and bleeding. Lorian's right hand was the same.

The crowds around them were aghast at the sight and weren't sure of what was going on. Some continued to celebrate, unaware of what was happening.

Kuring-gai was startled at first as it was an unusual wound.

"Are you alright? That looks like a freeze burn."

Lorian breathed in deep and then got to his feet.

"I'm okay, just a bit sick. I'm alright."

Kuring-gai slapped him on the back, "You just don't want to miss this moment."

Lorian smiled in reply. The moment seemed to pass but he

was in no mood to celebrate with everyone else.

"I'll get him to the barracks where he can have a rest," Dez offered.

"A sound idea," confirmed Nepta.

Kuring-gai nodded his approval.

Dez led the way through the street. The battle for Myr Edele was over now, the shield gone, the streets full of people filled with wild joy and celebration.

Dez looked up at the sky as they went. "So glad to see that neon blue gone. It's the only colour I've been able to see since you left."

A flight of fighters rushed past the city making Dez jump. He stopped to catch his breath. Lorian noticed his brother's right eye twitching. His hair had grown longer, his uniform was torn and stained.

"How have you been surviving?"

Dez didn't make any eye contact but swallowed hard.

"The hardest part was trying to block out the sound of those guns. Every day their rounds would hit that shield. It's stopped now but I can still feel the vibrations in my head."

"These tremors will pass, Master Dez," Nepta offered.

"When?" Dez snapped back.

"In time," she replied as gently as her program offered.

"Come on, let's get the hero a bed." He walked off down the street.

Lorian looked at Nepta for an answer.

"Battle-stress, Master Lorian, can be a dreadful thing to deal with."

"True."

They followed him to the barracks. Dez hardly looked behind to see if they were still there and didn't wait for them. He only stopped at the entrance to the barracks where a soldier took Lorian's details. Nepta had already put in the necessary information ahead of schedule.

"You know there were people killing themselves. They couldn't stand it any longer. I came close to ending it too, so close. But you rest easy, hero," said Dez, staring at his brother.

Lorian held back his emotions. He was in pain and didn't want to see this. "That's not fair Dez."

Dez held up his hands as he stepped back. "I'll go back to my hole and wait for the Dark Lord to come back and finish the job."

Lorian didn't have any words. He didn't know what to say as this reaction from his brother was not what he was expecting.

"Nepta, can you watch him tonight?"

"I don't need her!" Dez called out.

"Shall I do so anyway?" Nepta asked.

"Yeah."

"Rest well, Master Lorian."

Lorian never woke all night. He lay still, unmoving, his chest ballooning every few minutes as his lungs took in a huge volume of oxygen. It was the only physical sign that he was alive.

In the darkness of his unconsciousness, he heard a woman's voice.

"Lorian," she whispered. "Throw out all this darkness. Don't be afraid of the destiny I have chosen for you. All will be well in the end."

"I will take on this task," came a male voice that he didn't recognise.

He woke well into the morning. The light was soft and at first he had no idea where he was. There were muffled voices coming from somewhere else in the complex.

"When do you think the Axis will hit back?" asked one voice.

"Who knows," came the reply.

Lorian's face still ached as he got up. He looked about the small space that reminded him of his room back in Menenyr. *What had happened to Jesse?* he asked himself.

The male voice from his dreams still resonated. He didn't recognise it, but he was reminded of his father.

"Nepta?" he called for her on his commlink.

"Yes Sir, I'm glad you're awake. Are you better?"

"I am. Can you contact Dez? We're going out to look for dad."

There was a moment of silence before she responded. "As you request."

He ate as he walked through the city and back to Elsenmere Ridge. Dez and Nepta were waiting for him.

Dez appeared sheepish and Lorian wasn't sure what to say to him.

"I'm sorry about yesterday. It's just been . . . it's been screwed up here." He ran his hand through his hair but looked down at the ground.

"It's alright."

"There have been burial units out this morning," Nepta reported.

While the pall from the smouldering ruins of Axis equipment hung lightly over the fields where they had been left since their destruction, the bodies of the fallen were retrieved for burial by special units.

Lorian found he was still suffering from his wounds and his encounter with the Black Ash Prince. The healing paste had worked well, but it was the mental wounds he was having trouble dealing with. The creature's features had been seared into his mind as the great chill of his presence drank the warmth from his body leaving him weak. Every time he closed his eyes, he could see that terrible grimace.

Most of the conquering soldiers of the Bond had been withdrawn and positioned elsewhere around the Ophistar. A garrison had replaced the mixed units that had defended Myr Edele. Non-Merenmere forces were transported back to the fleet to be returned to Anueth as soon as the situation allowed. Survivors of Metora's original force were also returned to the fleet. Most were exhausted or nervous wrecks from the constant stress of the fighting and bombardment.

"What's the plan?" asked Dez.

The bridge leading out of the city was still a tangle of wreckage and not yet repaired sufficiently to allow vehicles to cross. Lorian began to walk towards it.

"Well, I guess we go looking. You up for that?"

Dez nodded while he was looking up at the ridgeline and fell into step next to his brother.

"Losa wanted me to come. She knew what this was about."

Lorian was confused, "Who's Losa?"

"My girlfriend. She wanted to come so she could meet you. I didn't want her digging up dead bodies. We've already got one damaged person in this relationship. Don't need two," he smiled.

They walked across the bridge and climbed Elsenmere Ridge. Lorian scoured his memory, trying to remember where the Black

Ash Prince had stood when he tried to bargain with Metora to hand himself over. His father had probably fallen here and he felt obligated to find him, if he had indeed died here at all.

Of course, he was also incredibly anxious over what he would do if he did find his father's remains. The thought of looking upon the rotting body made his stomach uneasy. He had seen enough death lately and had no wish to see more. Secretly, he wished his father had somehow survived, but the more jaded, the more war-weary voice inside him told him that was a fool's hope.

On the top of the ridge the grass was burned and there were holes in the dirt made from explosions and now filled with the bodies of soldiers, droids, and smashed equipment. In one of them he began looking closer, doing his best to bear the overpowering stench of death.

"Better alert someone about this Nepta."

"Of course."

"A horrible task," came the voice of Kuring-gai.

Lorian looked up to see the Khoru man standing at the lip of the hole.

"I wouldn't ask anyone to help me," he replied as he climbed out.

"I've had to do this too, looking through the dead after a battle. I'll help you."

Lorian nodded his thanks and continued along the ridge, followed by Dez, who had gradually started to slow his steps and tried to hide his nervousness by stopping often to look up at the sky.

"Do you remember what he was wearing?" Kuring-gai asked.

"It was a red jacket with black breeches."

Nepta moved ahead of them, scanning as she went.

"Sir, there is no one matching your father's features here."

"We'll look over there then."

They walked together across the burnt landscape, dropping into holes and climbing up again. They had to step over wreckage and bodies as they went with the fields on their left, the city on their right, and the great Mountains of Peril high on the horizon.

The group hardly spoke as it pressed on. Kuring-gai did most of the heavy work, lifting wreckage or turning over bodies.

By now, they had explored most of the ridge where Lorian believed he had seen his father standing. On a hunch, they decided to walk towards the eastern edge of the ridge. It was remarkably unscathed here, the grass disturbed by a fire but no punctures in the ground. Of course, the bodies clumped together were a reminder of what had happened. It felt like wherever they would go the dead would always be found. How long could he keep doing this?

"There is a chance Satern was taken elsewhere," Nepta offered.

"No, he's here somewhere. There'd be no point in moving them."

"True, the Axis would hardly be bothered shuttling around hostages once the deal was broken," said Kuring-gai.

Nepta began her scan and immediately jumped back in fright.

"Sir, I've found him, down there."

Kuring-gai began climbing down the ridge to where Nepta was indicating and stopped at a clump of bodies. Lorian could clearly see a dirty, red coat covered in mud.

"Don't come down here, Lorian," Kuring-gai warned.

"I have to," he replied.

Dez remained silent at the tip of the ridge.

Lorian moved slowly, taking only small steps downwards. Nepta had already joined Kuring-gai.

"Is it him, Nepta?"

"Confirmed, Sir."

Lorian sat down on the grass, his knees up against his chest. He was all cried out and his body shook as the emotions rushed over him.

A strong hand on his shoulder told him it was alright.

"I want to say I could have done more, but that's a lie."

"Your father knew."

"It doesn't make it any easier," he replied with gritted teeth.

"No, no, it doesn't. It's what separates us from the machines, but sometimes I wonder if that is true."

Kuring-gai was looking at Nepta, standing guard over her Master's body.

"Let's get back to the city. Nepta will have informed the burial detail," Kuring-gai suggested.

As the two reached the crest, Dez had already walked off and was some distance away.

"Dez!" Lorian called out, but his brother ignored him.

"Let him go," Kuring-gai said.

It took another two days for the fields to be cleared of the dead and the wreckage. All things mechanical were stripped for information and then crushed in the wrecking complex within the city. Weapons, communication equipment, and anything worth keeping was repaired and stored away. The dead Diamalords were buried in a mass grave far to the north.

It seemed the whole city and surrounding settlements far to the north and west in the exile lands came for the official burial ceremony. A large section of the field had been set aside and the names of the dead that could be identified would be carved in a giant wall in the weeks to come. The unknown would have their own memorial.

Metora and Lorian were part of the honour guard. The flags of all the peoples of the Bond that had sent troops to Ophistar fluttered about. Kuring-gai, Nepta, and Oberon stood close. With them was the Governor of Myr Edele, Takin Morr, and Chief Wolfcastle, who had managed to steal away from Anueth to oversee the status of the planet. There were already murmurs of his taking the throne, despite the grumblings from some section of the white Ophistar forces and the political arenas. The return of the Merenmere to prominence gave those who still remembered the civil war uneasy dreams.

Most of the planet's parliamentarians had fled during the Axis invasion and had still not raised their heads, Premier Dunn included. New leadership was needed.

Metora looked across the fields with its newly dug graves and the sea of faces, many teary and full of sorrow. This was now the most fought over piece of ground on Ophistar. This was one of the few times that he had walked across a former battlefield when all was quiet. Most battlefields he had fought on had been abandoned or he had moved elsewhere. It was quiet. The birds sailed in the sky and a gentle breeze brushed across the surviving trees and long grass.

For those three days after the victory, he had felt satisfied. The dismissive nature of the War Council had been thrown in its face and he could enjoy the victory and its vindication. With the dawn of this morning, he felt troubled but did not know why.

Chief Wolfcastle stood at the podium. He was not a man who liked speeches. Metora had written the words but he knew the day needed the words to be spoken.

"There comes a time when you are pushed to your utter limits. There is only so much pain a soul can endure before it strikes back. Those who fell here on this planet must not be forgotten and their deaths must not be in vain. This is the first step on the road back to peace. It will be hard and we all know there will be many more fields such as this one. As loyal citizens of the Sangreal, we must decide. Do we live under tyranny and wait for a future generation, if it comes, to free our children? Or do we do it now — us, you, me? This may well be our last chance. We all know we can't retreat anymore because there's nowhere else to go. If that Trunadim wants to control our lives, then he must beat us, and we will fight him all the way. Let it be said that free souls died here."

With the speech over, a woman dressed in swathes of green and gold to match her golden hair stepped forward and began to sing 'Ave Empore'. She stood by the open grave where the dead had been laid out during the night. These were the dead of the Merenmere and their allies, bound by pact and now bound in death to lay in the soil of Ophistar for all eternity.

With the ceremony over, family and friends remained behind to have their private goodbyes. Lorian and Dez remained at the grave-site. Neither had spoken to the other since the other day on the ridge. Lorian had sent him a few messages but they had never been returned. It took instructing Nepta to find him to satisfy Lorian that Dez was alive. He had feared the worst.

"Have you found what you're looking for?" Dez asked.

Lorian looked at him suspiciously. "What would that be?"

"This is what you wanted."

"I didn't want this," Lorian bit back.

"What do you want?"

"I don't know." Lorian looked back to the graves.

They remained in silence for a few moments. Lorian was angry that his brother would think that he would want this misery.

"I haven't had the years of war like the others, but it's been enough to change me," Lorian said.

"Change you into what? You and I are very different. I get that feeling that I'll be the one standing over your grave next."

"Then it will be your turn."

"We're all next. There's no stopping this."

Again, Lorian looked at his brother and shrugged his shoulders in frustration. He didn't have the answers to quell Dez's internal anger.

"What do you want me to do? Should I just jump in now?" He indicated the graves.

Dez remained silent. His right eye twitched now and again, no doubt a leftover from the continual bombardment the people of Myr Edele had to endure.

"This isn't the life I wanted," said Dez.

"Well, it's what you got now. Depends whether you want to fight for the one you want or let this existence destroy you. I want this victory to be the beginning of something . . . something that will end this war."

Dez began to walk away. "It is the beginning of the end, like I said. There's nothing stopping it. This is just a delay, just stretching out our final moments before we're all lying in a ditch. There'll just be no one to mourn us."

Lorian watched him go. He caught the eye of many of the people about them who had heard their conversation. He could only guess what they were thinking.

He put his hands in his pockets and left the grave-site. Nepta was waiting patiently for him not far away and together they made their way back into the city by shuttle.

It flew over the old battlefield on Elsenmere Ridge but he barely acknowledged the retracing of steps. He was still angry about Dez's attitude. Maybe they were all going to die and the situation was hopeless. Maybe they should fight on and hope for a miracle. The argument twisted inside his mind and was giving him a headache. The military side of him was also concerned about the next move from the Axis. Surely, they would turn up here and this fight would have been for nothing.

He would bring it up in the Council meeting. That was where he was headed.

"Nepta, find Dez and spend some time with him."

"What about the Council meeting?"

"It's alright, I'll manage. Looking after Dez is more important."

"Of course, Sir."

The shuttle arrived at the base of Crystal Tower where he got out and let it take Nepta back to find Dez. He hadn't even been to where Dez said he was living.

Metora had set up his headquarters in the upper levels of the tower. Many of the rooms on the former Governor's level had been taken over by the victorious allies. It was also one of the few levels that still had its windows intact preventing the high winds from turning it into a wind tunnel.

Lorian was glad to see the lift took them all the way up. Last time it only went halfway and everyone had to walk up the stairs.

Two female Merenmere guards stood on each side of the main door of the Governor's quarters. Inside the sparse room the leadership of the traitors, as Admiral Zuke had called them, were gathered.

Chief Wolfcastle looked tired and was continually rubbing his eyes but was able to break into a smile when Lorian entered the room.

"Lorian, we thought you weren't coming."

"I wouldn't miss it."

Gathered about were more officers that Lorian didn't know, though he recognised Colonel Halkinbraun. He nodded his acknowledgement.

Kuring-gai pulled up a seat next to him. He had a plate with food on it and was looking suspiciously at some of it.

"I don't know what this is, but it's good." Lorian looked at it, "Looks like cappella fruit and meat with something on it."

"Right, cappella fruit. Goes well with the gale bird and some durum sauce." He held his plate so Lorian could try some.

He barely put the meat and the sauce in his mouth when he started coughing.

"It's like eating lava," he exclaimed while reaching for a glass of water.

"Yeah, here's the whole pitcher. You'll need it," laughed Kuring-gai as he put the pitcher of water close by. Lorian immediately refilled his cup.

Metora entered the room followed by Oberon who went over to one of the glass windows where he remained aloof, watching the wild sea and beyond.

Lorian was still coughing from the hot sauce, which caught Metora's eye.

"That durum sauce is nasty stuff."

"I didn't warn him," Kuring-gai laughed.

Once everyone sat, they waited for Metora to begin. He held up a disc.

"I should start by saying that I have received my orders to return to Anueth."

"For what purpose?" Kuring-gai asked.

"It doesn't say, but from other communications it may well be to stand trial for treason."

Kuring-gai grunted his disapproval, matched by the cries of disdain from around the table.

"The whole fleet is ordered back?" Colonel Halkinbraun asked.

"No. Just me." He looked over to Wolfcastle. "I hope this hasn't been a waste."

"It hasn't. Stop doubting yourself."

"I've marooned an entire fleet here. I'd feel better about it if Imperial Command would give us the shield pods, engineers, and replacement fighters that I asked for. I should have known this would lead to further misery. If the Axis attack us again, this whole episode will be for nothing."

"Why haven't they attacked?" Lorian asked.

"I don't know. It troubles me," Metora replied.

"As I," added Wolfcastle.

"Maybe they know they don't have to do anything. We have to leave a fleet here to protect the planet, which then isn't defending Trinity," said Lorian.

Metora put his head in his hands and rubbed his temples, trying to quell whatever headache was boiling up.

"I've doomed us," he muttered.

"No," thundered Wolfcastle, as he lent back in his seat. "The fleet will remain here. We will prepare new troops to be sent back to Anueth. You will go home, but you won't be going alone. Lorian will go and I would suggest taking Kuring-gai and Oberon too."

"I'll go," concurred Lorian

"I'll go too. You're not going back to that nest of vipers by yourself," added Kuring-gai.

"Oberon?" Wolfcastle asked.

"I will return to Anueth," Oberon confirmed.

"I will remain here and get things organised before returning. Opportunities will come of this. The Axis disinterest, for whatever tactical reasons or darker plot we can only imagine, will reveal itself sooner or later. We'll be ready for it," said Wolfcastle.

Before they were able to go on to other business, Takin Morr entered the room. Lorian noticed he had lost a bit of weight around his gut and his face was a little leaner, his hair had grown, and his clothes were faded and torn.

"Gentlemen, how are we this evening?" he smiled widely and patted on the shoulder the men closest to him, which happened to be Lorian and Kuring-gai.

"Governor." Wolfcastle stood up to greet Morr, who now looked a little nervous. Maybe he was remembering his frantic words the last time he saw Metora. He almost appeared as a coward. Lorian thought he probably was indeed a coward and, now the Axis were gone, he was back to reclaim his old job.

"We need to discuss the city. I believe I should remain as governor. I have held this post for almost ten years with great success."

"You don't muck around, Morr," Wolfcastle replied bluntly.

"Well, this is an urgent issue."

"What did you do during the civil war?" Wolfcastle asked.

Morr was stumped for a moment, his mind wandering to the hypothesis that the exiles had returned and now they would seek revenge on those who turned against them.

"I was a junior Councillor under Lonen. I am not a soldier, my Chief." Morr was even more nervous and his body shook, revealing it to everyone.

Wolfcastle only smiled.

"You can remain as governor. I will be returning to the capital to begin preparations for the defence of our world."

Morr's euphoria had evaporated as quickly as it appeared.

"What do you mean? Is the Axis returning? I knew this would happen. Is our beloved planet going to be fought over until there are only ashes? Is that the end result of all this warmongering!?"

"Calm yourself Governor," Wolfcastle whispered menacingly.

"But how will we defend ourselves? Who will be in charge?" Morr continued his panicking rant while wiping the sweat from his brown with a cloth that had seen heavy use.

"There is nothing to worry about. Your only concern is Myr Edele. Can I count on you?"

"Yes, yes. I will return to my tower and begin the rebuilding process."

"Good. I want you to cooperate with the regional Councillors from the exile lands and Star Mun, not just your little piece of the universe. Agreed?"

Morr hesitated as he thought it over. "Yes, I will do as you ask, Merenmere."

Wolfcastle nodded, the meeting done. Morr turned away but then stopped.

"Anything else, Governor?"

"The shield in Myr Edele, will it remain operational?"

"If it makes you sleep better Governor."

Morr seemed to finally relax and his euphoria returned as he breathed out the nervous lung full of air he had been holding in.

"Wonderful. The people will be pleased."

"We'll meet again Governor."

Morr bowed before scuttling away and out of the room.

"I hope we can all play nice, *Merenmere*," Metora said mischievously to Wolfcastle.

"It'll take some of them time to readjust to the Merenmere returning to their old office of defenders of the planet. I just hope old wounds aren't reopened."

After the meeting, Lorian wandered the streets of Myr Edele which now filled with people and life. He was reading the reply from Imogen about how his little flight group were going.

With you away, I'm in charge. Kahil put in for a transfer. I supported it as I was sick of his whingeing. Trix says hello. We won't be seeing you for a while then?

I'm glad you are all ok. Did you get any souvenirs from the Dominator? Tell Trix, I miss her. Tell Kahil goodbye. I'm going to see my brother. He's been angry since I got here. No idea when I'm back.

Trix really, really misses you. Good luck. Talk soon.

That made him smile. Probably the first time he had felt any sense of happiness since coming back. Satisfaction? Yes, but Dez's reaction worried him.

Many of the shops had reopened, the markets had started back up, and there seemed to be new energy everywhere, unlike the last time he was here when there was only fear. Of course, life in the city before the siege was unknown to him. Many of the Merenmere symbols had been removed after the civil war and had not been returned. He hoped Chief Wolfcastle would be delicate in having Merenmere merge back into society. Most people appeared accepting of the situation they all now faced but there were always those jealous, resentful individuals who would never accept the Merenmere back into mainstream society.

He spent some time wandering around the streets until he was pleasantly surprised by Dez, who had sent him a message to come to his home and gave the directions. It was a small apartment in one of the smaller blocks in the centre of the city. Here there were burned buildings and rubble that was still being cleared.

Most of the glass was gone and there were ripped curtains and furniture hanging out of gaping holes. Their owners had gone and no one had returned.

He was surprised to find Dez's place was down instead of up.

The elevator was out, so he took the stairs down a few levels, passing people sitting in hallways talking quietly. In some levels there were children running about.

Dez answered the door after one knock.

"Come in," he muttered.

The apartment was small and had no windows or doors to look out on any scenery. It was devoid of anything to turn it into a home. Probably the reason he had not been invited to see it.

"What is this place?" Lorian asked curiously.

"They used to be storage areas but were converted for refugees a few weeks ago. It's home, but not for long."

"You're moving?" Lorian was glad his brother was getting out of this cage. That would also explain the austere nature of the room.

"We're going back to Tauclenne."

Lorian looked at his brother strangely. He had his mind's question answered when a young girl came out of the bedroom. She had long, blonde hair and blue eyes.

"This is Losa. She's from Tauclenne too. There's a group heading back to rebuild and, as much as I would hate to leave this paradise, I said yes." Dez smiled.

"Good. Nice to meet you Losa." Lorian smiled at Losa despite his surprise at this revelation.

"Nice to finally meet you too. Dez talks about you all the time," she replied.

"Really? What flowers to put on my grave?"

"Wild honeys?" he laughed.

It was the first time Lorian had seen him laugh in a long time.

"When are you going?"

"Well, we've packed our worldly possessions, which took only a few minutes. There's a transport leaving soon."

"You can see us off," Losa said as she took Dez's hand and looked lovingly at him. He squeezed it and smiled at her.

"Tell him," she implored Dez.

Dez sat down on a seat while Losa went back into the room. Lorian sat down a small box.

"What is it?" he asked.

"I've been cruel since you got back. I shouldn't have been, but I had to put up with more than just the constant bombardment which almost sent me mad. I saw men and women burn up as they threw themselves at the shield just to get away from it. People I knew well. I had stood there myself. One time I actually ran at it but stopped short." He breathed deep and avoided eye contact with his brother. "Then I had a few miserable arseholes accuse Dad of knowing this was going to happen and having done nothing to stop it, just so we could get back into the war. Can you believe that?" He shook his head in anger and frustration.

"That's a lie."

"But it can't become a rumour that grows into some phantom myth that our enemies use against us. I don't want these accusations to follow us and end up in the history books. You know what I mean?"

"I know its rubbish."

"I just had to tell you."

"You've got something good now." Lorian looked at Losa, who was now leaning against the doorframe.

"True," Dez smiled at her.

"Tell us what you've been doing?" she asked Lorian.

He shrugged. "Training in Menenyr. Oh, Metora and I got captured on the way back from here and ended up in Anarc. Luckily, Oberon got us out. I'm not sure how long I could have stayed in there. Umm, so more training. I met Princess Isla from Nunearanor and got a few hits on the Dominator. Got my leg cut up doing it and then ended up with Oberon in the Lacey Range blowing up battledroids." Lorian mused for a moment. "It's been a busy time."

Dez and Losa exchanged looks of surprise before Dez began to tear up.

"I'm sorry Lorian, I've been selfish, bloody ignorant of what's been happening to you. I didn't know. You never tell me anyway!"

They all remained silent but teary for a moment.

"My brother is a war hero, Losa. No, Merenmere believe the dead are the heroes and the survivors the guardians of their memory."

Lorian nodded sheepishly.

"It's time to go," Losa said.

They had a bag each which they grabbed and headed for the door.

"How long have you been staying here?" Lorian asked as they left the unit.

Dez put his arm on Lorian's shoulder.

"Since I got out of hospital. Being underground helped drown out the noise so a fair few wounded soldiers ended up down here."

They walked up the stairs until they reached the street. They continued in silence then until they arrived at the main transport hub. A number of transports were standing by being loaded with luggage and people.

"Which is our one?" Losa asked.

Dez pointed to a faded, light brown, two-engine shuttle that had many different coloured panels indicating it had been through a few reconditions in its lifetime.

Losa hugged Lorian. "I'm sorry we didn't get to see much of each other. You'll have to come and visit us."

"We'll be married with kids before Lorian gets back to us, or dead," Dez joked.

"I hope that doesn't happen." Lorian looked back at his brother who merely stared at him with empty, emotionless eyes.

"Are you staying in the city longer?" Losa asked.

Lorian shook his head. "No, Prince Metora has been ordered back to Anueth and I'm going too."

Losa looked to Dez while he looked at her deeply. Lorian felt intrusive standing there while they stared into each other's eyes.

"Time to go. Don't be a hero too soon, Lorian," Dez announced.

They shook hands. There was no embrace. They just walked off hand in hand without looking back. Losa waved before they disappeared into the shuttle.

Lorian waited for it to lift off and disappear into the west.

He had his own appointment to keep at the military platform. His heart was heavy as he made his way, ignoring the shops and the people, who all ignored him. Nepta was waiting for him at the same platform that had taken him away during the siege. He had been nervous and guilty then. Now he couldn't shake that feeling that Dez hated him for some reason. He wouldn't find out, because deep down he knew he wouldn't see Dez or Ophistar ever again.

RETURN

Any residue of the victorious mood had vanished as the shuttle left Ophistar. All thoughts were now on their reception in Anueth.

Metora noted that Lorian had barely said a word and had found some seats to slump his body across. Nepta sat by his side and powered down. He could empathise with his friend's distance and worries. He had the face of a heavy heart.

Kuring-gai had taken a seat in the cockpit with the pilot, leaving Oberon to crouch at the rear cargo bay. The Sangrillions used to have their own shuttle, built specifically to allow them to stand. Even the Sangreals' private transports were built to accommodate their guardians' tall stature. This left Metora with his own worries. It would be a cold and unfriendly welcome when they returned. Then the real pain would start. Most likely, the wheel turning towards his demise was already in motion. With Zuke at the controls, it was a certainty.

His mind wandered to where they would put him. Maybe it will be on a little battlestation somewhere on Trinity? One right in the path of an Axis fleet so, when his station was destroyed, they could blame him for failing the Bond and destroying the galaxy.

Or would they execute him for treason? *Would they?* Zuke would *want* that. Confined to the palace without any command would be the most likely scenario. Who knows? The thought of it all was giving him a headache, a common ailment of his lately.

He slumped into a chair close to where Lorian was looking up at the ceiling. In the dark place of his soul, he didn't know or care what they did to him. The War Council could be thrown into Grotfer as far as he cared. He should be listening to Wolfcastle more. He shouldn't doubt himself. His theories and practices about the conduct of the war had proved correct. The armies of the Bond could fight back. The Axis could be defeated by offensive actions. Just, nobody seemed to be listening. Now he felt he had made matters worse.

Kuring-gai sat watching the streaming light that surrounded the shuttle as it thundered through lightspeed. His skin seemed to have faded slightly and there were more streaks of grey in his hair than usual.

The people of Palaniri, the Khoru and Gunadar, aged quicker than other races. Generations ago, many of the Khoru had fled to Palaniri's twin planet, Chene, to escape the extreme policies the Gunadar were pursuing. Many remained to counter the aggression of the Gunadar. The Gunadar had then destroyed themselves as they attempted to cure the curse of an early death. Instead of a long life, they had transformed themselves into a bitter people. Exiled from Palaniri after their failed fusion tests that had put their whole homeworld in jeopardy, they had settled on another world, deep in the Dark Worlds, where they continued to use nuclear and DNA testing to extend their lives. In doing so, they had burned their new homeworld, turning it into a planetary windstorm that could rip the skin off a man's bones in seconds.

The Gunadar were forced to build their cities underground to avoid the nuclear fallout and storm, waiting for the day when they could find a new world. Kaw had finally conquered Palaniri and Chene, denying their use to the Gunadar, so their envious eyes had settled on Oneum. It had been conquered by Kaw during his initial assault, as his armies burst from the Dark Worlds, and never retaken by the Bond. Barely anyone escaped Oneum to build a new settlement on Anueth. Her youth was poisoned by Kaw's malice, her people forgot their king and Sangreal, her once tall trees were felled and replaced with long plumes of black smoke from the factories that provided most of Kaw's army of droids and fighters. Little news was ever heard from behind that blackened, industrial veil. It was a bitter tragedy that may never be righted.

The Khoru had to endure the final subjugation of their world. The Bond's military were too stretched across the Bond worlds to try to defend Palaniri against the masses of Axis forces and their allies. For a people of short lives, they knew they would never see their world again. Some held hope to take that final walk north, as their ancestors had done for thousands of years, to the continent of Forla Bandula. For many of the peoples of Palaniri, they would go north when they heard the whispers of their forebears saying it was time. Then they would travel into the forest of Warrawul and lay down in the arms of their forebears to sleep forever. Those who had died far away were always brought north and buried by special priests who were the only ones allowed to cross into the forest and then return. Many would want to take that final walk themselves when the dead told them it was time to do so.

Only the brave attempted to return to Axis-controlled Palaniri and try to reach Forla Bandula. There were pilots, called runners, who would take people there at great personal risk. Very few ever returned, and those that did and continued to risk their lives held special esteem.

Kuring-gai seemed to be in a trance, his body hurtling through space, but his mind even more distant. His thoughts were on his Tatika, his little ones — Fern, Bundar, and Josie, all gone now.

Metora had stood up and was now slumped in the doorway of the cockpit.

"I know. It's pointless", Kuring-gai finally said without looking away from the window.

Oberon turned his head to listen to the conversation.

"I've always heard that in the starlines you can see the dead, but I don't see anything".

"They are old legends from the time before ours when space travel was new and full of wonder," Oberon replied.

"My time to go north will come soon, but I won't be one of those who hears the voices of the ancestors and crosses into Warrawul. I'll be one of those lost souls, doomed to float the oceans of the universe forever."

"You won't be alone out there," Oberon said.

Kuring-gai continued to stare out of the cockpit.

"True."

"We all know someone lost in that ocean," said Metora, his mind turning to his sister, Mahren. Then there was his beautiful Isobel. All her pictures, all her property, he put away after she died. He couldn't bear the smell, the sight, or even the sound of anything of hers anymore. How many years had it been and yet the thought of her still pierced his heart? A part of him had really died that day. *Put her away, put her deep in your heart and never speak or think of her again* he would tell himself every time his mind flashed with her smile.

"I've fought hard for years. The grand strategy is beyond me, but I want you to win this war, to finish it." Kuring-gai stared hard at Metora.

Metora nodded his acknowledgment.

"You know strategy. You're one of the best commando operators in the Bond."

"But not forever," Kuring-gai smiled.

"I fear for your reception when we arrive on Anueth. I exist to protect. Political dealings are not to my liking," Oberon said.

"There's a lot of fear running through the War Council and the entire Imperial Command. I can't do anything about that anymore."

"Then we get rid of them and you take command, have someone proclaim you Sangreal, and finish this." Kuring-gai spoke with force and determination.

"You and I know that a true Sangreal would be elected. They would never proclaim themselves. That's how Iminus Kaw found himself falling into shadow."

Metora put his hand on his friend's shoulder to comfort him. He could see the man was frustrated, even afraid.

"I know, just . . . just, time is running out."

"The way things are, I'd just be another corpse for the Wrydluk to eat and my bones to be worn on Cryacur's head. Believe me, I've thought about it in my more frustrated moments, but I don't know if it would do any good."

"There has to be a way, brother," Kuring-gai implored.

A light began blinking, combined with a pulsing sound.

"We're approaching Delta 900," said the pilot.

"I wanted us to come back rejuvenated but I feel we're just going to our deaths," Metora replied as the shuttle came out of lightspeed. Trinity's defences extended across the cockpit window. At its centre, loomed the fortress of Delta 900.

They watched silently as their ship moved its way through the corridors between minefields and defences before coming into cleaner space, free of the material of war.

The shuttle continued its journey to Anueth and landed on one of the many platforms of Redsee fortress.

Nepta and Lorian followed the group out of the shuttle and stood at the bottom of the ramp.

"Someone was meant to meet us. Nepta, can you see what is going on?" Metora asked.

"Your arrival was announced moments ago. The Council members are assembling as we speak," she replied immediately.

"You did tell them we're coming?" Lorian asked Nepta.

"I sent a coded message prior to us leaving Ophistar."

Metora seemed to grunt under his breath before leading the way towards the main glass doors. A single sentry stood by, cloaked in the black of the Redsee guard regiment.

The doors suddenly opened and there stood a young female

officer, Sine Durlor, dressed in the dark grey uniform of the Jashir. She was clearly startled to see the group of men and droids standing there.

"Sire, I wasn't expecting your arrival. I was told the emissary from Mahnarosa was here," Durlor said, clearly embarrassed.

Metora barely raised a smile, "That's alright Lieutenant. Not your fault, just means less hands to shake."

"I did send a coded message," Nepta added, not wanting anyone to think she had made a mistake.

"I apologise. I was only following instructions."

"No need. Let's get out of this wind. It's playing havoc with my hair," he joked.

Durlor led the way back down toward the lifts. Metora slowed his step so Lorian could catch up. When they were shoulder to shoulder, he looked at his watch.

"What have I been saying? Games. Stupid games."

"It's an insult," Kuring-gai added.

"It's the cold dance of politics, Lorian. You're about to see the greatest show in the galaxy. Plenty of back slapping and maybe a victory dance. All the while, generals conspire behind doors."

Lorian shook his head in frustration at all this pettiness.

"Are there any good ones?"

Kuring-gai chuckled to himself. "Most of the good ones are dead, only the cowards are left."

"That is a harsh judgement," said Oberon.

"I'm still here," Metora smiled.

"And you Kuring-gai," added Lorian.

Kuring-gai laughed and seemed to rethink his words. "Of course, there are still some excellent commanders, but for every one of them there are two cowards. Satisfied Oberon?"

"I agree."

Lorian just shook his head at the sad fact that even a Sangrillion droid agreed the military hierarchy was weak.

The officer left them at the lift, heading off to other duties. The ride wasn't long and soon the doors opened to reveal a reception area. It was plain, with white walls, and a large viewing window. Most of the fancy furniture and fittings had been removed for safety. If you looked closely, you could still see the attachments on the walls that once held paintings.

"My Lords!" a voice boomed through the room. A tall creature with green skin and four eyes arranged in a horizontal line across its face appeared from a rear corridor.

"Welcome home."

The creature came closer and Lorian was immediately reminded of the Taarnok that guarded the Lancy Range on Ophistar. It was only now that he wondered what had happened to Darsulune and his kind.

During the time of the Sangreal, exploration deeper into space had led to contact with several alien species. Many of them had fled from the Dark Worlds as their own aggressors engulfed those systems. It was only after Kaw had launched his war from those very systems that the government of the Sangreal become aware of the identity of the aggressor. Iminus Kaw had vanished for years, obviously building his power base and using its resources for his own war of revenge on the Sangreal.

"My apologies for this embarrassment. I am Aide Porjume, at your service. I wish to convey my excitement over your victory on Ophistar."

"Thank you," replied Metora.

"I understand you have an audience with Admiral Zuke and the War Council? They are waiting to hear your blow-by-blow account of the battle. But first, the Elector has asked for a private meeting."

Metora hesitated for a moment. "Of course."

"Your friends are welcome to wait in the guest-chamber until your return," Porjume acknowledged the group standing next to Metora.

"I will be returning?" Metora asked.

The creature seemed confused for a moment.

"I believe so," he replied hesitantly. He was afraid that he had not asked the question correctly. Human communication was still something he was struggling to understand.

Metora gave his companions a resigned look before walking away with Porjume. He nodded for Nepta to join him.

"I wonder how big a pile of krick we're really in," Kuring-gai whispered as he watched Metora disappear into an elevator with Porjume and Nepta.

Quisto had prepared the briefing with Elector Dulian, Crowcraw, and Metora. The old man had been resting on a large chair overlooking the Anueth City skyline for almost two hours. He rarely travelled from Sentinal Tower and his meetings this morning with Redsee staff had left him exhausted. He had lain so still and quiet that Quisto had to check several times to see if the man was dead. Each time, he was only sleeping or barely awake, all the while ignorant of his aide going about his business.

Since becoming aware of the battle on Ophistar, he had said little. There were many government departments wanting an official word from Sentinal Tower, but there was only silence. The Elector remained withdrawn, tired, and seemingly near death.

Quisto hoped for this and there were moments he wanted to push the process along. It would be easy to accomplish, frightfully easy, but he had his orders to wait. An elderly Elector who was on the verge of senility was better that a new, strong, and capable Elector, someone like Prince Metora.

The old man would not be killed, but Quisto was increasingly afraid he would simply die of natural causes, forcing a new candidate into the office. This dilemma had been relayed by him weeks ago to a higher authority in Axis ranks. He hoped for a solution soon. There did not seem to be much time.

"What time is it Quisto?"

"Morning, Your Excellency."

"Oh. It doesn't feel like morning."

"Well, it is," Quisto replied unintentionally forcefully. His impatience babysitting a decrepit old man was beginning to bubble through his usual calm persona.

"Is Metora here yet?"

"Soon. He has been summoned. Are you comfortable with the coming conversation?"

"Yes. It is for the best I think."

"True."

Quisto smirked, unnoticed behind the Elector's back. Crowcraw epitomised the Bond — frail, delusional, and completely unaware of the danger they were in.

A cup of water sat on a table next to the Elector, to which Quisto added a drug, purely to keep the man alert for the coming meeting. It was the only way he had been able to convey to the public that Crowcraw was still the man he used to be.

An electronic voice indicated that Metora had arrived.

"Allow him entry," Quisto replied.

He stepped away to the side of the room just before the Prince and Nepta entered the room.

Crowcraw had drunk his water and stood, the drug taking immediate effect.

"Prince Metora! Welcome home!" he called out, his arms outstretched.

"Thank you, Your Excellency."

They shook hands. Crowcraw beamed like a proud parent welcoming home his son.

"Can I offer you anything?"

"No thank you," Metora replied, his eyes drifting to the man standing in the shadows just to his left. *The same man he had seen in Zuke's office. Now he was in Crowcraw's!* Once this meeting was over, he would have Nepta remind him to find out who he was and what had happened to Ubba Dani.

"I need to talk to you, my young friend, as I am sure you know of the tone of Admiral Zuke's reception. I thought I would get in first." The old man raised a brief smile.

"I can imagine."

"He is furious about the closed-door dealings of the Merenmere, and you. I too am perplexed by your actions. We must not let ego and pride divide us."

"It is not an issue of ego." Metora immediately defended

himself.

"Of pride then?"

"I do what I believe is right. I find it hard to listen to people who are wrong."

"Yes, it's part of your upbringing. A leader who is used to getting his way finds it hard to listen to others' counsel or orders."

Metora was taken back by this ambush of his character and upbringing. He felt like turning about and leaving the room but stayed out of respect and common sense. He already had Zuke offside and he didn't want the Elector of the Bond as his enemy too.

Crowcraw stepped away and resumed his seat. He didn't offer Metora one. None had even been placed for him to use.

"Have you thought about appointing a regent for Jashir? To lighten the burden that you carry."

"What are you talking about? A regent?"

Metora was expecting the Elector to want a report on the status of Ophistar, casualties, or when the fleet would return.

"Well, I've seen the pain you are in. Not only as commander of military forces but as Prince and guardian of your people. This is a . . . great burden at such a young age. To see so much death in your time must leave an impression on your soul." He leaned in closer towards Metora. "You can't go through the rest of your life as normal. Most military men who have seen such heavy fighting as you do not."

"You want me to renounce my oath and walk away?" Metora was appalled.

"Oh no, no, of course not. Unless you want to? All I am suggesting is that you accept a . . . a partner to carry the burden of such heavy responsibility, to help you Metora, that's all."

"What? A wife?" Metora joked.

Crowcraw laughed.

"No, a regent."

Metora became deathly quiet as he stared back at the Elector.

"There is no provision in the constitution for a co-regency, or in military law."

"Laws can be changed."

"Obviously you have given this a lot of thought and probably have someone already in mind."

"No," Crowcraw replied innocently. "There is no one ready."

"Then why bring this up?" Metora asked.

Metora looked to his left at Quisto, who stared back stone-faced, then back to Crowcraw. The old man laughed again. "I dwell on people I care about and yes, there are names, but that is old news. What if you died? Your appointed heir is only a child. Surely you can see the seriousness and practicality of the situation?"

Metora didn't reply. While it was true, his designated heir was a child, he trusted his remaining family and his officers to teach her well.

The Prince and Elector were locked in a stare, the younger leader looking behind the older one's apparent sincerity for a lie. There only seemed more words being held back. The Elector's lips trembled, but there was nothing more.

Finally, Metora broke the stalemate. "I will give the matter serious thought, Your Excellency."

Crowcraw smiled as an invisible weight seem to lift from his body. "Good, good."

Metora had had enough and wanted to leave. He knew agreement or compromise would be the quickest way out of the office. He bowed and the Elector acknowledged this respect with a nodding of his head.

"Now, enjoy your celebration. I will be seeing you shortly, hopefully to guard you against Admiral Zuke. But an old man can only do so much."

There was nothing else to say. Metora gave Quisto a final look before leaving with Nepta, the taste of bitterness heavy in his mouth. Something was not right in the Elector's office.

Outside of the office, Porjume was waiting.

"Did that go well, Sir?" Nepta asked.

"No. Not really."

"I'm sorry to hear that. The Elector seemed to be one of our allies."

"I don't trust him anymore."

"Is there anything I can do, Sir?"

Metora breathed deeply. "You know Nepta, I wish I could just disappear. I really do."

Nepta watched him walk away. Even a droid could see the massive weight on his shoulders.

Crowcraw fell back into his chair, his arms hanging limp on either side, his eyes closed, seemingly asleep.

"He is stubborn and his heart has been hardened through battle and heavy loss," Quisto said as he emerged from the shadow to be by the man's side.

"Yes. I hope he will come around, for his own sake," Crowcraw whispered weakly.

"Of course he will. He is an intelligent, wise, young man and he will see your plan is in his own interest."

There was only a weak acknowledgement. The Elector's mind wandered between exhaustion and moments of focus. What else could he do to save his world?

When he finally opened his eyes, Quisto was standing above him and there was a flicker of a sneer across his pale face, framed by the stringy hair.

"Sometimes I see cunning and self interest in those grey eyes of yours Quisto."

His aide only smiled and ignored the man's observations.

"It may well be best to approach the subject again in a few days." Quisto ignored the observation.

"Yes. You're right Quisto. Tell Admiral Zuke I have passed on my proposal."

Crowcraw had closed his eyes again, allowing Quisto to pull himself together. He so wanted to kill this man, out of hatred and fear. The Elector's moments of focus at the wrong time could prove fatal to both of them.

The old man's eyes remained closed and the gentle heavy breathing signalled he was asleep, allowing Quisto to finally leave his side. He would increase the old man's dosage of medication and keep a very close hold on him. He downed a small dose himself. The pressure of keeping up this charade was grating on his inner core. He watched the old man sleep. If it wasn't for the rising of the chest, he looked dead. That gave him some comfort. Surely this couldn't go on for much longer and the Dark Lord must strike? Soon, it must be soon.

Metora said nothing as he made his way to the guest-chamber where the others were waiting. Nepta attempted to lighten the mood with small-talk, but Metora wasn't really listening.

Inside the room, there was a commanding view of the city. Lorian and Kuring-gai were looking out of the window, pointing out locations of interest. Oberon remained close to the door.

They all turned to look at him when the door opened.

"What happened?" Kuring-gai asked immediately.

Metora stood there, his fist clenched, and his mouth twisted as he tried to bite down the fury that was building inside him. He walked straight up to the window and bashed both his fists on the glass.

"They want me to appoint a regent just in case I die unexpectedly. I'm sure they have someone in mind but they won't tell me who it is."

"What did you tell them?" Kuring-gai asked.

"I said I would consider it, but I won't be considering anything. Koree is the heir and that's the way it will be. It just makes me concerned for her safety and who they have in mind, if they really do have anyone."

Kuring-gai shook his head. "It's not enough we have enemies to our front, but we have villains at our backs too. A crazier man would eliminate them all."

"That is not the right talk," Oberon, who had remained quiet, now interjected.

"Yes, I know. But this is ridiculous," Kuring-gai replied.

"It gets worse, I'm afraid," a female voice spoke. Metora hadn't even realised she was there. Enin Wolfcastle, the youngest daughter of the Chief, was standing by another door. She wore the uniform of the Merenmere. Her dark hair was braided and her eyes were fixed on Metora. Her solemn expression and her line of work made Metora even more anxious.

"What is it Enin?" he asked.

"Zuke is pushing to have you disciplined for your actions."

Metora merely raised an eyebrow.

"Court-martialled?" Kuring-gai was more vocal.

Enin shook her head. "No, but there will be a full War Council hearing on what occurred."

Metora began pacing around the room, his face still a picture of the betrayal he felt.

"I'm so sick of these games. What's the point of carrying on when you have scum like Zuke who are only in it for their own petty enjoyment?"

Metora now slumped into a chair.

"Does this idiot have any idea that we are facing annihilation? I can't believe this is happening," Kuring-gai ran his hand through thick hair that seemed to have more grey in it than ever before.

"When does this begin?" Metora asked Enin.

"In a few days. It's completely confidential at the moment. Zuke has his spies, but so do we."

"You should tell him where he can shove his trial." Kuring-gai looked directly at Metora before turning his attention to Oberon. "Or better, you do it. You're the last Sangrillion droid and the last link back to the Sangreal. Surely you can put a stop to this."

"I cannot change fate."

"I've always fought for my fate, but I just can't keep going on like this," Metora replied.

"Yes, we must fight for our fate. Good always conquers over evil in the end, if there is someone willing to fight for it. It is those battles in which an individual's fate is revealed. Some will die, some will live, and there is always great pain and loss before the certainty is finally won. I am a droid built to defend the defenders of the galaxy, and now they are all dead. I only fight now to uphold their memory."

"So, should we even bother anymore? There are days I want to leave this place and I know you do too, Metora. The war is lost and we will all burn as the world is set on fire. It's only a matter of time. And with these idiots in command, there can be no question of any victory. Xendalin may have championed the same strategy but at least he had no stomach for this backstabbing rubbish. I always believed in fighting for our miracle, but time is running out, brother. Your strategy and you as Sangreal could end this. I believe in you. The people believe in you! Most of my people are dead and most of yours too, Metora! It would take a miracle now to save us."

Metora looked at his friend, waves of emotion rolling across both their faces.

"I'm not going to let them destroy you. It's not right," Kuringai said before leaving the chamber.

There was a moment of silence after he left. No-one spoke, no-one made eye contact.

"I've never seen him so upset," Oberon said finally.

"We're all hoping for miracles," Lorian said.

"Have we earned a miracle?"

"Have we?" Lorian shrugged his shoulders.

Metora shook his head, his gaze fixed on some invisible sight out of the window.

"Even if I was Sangreal, that wouldn't mean all will be right in the universe."

"There's worse to come?" asked Lorian.

"I don't know. The philosophers of old had their ways of predicting a future, but I'm not one of them."

Metora breathed in deeply. He had calmed down somewhat but had no real mood to hang around anymore. He wanted to go home and tend to his garden and walk in his forest. There he could give himself some peace and quiet before the storm, even see Koree, like he promised.

"Oh, Nepta, who is that aide to Crowcraw? What happened to Dani? He worked for Zuke last time I saw him."

"Dani was killed in an accident and his replacement is Quisto, formally Zuke's command attaché. Before that, he was in the espionage branch. There's no trace of him before that time."

Metora let out another lungful of frustration.

"What is going on?" he mumbled.

"I wish I could give you more information, Sir, but I have yet to be given access to more secure files," Nepta apologised.

"No need to feel sorry Nepta."

Lorian felt bad to give Metora more bad news.

"Nepta and I have been given orders to return to Menenyr."

"Good. You'll be safe there."

"And you?" Lorian asked.

"I'll be alright."

Metora sat up in his seat while Lorian and Nepta made for the door. Lorian looked back at the Prince.

"Don't feel guilty over Ophistar."

"I won't."

Lorian smiled before he and Nepta went on their way.

Enin came and sat down opposite Metora, "So let's pull those nuts out of the fire."

ENEMIES

For over an hour, Metora and Oberon had been waiting in the guest-chamber. Enin had left to prepare for what was to come.

Metora didn't even want to think about it, he didn't even want to be here in this place. There were moments he just wanted to leave, but the ice under his feet was still cracking.

The new room they had been ushered to was known as the Admiral's House, even though it was only a large rectangular room. It had always been the main reception area for the commander of the Sangreal navy but was little used now. The former head of the navy and now Supreme Commander of the Bond, Admiral Zuke, preferred to use the larger and grander Imperial Hall to greet his guests. Using the Admiral's House was either a demotion for Zuke, which seemed unlikely, or an insult to Metora, as if he wasn't worthy of coming to the Supreme Commander's own residence.

Inside the room was a large group of officers from all branches and nations of the Bond. Many began to applaud and there was a triumphant *Herr, Herr* for the victor of Ophistar.

Many of those cheering were the young officers and veterans. It was also plainly clear that, for every officer cheering, there were those who didn't. Higher ranked officers, many veterans of old campaigns, were stone-faced.

Metora was surprised to suddenly see Kuring-gai emerge behind him from the crowd.

"I've been told to watch your back, remember?"

Metora smiled. He was glad for allies in this nest.

Gradually, the room went silent, and he felt this was a moment for a great speech. He shook hands with excited and polite officers but received only curt nods from other men and women in the room. It made him nervous, and he really wanted to leave.

He had only made his way through a small portion of the room when the guards at the other end of the room snapped to attention. Great doors opened and Admiral Zuke and his staff entered. He was in his full-dress uniform, his back straight and proud. It was like he had just returned from vanquishing an enemy.

"The victor of Ophistar?" Kuring-gai mockingly whispered close to Metora's ear.

"Ladies and Gentlemen!" Zuke called. "Our victorious rogues have returned from Ophistar."

Metora did not like the smile across Zuke's face. It was clearly forced. The glint and twitch in the corner of his right eye revealed the dam holding back his rage.

"Quite a victory for out fledging fleet. The spear is still sharp. Kaw now knows just what we are capable of and when he launches his attack, he will be in quite a bother."

There was polite applause through the room. Metora quickly

scanned the officers' faces. He was surprised to see that the roles had not completely reversed. Those that had not applauded Metora had still not committed to lauding the Admiral either. They remained on the fence, more confused than loyal to any side. The enthusiasm from the younger officers was clearly not extended to Zuke, a sure sign that these men had made their decision on what direction they wanted the Bond to take.

Zuke stepped closer to Metora and his party so that they were only an arm's length apart.

"Metora, once again you have proven your skills as a strategist."

Metora nodded, ignoring the dropping of his title.

"Kuring-gai, always a pleasure. Let us drink to our new conquest!" Zuke called out and raised a glass given to him by an aide, "To Metora's new strategy!"

"Herr, Herr!" the room boomed with the combined voices.

Once it was clear that there were no more speeches, the crowd began to talk among itself. Zuke breathed in deeply. He appeared to be a man with much on his mind who had been struggling for some time to bottle it in.

"Well, well," he began in a whisper. He turned to Kuring-gai, "This is no concern of yours, you are dismissed."

"I don't think so."

Zuke's eyes bulged. "Do as I order . . . oh well, I guess it's pointless issuing orders to you as you don't obey them. The War Council is beneath your station isn't it, Khoru?"

"No, only you."

"Kuring-gai," Metora warned.

"Yes, careful, as I still have some authority after your little escapade."

Zuke turned back to Metora, "You have no idea of the damage you have done, do you? None whatsoever."

"What damage?"

"You have overextended our forces!" Zuke's voice had risen so that those close enough looked over.

"Do I need to remind you that resources are limited as we try to extend Trinity to cover Astra Septum?"

Metora was aware that over the years Trinity needed expanding to cover the slow orbital spread of the planets as they circled Grotfer. They would drift apart for 73 years, reaching a climax of distance before reversing the cycle.

"We never took anything that was anyone else's," Metora replied.

"Intelligence has reported further Axis fleets moving out of the Chene system, massing for a counterattack, I would think. All that you have done will be lost, our fleet with it. It can't be replaced."

"I already know this."

"Oh, do you? You're nothing but a brat."

"Enough," it was Kuring-gai's turn to warn this time.

Zuke continued, ignoring him, "What am I going to do with you? I think a suspension will suffice, at my discretion. I have the backing of the Jashir's administration if you wish to object. Confer with them if you like."

"But the deal has already been struck," Metora smiled politely, hiding his anger at his fellow countrymen and Zuke.

It was Zuke's turn to smile now. "It would have been Idraeli all over again."

Metora knew the story of Idraeli. He was a high-ranking officer in the army of Anueth during the first battle for Palaniri. As the Axis advanced in long columns towards the capital city, Idraeli had seen an opportunity to counterattack. Orders to the contrary were sent to him but he defied them and ordered his forces to attack. He was not informed, as many officers were not, of the reasons, just to follow orders. The Bond commanders were tracking a second column marching to reinforce the first and Idraeli had sent his forces to attack right where they would join. He quickly found himself outnumbered and outgunned. The euphoria of the attack was swept aside and it turned into a rout. In shame, and to keep his remaining dignity, he could commit suicide and have his name quietly forgotten. It was not forgotten by the troops. Many were furious at his actions in hindsight, but also fearful, as this would be the fate of all who failed.

Metora had no doubt if he had failed then he too would have been forced to die by his own hand rather than face a court and execution.

"I've seen you've been quick to claim the victory as your own," Kuring-gai pointed out, privy to information that Metora didn't have.

If a snake could smile it would look as Zuke did now.

"Victory has many fathers, failure an orphan," Kuring-gai said.

The two men's eyes were locked as they tried to stare each other down. While saying nothing, the shadow of Oberon towered over them all. Zuke was very aware of it as his eyes continually darted up and back to Kuring-gai. Metora wasn't even aware Oberon would be coming.

"My authority must be kept. I cannot allow troops to do just as they please, especially fighting the war their own way. We must remain united, otherwise we will be divided and destroyed. You know this to be true."

Metora wanted to tell him that the dividing had already begun, but he was tired of arguing and Zuke wouldn't say he believed him even if he did.

"I will have your suspension certificate waiting for you by the time you return home and formal proceedings will begin soon after. You are also banned from discussing any of these matters with anyone. I really don't think your behaviour is at the standard of a general or a prince."

With that, Zuke turned his back on the three and moved away through the crowd.

They watched him, stunned at his words and revelations.

"I've had it with these pompous bastards," Kuring-gai was barely able to contain himself.

"Generals playing politics," Metora mumbled in reply.

He hated these dealings with a passion. His only mindset was victory and there were too many people looking out to save their own backsides or profit from others' misfortune. He had no doubt that Zuke was manoeuvring his way towards being nominated for Elector despite not revealing his hand yet.

Metora did not know much about Zuke's past. He didn't have much to do with Imperial Command matters. Zuke was probably only a child when Kaw first tried to overthrow the Sangreal. When he joined up, did he fight with zeal, or see it as an opportunity for advancement? Metora didn't know, but he would find out.

The three figures left the Admiral's House, slipping out the way they had come in, though it was hard for Oberon to somehow make himself invisible.

There was no chatter. Metora was deep in thought. He could now understand the warnings from Runamore in the years before the war. The philosophers had foreseen the doom of the Sangreal as more people became self-centred, greedy, and materialistic. It had even affected them. The pre-war culture of the Bond and what it had morphed into were alien to Metora. He knew only the way of the warrior. He could only read it at night when he was alone.

People's apathy and self-worth destroyed the common bond, humility, and the search for the simple life that had been the cornerstone of the Sangrillion Empire since the time of the Ethereals.

Power, wealth, and social climbing were the dreams of old generations. Souls like Kaw exploited those desires and few saw it for what it was. A charlatan dancing in the shadows, whispering pleasing words into soft, perfumed ears that demanded to hear more and closed its mind to anything else. Now, in hindsight, it was all too clear. Who was to blame when it was the movement of the time?

Now it was the cause of following generations to right the wrongs and finish off what had been started centuries ago.

Metora looked at the old men standing about him, their accusing eyes on him as he moved through Redsee so he could return home. It was their parents and grand-parents' generations that had caused this war. They had done nothing to stop it and now were telling him how to run it. In the past, the Bond had managed to survive and this had eased their guilt, but they now believed it would all be over soon. Was it anger veiling guilt?

The spiritual descendants of Rhianaihr, the first Sangreal and founder of the Order of Light, had abandoned this world and hid their home in a thick mist. Had it disappeared into the waters? Had it been simply destroyed as a last act of closure? There was no answer. All he had was the belief that somehow he would find a way to end this war. Alas, there were mounting days when he wanted to do as the Order had done —— vanish from this world and find a peaceful place to lay and rest.

Metora had returned home while Kuring-gai had decided to return to Dunmarra, the great Palaniri fortress. Oberon walked with him through the streets of Anueth City as they headed for the shuttle terminal. It was becoming dark and few people were about. Energy had been rationed for years in the city and many of the businesses and places were closed. As they walked, many of the lights went dark, making Oberon's bright blue eyes shine ever brighter.

"Why didn't you leave when the Order left?" asked Kuring-gai.

Oberon looked down at the man for a moment and said nothing. Kuring-gai stopped and looked into those bright eyes.

"You would have had your orders at the time but now, with them gone, why do you stay? Is it your will? Or . . . were you ordered to stay behind?"

"I have my orders and my will."

"I thought you were fighting for their memory, nothing more?"

"Would you prefer it if I did leave you to your deaths?"

"No."

Oberon continued to walk and Kuring-gai knew he would not get any further information from him.

They were silent as they continued. A passing patrol car would slow as they approached, no doubt their crews amazed to see the droid.

"What are we going to do about this situation? We're running out of time."

"Have you heard your ancestor's song?"

"No, not yet, but I think it's coming. I don't want to hear it Oberon, I'm not ready, things are still to be done. I can't leave Metora to fight in this snake-pit. What sort of friend would I be?"

"A loyal one."

Kuring-gai smiled.

"Enjoy your time at Dunmarra, spend time with your family, revel in their laughter and songs. Many scouting patrols have returned from deep space and I believe Mahalia will return soon."

Kuring-gai's heart beat fast. He hadn't seen or heard from his favourite niece in months. Another soul to worry about.

"Brutal times are ahead. Perreder has invited me to visit, which I will do soon."

"I'll tell him."

Oberon watched as Kuring-gai boarded the shuttle. He knew of the private pain of the Khoru warrior. His wife and children had been killed years before. They had been betrothed when they were little by their Elders. They always seemed to know when two souls would belong to another and would often travel across the continents meeting little children who they would try to pair up with their other half.

The Sangrillion droid left the terminal. While he walked, he multi-tasked as he researched a way to help Kuring-gai and Metora. He was linked to surveillance equipment which saw that Metora had sought shelter and was pacing about his room.

Lorian was sleeping soundly within Menenyr. All seemed well, but he knew better. Appearances can be deceiving. He didn't trust the city he had returned to. There were too many reports about assassins, spies, and a code that was beaming out from the city towards Axis-controlled space.

REVELATION

Kiam and Gilkasha were the guardians of the planet Kiam. They had never known how they had come to be there but trusted the Spirit and its wisdom. There was no memory that they had known any other place. Gilkasha had named it after his companion, for Kiam's beauty matched this world and she was one with the land and water.

For over a thousand years, they had roamed every continent and sailed every sea. The Spirit had taught them many skills of building and writing which they had in turn passed on to the people of this land. They were loved and honoured by the people and they returned that same love and honour.

Then the Spirit had asked them to produce children, which they had done. The Flame Trees were born and they were blessed with the same strengths as their parents. They had helped guide the people and turn Kiam into a thriving peaceful world.

It was almost sunset. Kiam was looking over the vast land from the balcony of their home. While the Ethereals had mastered lightspeed travel, they would still communicate telepathically.

"Kiam," came the voice of Ashlar, the strongest of all Ethereals.

Gilkasha had also heard it. Ashlar's voice seemed strained and broken.

"Thara has fallen," he continued.

Both Kiam and Gilkasha rushed to a purpose-built solarium to communicate with their brothers and sisters.

There was a ghostly image of Ashlar. He was seated and his head in his hand.

"What do you mean? What is this?" Kiam asked, shock and anger in her voice.

"He's on a murderous rampage. I had warned the old spirits about his intentions, but he's broken now."

"What do we do?" asked Gilkasha.

"There is no going back for him."

"Where is he?" asked Kiam.

"I believe he's coming to you. Do you think you can hold him until we arrive?" asked Ashlar.

Kiam nodded.

"Alright, let light be on you." Ashlar's image vanished.

They had waited and then mourned when they had received word that their fellow Ethereals, Latora and Nava, had been poisoned on Taranova while, on Mahnarosa, Soren had had his arm blasted off and Indra had been set upon by unknown assailants. They were both barely alive.

It was sunset when he arrived.

Kiam looked to Gilkasha. "He's here."

"He should be destroyed."

"I can't understand what has possessed him."

Gilkasha's grunt was half laugh and half frustration. "He was always proud and unbalanced."

"But never violent."

Gilkasha put her hand on her shoulder. "He has come to destroy us and claim this world for his own. The two of us will bring him before the Spirit and then his fate can be chosen. Agreed?"

She nodded. Hand in hand they went out into the fields to face him.

He was waiting, his eyes lit like red coals and his face twisted with venom and contempt.

"This will end now, Thara," Kiam called out.

Thara said nothing in reply but went on the attack. He was armed with a long spear that fired great, red light that blew holes in the ground where Kiam and Gilkasha had stood.

They split their attack, coming in from the sides at the same speed to meet in a collision of violent fury as all three fought, fists to fists.

Thara knew it would be difficult taking on both Kiam and Gilkasha but had not expected them to fight so hard. Gilkasha took his spear and broke it over his own knee while Kiam threw his body so far north that he landed close to the lava fields of Mount Ormum.

As he picked himself up, he knew their plan — force his surrender by driving him into the lava. He laughed to himself at such folly. He would not be that easy to subdue or destroy.

Again, Kiam and Gilkasha split their attack, swooping in from the flanks. The Ethereals had always been one with the lands and had control over nature. Thara used his powers to pull boulders of rock and lava from the fields that were spewing from the ground, woken by the unnatural war that was now waging.

Each was thrown towards Kiam and Gilkasha, which they dodged, but more came with growing frequency.

Thara'a attacks had the desired effect. He had gained time to think. The odds needed to be even and separating these two would be the only way he would win.

A great wind blew up, knocking him to the ground. Instantly, Gilkasha was on him, his weight pinning him to the ground.

"You need to stop."

Thara was furious and determined not to be beaten. The great demon that now clung to his soul lashed out with spite and hatred.

Gilkasha was thrown away. Thara quickly got to his feet and attempted to push him into the lava that was creeping closer. Kiam was wise to this move and threw rocks and dirt that again had Thara on the ground. He found himself being pushed closer to the lava flow.

Breaking the hold, he retreated to regain his breath. One small community was burning now as the lava erupted from the ground. Its people would never return to this place.

Kiam and Gilkasha crept forward, using the smoke from the burning buildings as cover, but Ethereals could always sense each other.

Thara had decided to take on Gilkasha. He was closer and had moved forward of Kiam. Dozens of small clumps of lava rose from the fiery river and were thrown rapidly at him by Thara. Even with the power of the Ethereals, he could not stop all of them. It took just one to pierce his chest and Gilkasha fell dead, his heart burned from his body by firestone.

Thara laughed at Gilkasha's sister's tears as she cradled her dead husband's body. He hated humanity, its kindness, and its dreams. The power that he possessed meant their only purpose was to be his slaves.

Kiam's tears had no effect on the searing heat that cut flaming rivers through the land, burned forests with firestone, and evaporated streams and glens.

Furious with grief and anger at her brother, she focused her own magic and collected the fallen stones. She built up a wall in front of Thara's approach. He thought it was a way to block him but when it started moving towards him, he knew it was to crush him.

He blew many of them apart but there were too many and he was struck on the chest and arm, throwing him to the ground.

Kiam then moved forward to end this mess when a mighty river of lava burst from the ground and flowed between them, leaving the two to stare at each from afar, both now too weak to finish the other off.

Thara left the battle scene without knowing the fate of Kiam, who he last saw on an island, surrounded by lava, with the body of Gilkasha in her arms. She was broken and he needed to regain his own strength to take on the others. He resolved to end her when he had finished them. That would be easier.

Plexus hovered over the hot plains of the equator of Kiam. The planet had been quickly conquered in the initial strike by the Dark

Lord as his armies burst out of the dark world and fell upon a surprised and bewildered Sangreal world. Her stunned Queen, Juney, had tried to form a guerrilla army while attempting to get as many people as possible off-world, but it all only lasted a few months before they were consumed in the fire and never heard of again. It had never been retaken by the Bond. They had never even tried. The planet's multiple moons and orbit made it difficult for any fleet to approach unseen and deploy for combat. All the moons were now dotted with battlestations and fortresses making it a suicidal mission for anyone daring to attack.

Since then, there had been relative peace on Kiam. The old buildings had been torn down and factories built. Striketroopers were built and trained in safety. Diamalords had their own instructional units. Massive shields and space stations guarded the approaches and shipyards. All was quiet on Kiam and Cryacur could only guess why he had been sent here. The Dark Lord had assured him that this business was old, long forgotten, and before the Sangreals and of the time of Thara.

There were only ever twelve Ethereals, all of them killed by Thara or his stooges thousands of years ago, and their graves were only known to those who dwelt in Runamore. Unknown to them, Iminus Kaw had found four of them and had been satisfied the stories were true and that the Ethereals were gone from the universe.

The Ophistar boy's blood had changed everything. Could a grave have been missed? Perhaps the Dark Lord had not found them all. To end the matter, he had sent his most trusted servant to find them.

The hot plains of Kiam were dotted with volcanoes that came

to life once a year, spewing ash, smoke, and lava across the land.

The boots of Cryacur cracked the dried mud that covered the hardened lava flows which covered the land. He had no information other than rumours from the population of where the grave was. There was a cave at the foot of a mountain which the locals would not venture into.

It was hidden in a ravine that seemed to be safe from most of the lava flows. Trees grew in the ravine and there was the colour of flowers and the smell of their scent in the air. He knew this would be the place.

A large boulder covered the entrance. His escorting Striketroopers quickly destroyed it allowing him access.

Taking one security drone with him, he entered the darkness. The tunnel was filled with plant life that recoiled from him as he passed. Some of the flowers withered and turned black.

The hovering drone's light was a long stab into the darkness of the tunnel. It was quiet but for the rustling of wilting flora.

Finally, the tunnel ended in a large chamber. The drone's light revealed two beds cut into a large rock that lay at its centre. On each was a body, seemingly uncorrupted by death. There were flowers everywhere that reacted the same as those in the tunnel.

After the drone had circled the chamber and deemed it safe, Cryacur approached the dais. He could see it was a man and woman. The flowers that grew around them recoiled in revulsion as he came closer.

The man seemed asleep. His hair was blonde and his face without lines. Cryacur looked for any damage in the man's chest but could see nothing to confirm it was Gilkasha. Surely it could be no one else.

He looked over to the woman. Her face was covered by the lightest white linen. Suddenly his drone was flung against the wall and exploded, its light replaced by an eerie, soft gleam that filled the chamber. Before he could react, the woman rose quickly from her grave and grabbed his throat and squeezed. Her body was so bright that it drained all energy from his body, buckling his knees and forcing him to the ground. There was no point in struggling as her grip on his throat was so strong.

"Your Master has forsaken redemption and his doom will see his soul entombed for eternity, as is the first enemy! You creature with no soul, cast together by blood and bone, born out of malice, and who knows no love, your fate will not be revealed today! I have a message for thee. Tell your Master that the curse so branded on his heart still sings his doom and the crown he wears with foolish pride will be cleaved from his head, for the champion has come!"

The Black Ash Prince had no chance to retort or react. He was thrown from the chamber, straight through the rock. He landed in the ash field where he threw up a great deal of dust. The hole in the cliff was gone, now replaced by rock, and invisible, entombing Kiam Lune and Gilkasha once more.

Cryacur climbed to his feet. The brightness of the chamber was gone, replaced with the heat of the hot plains. He rubbed his throat, quelling the throbbing pain as he stared at that cliff for some moments, musing over his anger and deliberating whether to destroy the mountain. Nonetheless, there were things to be done. He could tell the Dark Lord that Kiam Lune and Gilkasha had been found, and they were dead.

His ship arrived to take him to his next target. Rarely had he ever felt fear, but the words of Kiam made his own cold blood just that little bit colder.

The morning did not bring much joy for Metora. He had allowed himself only a small sleep in. Knowing there was a literal mountain of correspondence waiting for him to go through forced his hand.

Gregor had laid out breakfast with a communication board that held all the reports, requests, and other correspondence that had been sent since he had left Anueth.

Some of them had been marked urgent. The first was an official order from the War Council to appear before them tomorrow in a full assembly.

That wasn't good news. It was rare for all members to come together in the chambers. Usually, that was for very bad news, or when someone had done something very bad. Obviously, for Metora, it was the latter.

The second was from Enin Wolfcastle and it confirmed his fears. He could only breathe out in frustration. Worry flooded over him. He was so sure his strategy was right, but things weren't going smoothly. There was no doubt his name would be cursed by those who survived the final firestorm after Trinity collapsed.

On a positive note, he would be returning to his home. He would be able to relax there. As Metora scanned the list of names and agendas, he became more alert upon seeing a particular message. It was simple and direct. For a few moments he thought it over and then he contacted Oberon to meet him at the house. This day may turn out to be good after all.

The Prince didn't waste too much time in the palace, quickly dressing and grabbing some things before leaving.

As soon as he entered his home, he felt the outside world to be locked away. Everything had been repaired since the time a Wrydluk had entered his backyard causing a firefight.

The gardener, Oden, had certainly cleaned up the yard and planted more trees and plants. All traces of the firefight had been erased.

Metora went to the tree where the commodins lived and noted with joy that there were newborns among them. The mothers brought them out for him to see and hold. With the lightest touch, he patted and kissed the little heads of the mothers, who purred in return. He was now a proud grandfather and he shared the joy of the little creatures that seemed to have recovered after the stress and horror of the Wrydluk.

"Good morning, Prince Metora," Oberon said from behind him.

"Good morning, Oberon. Come see my new grandchildren," Metora beamed.

The droid stood close to Metora and the commodins looked up but had no fear. They were used to seeing the Sangrillion droid in the garden. Oberon's great eyes scanned the little family of grey, furry creatures.

"You will soon have to build new housing for them."

"True. Oden has planted another tree and I was thinking of putting the older ones in the forest, but I would worry about them. I might even take some for Koree to look after."

"You have news?" Oberon changed the subject.

Metora breathed heavily and put the commodins down so they

could run back to their homes.

"I've been summoned to a full War Council sitting tomorrow."

"So, they are pressing forward with charges."

"Well, considering the virtual treason I committed, why would there be another other way?"

"The army and navy will back you."

"Yeah," Metora replied quietly, "Let's take a walk through the forest."

Metora led the way along the path that led towards the great forest that bordered the rear of his home. There was no talk between them until they had the great canopy of the trees above them and the outside world was blocked out.

Birds chirped. A light breeze danced with the fingertips of the tallest trees. There was no war here in Metora's sanctuary.

"Have I done the right thing?" Metora asked.

"I believe so. It will make our military position a little more stretched, but the advantage to morale cannot be won any other way. Only victories against the Dark Lord's forces will build up the strength of heart."

"Will you come to the hearing?"

"Of course. Kuring-gai will attend also."

"Where is he today anyway?"

"Resting. He is approaching exhaustion."

Metora only nodded. He knew the stresses much of the Palaniri had and he faced losing another friend again.

"There's more. Do you know of the Councillor, Joviann Lor?

"She is a new Councillor from Oneum."

"She has requested a meeting far outside of the city."

"Where?"

"Here."

They continued, moving on through the forest. This area was restricted. It formed part of the Jashir estates that were bought for Metora when he first arrived on Anueth. Over the years, Metora himself has gradually increased the number of trees and tracks. He knew this place well.

"There is a figure approaching ahead," Oberon warned.

"Male or female?"

"Female."

Very quickly Metora could see a cloaked figure ahead of them with her back turned. Her hood was cast back, and he could see it was an older woman with long dark hair. She looked up at the trees and seemed to be listening to the sounds of the forest, a satisfied smile indicating her love of her surrounds.

She smiled when she was noticed and didn't take her eyes off them all the way until they were face-to-face.

"Joviann Lor?" Metora asked.

"Yes."

Her eyes were blue and were transfixed at the sight of Oberon.

"This is a magical place, Prince Metora. I can see why you come here to forget about the galaxy and its troubles."

"It's my little sanctuary."

"I'm glad you agreed to meet me."

Metora indicated a fallen tree that they could sit on. He had no fears. Oberon was alert and would take care of any trouble.

"I hope it's to your liking."

Joviann laughed, "I'm used to roughing it, as they say."

"So, where do we begin?" Metora asked.

"Admiral Zuke and Dulian Crowcraw."

Joviann waited for a response from Metora about the two banes in his life, but he had nothing to give except for the sour look on his face.

"I can see they are not to your liking. There are members of the Council who do not share their view and are more . . . inclined to your side of opinion. I should really begin with more about myself. I'm from a poor family on Oneum. Having an interest in politics at a younger age and love of all things of nature," she looked up at Oberon, "I was accepted into Runamore when I was six years old."

Oberon seemed to raise his height even higher at the revelation.

"You are a member of the Order of Light?" he asked.

"Yes, a junior member during the dark times. I fled with the survivors of my order into woods like these. There we regrouped and mused over what we should do. Some simply wanted Kaw to do what he pleased, believing it was a just reward for people's apathy. However, others were true to the ancient oaths and resolved to be the pillar of the galaxy once more. We stay secret but want to become more than a memory that people pine over, a gentle wind on the surface of a clear lake creating ripples that will eventually become waves."

"Where did the Order hide?" Metora asked.

Joviann merely smiled, "That is a secret, my dear."

"What about, how many of you are there?"

"Too few to fight a war or persuade the War Council, I'm afraid, but we will help you where we can. But we will need your help too."

"But if the Order makes itself known, that surely that will unite the Bond?" Metora said, looking to Oberon for his support.

"This is true, but it could also be destroyed quickly, especially if they are few in numbers," Oberon replied.

Metora appeared to accept the Sangrillion's reasoning.

"So, what can I do?" he asked Joviann.

"The Elector is old, and we don't trust his advisors. There is some veil about his aide Quisto. The records on him are scattered, but with the recapture of Ophistar we found mention of him during the civil war."

This raised Metora's eyebrow.

Joviann continued, "He was instrumental in making the war happen. He even killed the Chief on Elsenmere Ridge. This information has been buried and the only record is from the history of the battle hidden in the archives of the daughter of the Chief. Someone wanted this never to be known."

"But he doesn't look much older than me? How could he have fought then?"

"We can't explain it, but a man with the same name and description fought in that war, that is certain."

"I knew it. How can they be so stupid?" Metora said to Oberon.

"It would fit with the Dark Lord's strategy of spies and political disruption," said Oberon.

"Kaw has himself a spy right at the hand of the Elector of the Bond. Incredible."

"There's more. They have a candidate for a new Elector. As we speak, they are manoeuvring into position to have this person elected once Crowcraw is dead."

"Dead?" Metora mused over the revelation. "It all makes sense. Kill Crowcraw and have a puppet installed, then . . . it's all over. The whole political and military network would be paralysed. Units in the wrong place or misused, budget cuts, weak commanders promoted into command positions to weaken strategic and tactical moves. It's classic Axis fifth column tactics. What about Zuke? Is he an agent?"

"No, it would make it easier to explain his actions, but he can be easily manipulated. His passion for hating you is his undoing."

"I don't know what to do about him," Metora admitted.

"You have allies in the Bond, and you have to weather the storm. The problem is the fear gripping the War Council. They are counting the days until this 'endgame', as they call it. It is already fated for failure in their eyes."

"I was hoping the Ophistar offensive would ignite some passion, but it's done virtually the opposite," Metora cried out his frustrations.

Joviann merely smiled again and placed her hand on his knee. "It has shocked many in the Bond that the fleet can reach out so far and win. It's like going out in an acid shower and not getting burned. The Dark Lord is making his plans and so should we."

"Should we warn Crowcraw?"

"He is old and making him aware of it allows Quisto to know too."

"Then we should go to Sentinal and kill him." Metora looked at Oberon for further reassurance.

"No, that would create further tension and trouble for you. We are aware of what's going on within both towers and so we should prepare. We expect the death of Crowcraw soon and it may well be for the best. It will reveal Kaw's candidate and you, my friend, will have to be a good boy, as your support will be crucial."

"There are some who wish Metora to be Elector," Oberon said.

Joviann looked seriously at both of them, "There may well be advantages to that, but Metora's strength lies in the force of arms, not political games."

Metora managed a laugh at the blunt assessment of his skills.

"So, I'm a thumper not a thinker?"

"You know what I mean. You are the finest warrior of our age and master of the art of war, but politics is a dirty game and, during war, politics takes a backseat. People trust generals not politicians. The Order sees this as a step to regaining the prestige of Runamore. The Sangreal always had a champion to fight wars. Rarely was the Sangreal a warrior themselves."

"I don't like the idea of Kaw getting his claws into the Bond. True, if Crowcraw dies we will see his candidate, but we need to make sure this person is shut down and not allowed to interfere in military matters."

"I share Metora's apprehension about the Dark Lord's pawn," Oberon stated.

Joviann said nothing but looked at the ground, seemingly lost for words.

"What has brought all this about?" Metora asked, "The Rhianaihr left years ago and we've heard nothing and have received no help either. I thought you'd gone to another galaxy and started again."

"I'm told that something has stirred. I don't know what it is. I follow orders too. The Order of Light has not given up on protecting the systems of the Sangreal. I will see you in the Council chambers, Prince Metora."

With that Joviann stood up. She bowed before Oberon before walking back along the track she had come from.

When she was gone, Metora looked up at Oberon. "What do you think, Oberon? Is she the real deal?"

"The records do not show a Joviann Lor being a member of the Order, but she may have changed her name as protection."

"True. What a thrill to have the Order return. It may well be the strength we need to beat Kaw." Metora was beaming. He was glad for the help and in his heart knew that they were on the road to victory. He wasn't sure how, or when, but his faith had returned. There was just the matter of the Council meeting to attend to that brought him back to reality.

SECRET BUSINESS

The Axis reconnaissance fighter burst out of lightspeed, much to the surprise of Specialist Jonden.

"Damn it," she exclaimed to herself in a whisper as her systems lit up on detecting the intruder.

Jonden's surveillance hub was buried deep inside an orbiting asteroid that had been hollowed out of the rock. A specially designed, inner sphere kept the containment level while the asteroid spun in its orbit. Two other crewmates, Vivan and Marla, were off-duty in the lower levels, so it didn't get too lonely. The three-month rotations at times became a drag, however, as communication between Artari, as the asteroid was codenamed, and the outside universe, were strictly regulated to avoid detection.

Usually, they passed the time with little activity in their little piece of space. Vivan and Marla spent most of their time doing boring system checks. Vivan had plans to study engineering, while Marla was a combat veteran. She had been injured during the battle for Ophistar and ended up here, recuperating from her wounds. Being surveillance-trained made it a good place to heal and she didn't mind that one bit. Jonden was also a combat veteran who had lost a leg a few years ago. It had taken her months to get over the sight of her leg laying a few metres from her. The physical wounds healed quickly but the mental scars took longer. These little postings made her feel good, still valued, and useful to the Bond.

It wasn't unusual for Axis recon fighters to appear in deeper areas of space that were usually beyond Bond or Axis influence. The old systems of the Sangreal were surrounded and the Axis were now on the lookout for any ships escaping or trying their luck on the blockade.

Usually, it was small recon fighters like this Takeon that turned up. However, in other areas, larger ships, even the big battleships, were turning up on patrols.

It had been a few weeks since the last Axis ship showed up here. It had taken a few shots at the clusters of asteroids that were about and then disappeared. Vivan had been on duty then and had wondered whether Artari would hold up if targeted. Command had informed it could. It had no defences of its own and was purely a surveillance base.

Jonden was smart enough to know that the Bond didn't want Axis units sniffing around here. They were under strict orders not to shoot back, not to make unauthorised communications, and not to do anything that would give the Axis any reason to know they were there. They were to watch.

Therefore, she watched this Takeon glide about the asteroid field. It came close to Artari, too close really. Jonden found she was biting her thumbnail. It shot past, then looped back a few times, then vanished. She began scanning the system, making sure there were no others, or the same Takeon backtracking to catch people coming out of their hiding spots.

"Marla, we just had a visitor."

"Just one?" came the reply.

"Yep, I don't think he's coming back, so I'll call it in."

"Didn't use us for target practice?"

She laughed. "No, he must be taking his job seriously, or it was a droid ship."

"Yeah, no worries, call it in."

Deep underground on the planet Armana, Captain Mahalia Gray was checking the last of the approvals for her flight path. Being in the command centre with all its array of communication equipment and operators, she was privy to the communications coming in from Artari.

She had been here a few days, resting after coming in direct from Anueth. It was important that she didn't make the run too many times. It was a delicate dance, trying to dodge Axis fleets, and now these nosy recon fighters had started turning up sporadically.

It was a question of how many times they could run the blockade without the Axis becoming too suspicious. Orders had been not to engage with any Axis forces that were appearing in the running lanes. Better to remain silent then stirring up trouble.

"Concerned?" Captain Humel Crowcraw asked. He was the eldest nephew of the Elector and was still suffering from the burns he received in a cruiser crash almost five years ago. Humel was a great organiser. The physical and mental scars he had received kept him out of the ranks of the frontline, but he had found new purpose here on Armana.

"Not really," Mahalia replied. She had come to depend on Humel and he had become a surrogate uncle as he guided her on the best way to accomplish their mission.

"The few recon fighters coming this way tells me we haven't triggered any concern in Axis ranks. That's good." He smiled as he spoke, despite the scars across his face.

Mahalia had seen photos of Humel before his injury and he seemed a plump older man who admitted to loving his fair share of food and wine. Now he was a slim figure who wore a special mask that hid most of his face to shield it from outside contamination.

"We need to keep it that way, but these shuttle runs every quarter aren't achieving much. I've been thinking about increasing our runs, or at least doubling the ships during each run."

Humel thought it over for a moment. "There's room here but we'll need to start making plans on expanding without raising suspicion. It's too early to start moving on the surface. Still, doubling the shuttles would be better than increasing the number of runs. At least for now."

"I'll bring it up when I get back."

"I think it's safe to go."

"Okay, I'll get going." She hugged him.

"Good luck," he said while looking at her deeply.

"We're not having this conversation again, I'm going."

"See you next time," he waved and headed to the large shuttle in the hanger as she left the command centre.

He had told her plenty of times that he should be in Dunmarra heading up the operation, not here on Armana. Look at him. Physically he thought himself useless and that no person would want anything to do with him. He should be left behind to die as part of the rear-guard, not out here where it's safe.

Mahalia climbed into the cockpit alongside Dury, an older pilot from Jashir. He was a bit loose, as the term went for those who had seen years of action and were now erratic and without a care in the world.

"You ready?" she asked.

"We are ready. I heard we had a visitor."

"Yeah, but that's not unusual. We just don't want any more."

She took the controls of the shuttle and caught the last sight of Humel as he watched from the hanger door. He waved and she waved back.

There was no waiting to exit the planet's atmosphere before going into lightspeed. They couldn't risk it.

"Ready for jump," Dury called.

"Go."

The shuttle vanished into lightspeed, headed for its first of five markers where they would change course as they dodged Axis patrols and bases. The different course each ran was designed to hide their point of origin. Some markers were far from the war zone. The last one always made her nervous, but Dury seemed to love it.

He was smiling to himself and when he looked at her, he would raise his eyebrows in excitement.

"How close you gunna get it?"

"We'll see," she smiled back.

The shuttle came roaring out of lightspeed virtually on top of an Axis cruiser that was close to Trinity.

Both Dury and Mahalia cried out in shock, which quickly became cackles of laughter.

"I think you made the Captain shit himself!" Dury laughed.

"Exactly where I wanted it to be," she laughed back as she twisted the shuttle away from the totally surprised cruiser. It was a favourite tactic among some pilots but something that was difficult to achieve. Bringing a ship out of lightspeed metres from another ship gave many a pilot stomach cramps but, when it was done properly, it allowed a ship to zip past before the opposing one could even react. This time it was just a happy accident.

"He's a bit close, isn't he?" she said.

"Yeah. I think more than just the Captain would have shit their pants."

Trinity loomed up ahead. Blaster fire burst out from its battlements as they kept Axis fighters away from the shuttle. They had come out of lightspeed not far from the outer edge of one of the main lanes. Normally she came in even closer. No doubt the Axis cruiser was keeping an eye on this part of the defences. They'll probably send another, bigger ship, or more of them, to replace this one. Next mission she'd use a different lane, but the Axis were slowly shutting down each one. It would be something she would bring up.

"Home sweet home," Dury said as the blasters went silent and the shuttle began moving into the protection of Trinity.

Mahalia would much prefer to rest but she had her orders to come to Dunmarra and report. There were further missions to prepare in a short time.

Dury put the shuttle down in an old industrial complex. Much of it was overgrown and the buildings were old. During certain times of the year, it was used as a training ground.

"You rest up. I'll see you in a few days," she said as she climbed out of the cockpit, patting Dury on the shoulder as she went.

"Yep, you too," he replied as he brought the shuttle down on the tarmac.

Mahalia jumped out and ran towards one of the buildings that housed small shuttle craft. She made it from the tarmac just as it swivelled open to swallow up the shuttle and reclose.

She piloted the small, single-seat craft close to the ground. It wasn't a military craft and retained its red and gold paint, though it was wearing off quickly. She kept the hood down to enjoy the air through her long, dark hair, catching her green eyes in the mirror — her father's eyes and her mother's hair. Her mother was from Palaniri and now lived at Dunmarra, while her Oneum father had vanished years ago.

These quiet, solo moments were rare and she relished the chance to roar through the countryside. Being a pilot, she rarely got to see what other planets' surfaces were like. She'd been to Mahnarosa and Taranova, but never to Palaniri or Oneum. She'd been born on a cruiser out in space, so she felt space was her home, but the people who cared for her were here on Anueth.

Dunmarra lay far outside Anueth City. Many of the planetary enclaves were scattered around the continents to create room and as independent fortresses in case of invasion.

Much of the Palaniri fortress was below ground. Only the

many landing platforms, communication towers, and gun towers were on the surface, all surrounded by trees and wild bushland.

Her little craft flew low over a lake as she came in. The blinking lights from the towers ahead showed where to go. She pulled the craft onto a small platform where a number of other craft were parked.

The elevator took her down a few levels and brought her out into a large hanger area filled with mechanics and various fighters, all in some sort of repair cycle.

Perreder was somewhere in here. This meeting wasn't official, strictly secret business known to only a few of the Bond leadership.

As she walked through the hanger, she exchanged a few waves with familiar faces. There were a mix of planetary people here and she was surprised to see a few beings that were not from the Bond worlds.

Up ahead, she saw a group of officers and with them was Perreder, his girth and grey beard making him instantly stand out from the group. They were all busy talking and didn't see her approach.

"Am I interrupting?" she cautiously asked.

They all turned with bright smiles. Perreder gave her a hug, probably the most hands on of all the leaders she had dealt with over the years. She didn't mind.

"Welcome young one." He had pools for eyes, but they seemed filled with joy.

"Everything is going well. Did you get a chance to read my report?" she asked hopefully.

"Of course, we'll be talking about that, but there is something more important here for you." He smiled, then turned to his right where there was an older man with greying blonde hair. Her father.

Mahalia covered her mouth in shock. "No," she managed to exclaim.

Dekra held out his arms. "Mahalia."

She stepped towards him, and they embraced. "Fresh from Anarc. I thought I'd never see you again."

"You two have much to catch up on," Perreder exclaimed, "The days are yours."

Mahalia couldn't wipe the smile from her face, while Dekra wiped her tears of joy. Perreder watched them, his soul happy for them.

"So, what do we think about her suggestion? I think it can be done as long as we continue to keep our veil of secrecy and our careful schedules," suggested General Jumgarah, an older, female, Palaniri officer.

Perreder was thinking it over. "I think the same."

Alpha's office was among the Intelligence Agency, deep within the fortress of Tere Kaw, spartan but for several pieces of art, in particular the head of Larkudura. The latter had been an old enemy from his homeworld who he had hunted down and killed years ago. There it was, still preserved, with his anguish and pain frozen on his green skin features. Now lit only by soft light, most of the office was dark, for Alpha didn't really like the light. He was a master of shadow and subjugation who put his Master's ideas into plans.

He had spent the morning going through files on members of the Axis whose loyalty was in question. A routine purge was in the winds, but he questioned the timing with the Dark Lord's attack seemingly close. Could they afford to lose these officers? Maybe they should be put into suicide squads? That made him smile.

Now he was looking through recruitment files. Many Diamalords were eager to volunteer for espionage missions as they brought great credibility for promotion as well as personal ego. He was careful who he vetted. No one was to manoeuvre their way into his job.

"Sir, Master Kaw has ordered your presence in the command centre," came the computerised voice of his assistance droid.

"Understood," he replied and rose from his chair, striding from his office and into a lift. His brother, Omega, was already there. Alpha had remained uncommitted to Omega's interest in joining the Gorgoth.

"Where have you been?" he asked, though it came out as more of a demand.

"Interrogating," Omega replied. His voice was deep and brutal.

"Good." Alpha was satisfied his brother had returned to doing what he did best.

"We must be careful of our position here. The Dark Lord does not care for failure and we have never failed. You wanting to give it up to become a mindless killing machine when we still have work to be done did not impress me. Look at our Master, Omega, driven, full of purpose and controlled anger. What does a man go through to become that? I only know of rumours. Perhaps a woman, a wild childhood full of fear and hatred? The Sangreals believed that life creates what it needs, so why did life create a man like Iminus Kaw? And what a man. How many times has he been broken and yet come back from the dead to strike back at those who have harmed him or deny him what he wants? What do you want brother?"

"To enjoy myself."

Alpha chuckled at his brother's honesty.

"Indeed."

The lift opened and they exited, going through a control point guarded by four Gormarr with Diamalord commanders. These were not droids but human troopers. Sometimes it was hard to tell under the polished, black armour, but the height differences usually gave it away, plus the human mannerisms of speech and body movements. Droid Striketroopers did not carry these traits. The individualist designs of their capes also showed human design. The Gormarr themselves were trained in the same hellhole that the Gorgoth emerge from, all of them willing disciples of Kaw's sorcery. Droids could not be taught such craft.

The main door to the Dark Lord's throne room opened and they entered.

Kaw stood by a control centre and looked to them as they entered. He extended his arm out in a form of greeting.

"Does he enjoy himself brother? A man full of purpose, commander of the greatest of all forces this galaxy has seen, ready to see that purposed fulfilled. What do you think brother?"

Omega merely smiled.

There were a number of other droids with Zigma, along with officials and officers, which was unusual. Kaw normally kept his throne room locked down to many people. Alpha had been here numerous times and quietly felt privileged to have done so. It showed the confidence his Master had in him.

Kaw moved from where he was and strode up the dais to sit on his throne. The brothers waited at its bottom, bowing as their Master took his position.

There was already a female figure kneeling, who now stood.

She was an older woman of average height. Her naturally blonde hair had streaks of dark red and her eyes were bright green. The white of her pants and jacket were a visual clash to the darkness of the throne room.

Nash Beren had served for years in espionage cells in various planets. She was a gifted diplomat, highly intelligent, and determined in any mission given to her. However, unusually for many of Alpha's operatives she had become pregnant and had spent time raising her child. Her name had come across his desk almost a year ago and he had his agency contact her.

Their Master had a deep passion for insurgents and shadow games. Alpha was not a military man but he had seen the frustration of many officers over the continued failure of many of the great offences. Torm Dor, the great encirclement strategy, had worked, but Trinity was still a difficult obstacle to overcome. And so, he had developed another solution. The Bond was already rotten and weak. It just needed more of a push for it to fall over.

For most of the year he had Beren training for her new mission. His proposal had been put before Kaw and now she had been presented to him.

"Do you think my armies will not break Trinity?"

"They will, my Lord, but it will not be easy. Our agents have had great success in the past assisting in conquering other systems. Nash Beren will not fail in her mission."

Iminus Kaw watched them, his eyes hidden under the frame of his cloak and the metal grill that covered the lower half of his face. Nash stood firm, a wry smile across her face.

"Have it done."

"Your will, my Master," Alpha replied as he bowed low. Omega and Beren copied him.

Then the three turned and left the throne room. Behind them, Kaw's throne swivelled around as the massive screen behind him came to life and filled with the face of the Black Ash Prince.

TRIALS

What more could he do? Metora thought to himself. He felt so angry and exhausted that he could do little else but stare at the arranged chamber that would hold his accuser Zuke and other members of the Council.

As they entered, he stood with his defence team, just a single lawyer, Enin Wolfcastle, daughter of the Chief himself. She had been wounded in battle when she was younger and been unable to return to full duty. While recuperating, she had taken up studying law and offered her services after her father had discovered Metora's predicament.

"Are you nervous?" he whispered without looking at her.

"Are you?"

"I've got better things to do."

"Well, this is my first time in such a high-profile case. I hope I don't stuff it up."

"You'll do fine, Enin."

Metora continued to watch the men and women file in, thirteen in all, including Zuke. Many wore decorations and he recognised some, like Hiro Null and Wearah Zeep, both from Mahnarosa and former combat officers. Both he had known through the years. The others he had the briefest knowledge of but believed he could count on for support. There were others on the Council who owed their spot to Zuke, and they were his biggest worry. Officers like Garish and Hera Farnbar, husband and wife, were close associates of Zuke. Promoted above their abilities, their continued bad investments in technology had served no purpose but to line their own pockets.

Metora could not fathom such people. Complete annihilation of their way of life was at stake and had been for almost two decades, yet their concern was for following orders and selfish monetary schemes.

No doubt all of them had been reading the report prepared by his staff and sent yesterday about the battle of Ophistar and its future use to the Bond. There was also the counter claim from Zuke. It bit deep, calling Metora hot-headed, even incompetent in managing large forces of troops on the strategic and tactical level. It was either rumour or exaggeration and if the world were to end in three seconds, he would gladly rip Zuke's head off.

The more he thought about all this nonsense the more he hated this place. Would it change if he were Elector? Would he even care if he was? He hated the machine that the Bond had become.

His mind-wanderings were interrupted by the call to order from Zuke, who ran proceedings. Metora and Enin sat once the Council had. Metora immediately began to shift back into his thoughts but couldn't completely ignore the opening statement from Zuke as he half-heartedly listened.

"High treason, endangering lives, endangering the security of the Bond, overextending the military strength of the Bond in a way that could weaken our position, these are the points I have made in my report to the Council. Prince Metora has acted recklessly in using our limited resources for his own person agenda . . ."

Metora had had enough. He couldn't hold his anger any further.

"Personal agenda? You dirty arse. I'm the only one ready to stand up to Kaw. Your lot want to discuss every minute detail in committees that are only pursuing your own agenda, Admiral."

Enin tried tugging on Metora's jacket, a silent plea for silence that he ignored as he wasn't finished.

"The extinction of our world is on us. There's no escape for us with this mindset. Wake up!"

"Again with this argument!" Zuke exploded. "This is what I have detailed in my report to the Council. Repeated arrogance and disdain for authority. We are here debating your future and you have completely shown to the Council the accuracy of my opinion. I should just sit down and let you go. You have to remember that you must do as I order."

"Even if that means we all die?"

There was silence.

"We will hold on," Zuke said with clenched teeth.

"For what? For Kaw to get too tired or find some other galaxy to conquer? You must be out of your mind to think he will stop. The Axis fleets are ready. The battle for Ophistar was only the last act."

Most people in the room were open-mouthed in shock as the

Prince of Jashir and Admiral of all Bond forces were now locked in a heated argument. Their eyes darted about nervously wondering where this was going to go and who would put a stop to it.

"We are not here to discuss the strategy of the War Council, only your actions."

"Then it needs to be discussed."

"Why? What is this really about? You want to usurp me, Metora?"

Metora stared him down. "No. I should have the chance to explain the time it has gained us."

"What has it delayed? Nothing! By your own reckoning, the recapture of Ophistar will be pointless, we will be swamped and Ophistar will be recaptured anyway."

This was true. It had now dawned on Metora that Kaw didn't need Ophistar anymore. It was a bitter pill to swallow. Had he really let a real chance for the people of the Bond to survive slip away?

"First we will discuss your actions, and then we must consider the actions of members of the Bond who are still refusing to return to Bond space."

Metora knew this. Zuke was trying to get the fleet back from Ophistar, effectively abandoning the planet to the Axis.

Metora moved to sit down, a sudden sense of glumness came over him as the pendulum of victory swung Zuke's way.

Enin stood up, "Councillors, Prince Metora has served this Bond well and his opinions and actions should be heard. We apologise for our passion, but we should continue." She looked at him, pleading with her eyes for him to stand down and apologise.

"We can move on when we hear it from him." Hera Farnbar pointed her stubby fingers Metora's way.

He understood and took a breath. "I apologise to the Council, I'll sit quietly."

Hiro Null spoke first. "This is true. So, let's all cool our heads."

Enin sat back down and leaned over to whisper in his ear, "What do you want me to do? They want to charge you with treason. This is a death sentence normally. It's only your rank and station keeping you alive."

Metora knew he had crossed a line, well, at least was close to it. It was clear on the faces of his allies. Some were frightened, some faked it, some were accusing or held sympathy, even a plea for him to stop.

"Can we work out a deal? I'll stand down as commander of the Jashirn forces, take a holiday, self-imprisonment, anything, just to get this over with."

"Are you sure?"

"Enin, I've had enough of all this rubbish."

"Ok, I'll raise the point. Hopefully we can stroke Zuke's ego enough to satisfy him."

Metora nodded his agreement and returned to his mind-wanderings.

"Councillors, Prince Metora has offered a deal, if we can discuss this during a recess."

The Council members looked surprised. "Agreed," Null said.

Metora didn't move. He really needed someone's advice as he felt completely lost. Kuring-gai had become a close friend over the past few months but he was not political motivated, despite his kind heart. He would ask the King of Anueth, the man who had virtually raised him since leaving Jashir.

Inside the chambers reserved for their use, Enin was the first to talk.

"What was that?!" she said with a mixture of anger and admiration.

"I was a bit angry," he replied as a half-hearted apology as he tapped in the request to speak to King Leigh through Nepta's net. The droid had been waiting patiently in the chambers for them to return.

"A *bit?*" Enin laughed.

"I take it things aren't going well?" Nepta asked.

"Oh, a bit, Nepta, they're going well a bit," Enin said as she slumped into a seat, her computer tablet on her lap. She thought for a moment then began to get to work silently.

"Sir, there's been no reply from the palace. Oh, wait, now it's here. Yes, the King is at the shipyards reviewing crews."

"Damn it," he looked to Enin, "What do you think?"

She shrugged, clearly annoyed at her client's behaviour. "What do you want to do?"

Metora looked up at Nepta. "I really hope I'm not messing things up, but it has to be done. For my own sanity."

Lorian and Kuring-gai had waited outside of the sealed Council room, hoping at first to get in to offer their support to Metora. Finding the way blocked, they had waited for him to come out, but there was no sign of the Prince.

Kuring-gai didn't like to hang around too long so he

convinced Lorian to take a walk along the promenade to get some fresh air.

Lorian hadn't had a real chance to explore the capital city, while Kuring-gai knew it well. People were out going about their business, as they always seemed to be in cities.

He had been telling Kuring-gai all about Menenyr, his new duties, and the new friends he had made since joining.

"Good, very good," he laughed even though, with Metora's predicament, it was possibly in bad form. He was enjoying hearing the youthful experience of Lorian's joy at his new life. It made him forget his own troubles for a little while.

They came across a café type eatery where several soldiers were sitting about drinking and eating. They found a table and received two drinks from a server droid.

"What will they do to him?" Lorian asked.

Kuring-gai shrugged.

"I feel sorry for him. He's still passionate but there's a lot of anger there. And despair, lots of despair."

"I see a lot of that."

"Sometimes I just want to leave and go home. It's hard to keep going. But I'm loyal to my people and those who want to keep fighting. I can't abandon them."

Lorian deliberately lowered his voice as he didn't want anyone else to hear.

"Do you think we can win?"

Kuring-gai shrugged again, "Part of me doesn't care anymore. We're finished."

Lorian was shocked and saddened at this revelation. Kuring-gai must have seen it in his face.

"You never know, we might get that miracle."

"Looking at the odds, it doesn't look good, does it? Better to die on our feet than live on our knees."

"I'll drink to that," Kuring-gai clinked his warm brew against Lorian's glass.

"Hopefully I'll get back and walk into Warrawul where my fathers wait."

Lorian was aware of the great forest where the Palaniri buried their dead. He found it a fascinating story how a people could sense death and travel to Forla Bandula, and then into the forest, never to be seen again.

"I've been reading about Palaniri and Indra."

Kuring-gai smiled, "A mighty Ethereal. We're all descended from her, and we curse her children that poisoned her and gave us this pain of an early death. Those stupid Gunadar. They can burn on whatever world they've ruined."

"A few thousand desert every year."

"Yes. We do our best for them."

"Fate is a curious thing, isn't it? Look at us. We were prisoners on our own planet, but we came back. We were patient and planned, then opportunity came along, which we took. If the Axis hadn't invaded, then Ophistar would still be neutral and the Bond wouldn't have been given a second chance."

Kuring-gai eyed the young man deeply.

"And if Thara, all those thousands of years ago, hadn't turned into a wicked creature, then what would today look like? Feels like a beast feeding on itself for generations, and now we are left at the end of all this mess."

"I believe we can win."

Kuring-gai was impressed. If only there were more young ones with fire in their bellies who had the rank to change the cause of the war. It would be a tragedy to have the Bond crushed, but a greater sin to throw away the chance for victory through incompetent leadership.

"You've got my attention."

Lorian let go an embarrassed laugh, "That's the question, isn't it? There's too much defeatism in higher places. People are afraid. We must regain our fire and know that there is hope. There is a will out there in the universe, even rules, just like there is in war. If you follow the lore, then you can be certain of victory,"

"What have you been reading?"

"It's an extension of my studies. Warriors have schools of thought. Even the old Rhianaihr had the same. Those old leaders lost their way. They forgot the lore, Kuring-gai, just like if you or I ignored the rules of war. Then we lose, right?"

"True. Victory needs sacrifice, rules, belief, plus a bit of luck."

"Luck plays a part. Imagine all those battles that would have gone the other way if certain things just didn't happen the way they did. Like an army arriving a few minutes too late, ships breaking down or getting lost and not ending up where they were needed at the right time. Chance is a funny thing."

"Metora has told me you are a gifted strategist. Now I see it for myself."

Lorian smiled. "Not much use for a flight Lieutenant," he shrugged.

This brought a chuckle from the Khoru veteran. "It's hard to be an optimist in an ocean of pessimism. What do you think of the vanishing of the Ethereals magic from the galaxy? Why don't we, as their descendants, possess these skills?

"I don't know, I've never thought of that. The Ethereals were created for a reason, and they had special skills we don't. Their children, on the other hand, did have those powers, but their descendants are rare, probably all dead."

"Indra would write that all our souls went back to the Spirit. She was secretly jealous that we did while she was bound to life and her duty. I hope her soul found its way back to her father. Sadly, that power died with her and we'll never get it back."

Lorian had never discussed his inner thoughts with anyone. He rarely had the chance on Merenmere, as he was too shy to express it. Sitting here with Kuring-gai, he found new courage to engage in such a debate.

"It's a funny thing, belief. Two people could have opposite views that clash with each other, but both believe they are right. Who wins? The strongest? The most cunning? Is our universe created on 'good always conquers over evil'?"

"Does evil thrive when the good do nothing?" Kuring-gai offered with a smile.

"Exactly. And how about nations at war, with opposite ideals. How does the universe decide who wins? Or the ones who follow the universal lore?"

Kuring-gai stared at the boy with incredible eyes.

"Where have you read this?"

Lorian shrugged, "In the library. But I've been thinking about it for some time. It's just that other people have asked these questions before me."

"Yes, they have, many people and long ago too."

"It gives me a headache," Lorian laughed.

"True, but it's all good, sins of the fathers, Lorian. You are talking about the Mable Cycle. Philosophers have long believed this very thing, that evil and good follow each other, just like the movement of the stars and planets through the universe. There are times of calm, and then there are times when evil will dominate, then good conquers. We saw it with Thara, then a thousand years of peace, then Kaw. Did Thara get what he wanted? No, he lost it all. Did he follow the universal lore? The question is, will Kaw get what he wants, or will we be the generation that brings about his downfall, or will it be in decades to come? And will there be another Dark Lord in another thousand years?"

Lorian took in Kuring-gai's words and was not surprised that someone else had already had a thought process and probably answers to the things he was thinking. He now had more to study.

"If the Rhianaihr still existed, they would have snapped you up."

Lorian smiled at that idea. He probably would have been part of the Order of Light. Yes, he would have liked that, but it was not to be.

"I hope you get to cross into Warrawul."

"Thank you, brother, and what would be your paradise?"

"The Merenmere believe that Ashlar holds our destiny. I don't know. I just hope everyone finds theirs."

"That is an unselfish thing to say."

"Well, maybe someday Ashlar will tap me on the shoulder when its time. I try not to think about it."

"Good. That's a wise thing but also a hard thing to do."

Kuring-gai nodded slowly. He was intrigued by this young

man. Wise for his age yet still naïve to the universe's suffering. Completely clean of all baggage and problems older people seem to accumulate before they die. He hoped the universe would not crush him.

The crowd around them started moving, a sign that the hearing was resuming.

"Time to go back and see what the damage is," Kuring-gai announced.

Metora has spent the rest of the recess sitting with his tablet, seemingly withdrawn temporarily from the galaxy as whatever he was concentrating on gave him some escape. Enin had worked a draft of a proposal as she conferred with Jashir commanders. Many of them were not happy with what had transpired earlier and begrudgingly agreed to the conditions. Colonel Halkinbraun was even vocal about his distaste for the whole process. In the end, it was done. Now they waited.

Metora's distant mood continued while Enin was kept busy with correspondence with the War Council. Finally, he seemed to pull himself somewhat into reality by closing down the tablet and looking out at the city, still seemingly far away, contemplating his actions and regretting them, then convincing himself they were right, then countering that, and on and on until he felt physically sick from the stress. He was ready to accept his punishment as in this hour he no longer cared.

Enin finally returned with a smile of triumph.

"Sire, you're in luck. I've got us a deal."

Metora came alert and sat up, "What's their decision?"

"An apology to be made today, then suspension, with you stepping down permanently as head of Jashirn Forces."

"Do they have a replacement?"

"Not that I'm told."

Metora had no doubt Zuke had been franticly trying to find *his* man to fit the position. The wily old Admiral would then have control of the armies of Jashir. Metora could almost hear his crying out *at last!* as he laughed with pleasure.

"How long will the suspension last?"

"Zuke's discretion."

Metora let out a breath of frustration.

"I'm sorry. It's the best I could do."

"It's not your fault, Enin. You did good. So, let's get this show on the road."

They didn't have to wait long before Zuke appeared at the head of the table, now looking very pleased with himself. The hint of triumph was quickly veiled by a false sense of solemn duty as he called Metora's name.

"Please stand."

Metora did so.

"As outlined by the actions on Ophistar, this court of enquiry finds you guilty of reckless treason. You are to step down as Commander-in-Chief of Jashirn forces, effective immediately. You are also suspended from operational duties, effective immediately. Is there anything you wish to add, My Prince?"

Metora stared at the older man. It was clear this was an indication that it was time for the apology. The Prince gathered his thoughts.

"Councillors, my actions have proved to you to be reckless,

and it seems a pointless exercise that has led to the weakening of our position. I have wasted the lives of my warriors and ships. The Admiral's orders, I have disobeyed and ignored. I have let my passion outweigh critical and deliberate safe tactics. But I would do it all again."

There was an immediate outbreak of huffs and mutterings mixed with a few chuckles from the assembled crowd and Council. Metora never took his eyes off Zuke, whose former victorious self was now full of scorn.

"Then the Council must deliberate further on your future, Metora," he finally replied.

Enin was quick to jump to Metora's defence, "Admiral, you can't. The Council has already made its decision. It is beyond its power to simply chop and change matters to suit a person's ego."

"How dare you!"

"Councillor is correct," a female member of the board spoke. "Judgement has been passed and cannot be altered. We will not alter it."

Many of the Councillors expressions reflected frustration and a desire to have the matter dealt with, as they thought it had been before Zuke's sudden desire to go around again.

It seemed to end the matter, but the whispers went on. Zuke had been restrained but he was still biting at the bit. He sat back down in his seat, his eyes red hot coals full of hatred for Metora.

"I think we're done, but that probably didn't help," Enin whispered to Metora.

"It was worth it," he whispered back.

"Council is dismissed," Zuke finally said before quickly leaving the chamber followed by the other Councillors, some of whom were openly chuckling to themselves.

Metora sat there for a moment, just taking it in. There was a sense of a burden being lifted, but he wasn't sure what that was. Was it being fired from his post? Or finally, and publicly, telling Zuke what he exactly thought? Whatever the reason, he felt relief.

Nepta followed him from the room and out into a public foyer where Lorian, Kuring-gai, and Enin were waiting. Kuring-gai was laughing with Enin. No doubt she was telling him what had happened.

"Did that feel good?" he asked.

"It did, but I hope I haven't made things worse. I don't know how the troops will take it. Word will get out eventually."

"What will you do now?" Lorian asked.

Metora only shrugged, "Rest at home. What else can I do?"

"Conspire?" Nepta asked.

They all looked at her, wide-eyed. Metora laughed.

"Maybe she's right," Kuring-gai added with a wily grin.

Metora didn't want to be drawn into the subject and shook his head.

"Oh, that's how you start trouble?" Enin quizzed the Palaniri man while also eyeing off Nepta. "I'll be heading back to the office. You'll be okay?" She asked Metora.

He nodded, "Sure. Thanks for your help and putting up with me."

"Well, you know where to find me and I don't think this will be the last time."

After Enin had said her goodbyes, they began walking from the foyer to the shuttle hanger that held Metora's craft waiting to take him wherever he needed to go.

"You probably won't see me for a little while. Might be good to keep a low profile."

"Zuke will be pushing his people onto your command staff like a disease you can't cure," Kuring-gai noted sourly.

"Well, they'll push back. I need a break anyway."

"You'll be back refreshed and with new ideas. Maybe it's a blessing in disguise," said Lorian.

He already had plans to wander in his forest for hours and check on his many animals and plants. There he could be away from the war for a little while until it erupted again, as he knew it would.

"They'll call you again," Kuring-gai said.

"I know. But whether I'll be there to answer it is another tale. Stay safe you two."

With that, the Prince boarded his shuttle and left the building.

Metora's first stop would be the Royal Palace where he would collect some things. He would also alert his staff of his intentions to return home. Then? Then he would go and see his little niece. He promised her that he would see her.

He was greeted in the palace's hanger by Halkinbraun, who had a deep grimace on his face.

"This is a disgrace," he spat his contempt.

Metora only smiled. He didn't have any more words but was encouraged by the soldier's defiance. There were tears and tense words of rebellion. They moved quickly through the halls of the palace as Metora wasn't intending to stay long. He would relax at his house before making his next decision.

"We can discuss all this later, Colonel. I need a rest, I really do."

"I understand."

King Leigh appeared behind them and put his arm around Metora's shoulder.

"You've had a rough day. I'm sorry I couldn't talk when you needed me."

"What's done is done." Metora replied.

They continued to move through the palace's corridors, passing guards as they headed to Metora's quarters.

"You're leaving? Is that wise?" the King asked.

"I don't know. I just need a rest."

"Sire, your shuttle is ready, and I have alerted Bannade House."

"Thanks, Nepta."

They had almost made it to his quarters when a strong wind came up and rumbled on the outside windows. The room suddenly became darker and all of them could taste charcoal.

"What is it?" Leigh asked, but only received blank stares.

There was a sudden crash of glass coming from the mirrored room.

Guards ran in first, followed by Leigh and Halkinbraun. Metora lagged behind, a mixture of curiosity and annoyance as he was keen to be on his way.

There was a figure, tall, cloaked in grey, with a ruined crown on his head. Great shards of glass covered the floor where one of the panels had been smashed.

"It's him," Halkinbraun whispered.

Metora was not sure who he meant, but then came to the realisation that it was Iminus Kaw himself.

Kaw's head slowly turned to face them. His eyes were burning coals cemented within a white, porcelain face framed with long white hair, both devoid of any colour.

"Look at me! The work of your fallen idols," he growled.

He seemed to grimace in pain and when he breathed the air itself seemed to be smoke.

"Now you know what it is like to be betrayed. Don't you just want to burn them all," he smiled menacingly, a long-pointed finger directed at Metora.

"What . . . what do you want?" King Leigh stammered.

Kaw looked at them. "I was threatened with ancient foreboding, so I will threaten thee. *Where is this champion?* So I can crush the life from its body and throw it at their feet when they think they can destroy me."

"Who?"

Kaw grumbled in contempt, "I never believed it was you, Metora, but perhaps I need to look at you in new light."

They eye-balled each other for a moment before Kaw struck. Great bolts of fire shot at them, striking Halkinbraun and Metora, who both fell to the ground. Kaw came in close to finish them when Oberon entered the room and began firing at the great mass of Kaw's form. He recoiled in pain, retreating to the mirror side of the room.

"You belong to me, Sangrillion!" Kaw screamed.

"No."

"There is no champion, no more Flame Trees, and no hope for your corrupt bond of men. Liars! All of them! Darkness is where power lies. Your time is over. Now it is my time. Even you cannot beat all my sons, Oberon."

Metora, wounded, managed to stand up.

"Like a disease that will not die," Kaw spat his words at Metora. "Your brother will seek you out, or maybe my Prince will be the one to break your body into pieces. Look at your final despair!"

Kaw raised his hand and the black curtains that covered the remaining mirrors were burned away to reveal images of burning cities and piles of burning corpses. Great ships on fire fell through the sky and crashed into the ground. Images of the Gorgoth hunted down people and killed them where they stood. It was dreadful bloodbath that was only ended when Oberon fired at all the mirrors smashing them in a wave of glass.

Kaw laughed. He held out an open hand and mimicked crushing invisible object within his fist.

"We will fight on." King Leigh, determined, faced down the Dark Lord.

Another crack of lightning broke from Kaw's hand and burned right through the King's chest. He fell to the floor.

"You have nothing in your arsenal to defeat me. Throw your bodies at us. Throw your hope away! Then you will understand my thirst for revenge is stronger than your will to live!" He laughed and looked at the broken glass.

"Now no one will know their fate, Oberon."

"You already know yours. Leave now."

"No, I want to watch Metora die, and then I will be satisfied that the lies of the Ethereals still ring after a thousand years."

Oberon stood guard while several guardsmen helped Metora and Halkinbraun from the room.

Oberon's arm was out, giving Kaw a quick, *come on*, motion with his fingers. The Sangrillion had no fear of Iminus Kaw, but the Dark Lord would not take the bait.

"See you on the battlefield, Oberon."

Kaw vanished, leaving only the clinkering of broken glass and the scent of burning.

Metora slumped in a chair looking at the dead body of Halkinbraun. The fire bolt had struck his shoulder, while Halkinbraun had received a hit to the head, killing him instantly. Royal guards carried King Leigh's body in. Nepta followed, her silver glaze burned and damaged as she had been thrown against a wall.

"He's gone," Oberon declared as he came in.

"I'm going back home. Are you able to stay there for a few days?" Metora was afraid and didn't want to be alone. He didn't want to stay here either. His emotional walls were crumbling and this was not the place for them to collapse completely. He would do that in private because he wasn't sure what would happen when they did.

"I will."

Lorian dreamed. The woman danced across a lake, her toes grazing the water with a light touch which sent a ripple across the water. Her white skirt was a heavy wind flowing around her as she twirled about.

Deep from the brooding lake, a blackened hand shot from the glassy surface. It was broad, scarred, and with one deadly strike it gripped her throat. A massive head emerged from the water, its eyes red as boiling pools of darkened blood. Without a sound, without a cry for help or victory, the figure pulled the dancer under the water and neither emerged as the lake settled to glass once more.

When Lorian woke, he was more annoyed than frightened. These constant dreams meant something; they weren't spawned from some personal fear deep in his conscious. For a moment, he took a breath, trying despite being still half asleep to find a meaning to the riddle. There had to be an end and for some inexplicable reason he was drawn to Runamore, the old fortress of the Rhianaihr, lost among the fog of the lake of souls. He would go there. Tonight. Now.

He dressed and left his dormitory, heading straight for the flight wing where he climbed into a speeder.

It was cold in Anueth now as the systems of the Bond moved away from Grotfer during the winter season, part of the cycle of Astra Septum. It rarely snowed in the city, but to the west, where Runamore stood, it was moving into a deep freeze. The moons of Anueth glowed bright on the mountains surrounding the city as he came out of the fortress heading west.

"Destination inhibitive," said the computer's voice on the speeder.

"Why?"

"No coordinates."

"I gave you coordinates. Lake of Souls, bearing 25 by 750."

"Destination inhibitive," the computer responded again.

"Give me manual," Lorian said as he began to take the speeder's controls.

He had wanted to use the time to study the layout of Runamore as it was known before its disappearance on the speeder's computer. Now he had to fly.

As he cleared the mountains and saw the massive blur on the radar screen that signalled the thick mist across the lake, Lorian took a moment to gather his thoughts. It was crazy to fly straight into the fog so he looked for a place to set down so he could figure out a way to get to Runamore.

Finding a small field, he put the speeder down. The ice on the grass cracked under his feet as he took a few steps away from the craft, his viewfinder to his eye scanning the mist.

"Nothing," he said to himself as he realised his scanner could not penetrate the natural field sitting over the lake.

Then he got an idea. The speeder, an AX560 type, could move over water. It was slow, but he didn't care.

Reboarding it and setting off, he set it down at the lake's edge and hoped for the best. Satisfied the speeder would float, he began to move the craft cautiously into the mist.

It was impossible to navigate. The stars had disappeared, he had lost sight of the mountains and moon, his radar was a simple blur, and he couldn't see any further than the bow of the speeder. He could only rely on dead reckoning and hope he was able to at least make it back alive.

There was nothing for Lorian to do but press on, despite his rising panic. When the loud rumble of thunder and the crack of lightning were heard about him, only then did Lorian begin to really doubt his strength to go where no man or droid would choose to go.

"This was really stupid."

The lake's water began to churn, pushing the speeder on a steady climb up and down small waves that were gradually getting bigger.

More lightning cracked across the sky and penetrated the mist. Then it began to rain and the water churned more violently. Lorian wasn't sure how tough his speeder was but knew it would not be able to handle a wild storm. He was also beginning to get sick from the motion.

Frustrated, he decided to end it and began to pull the speeder into the air. It wouldn't go, however. A wave came crashing over him, flooding all his instruments, and almost forcing him from the seat.

Now he began to panic. Two more attempts to get his speeder off the lake failed and he knew he was doomed.

He gripped the speeder's controls and hung on as the little craft was pummelled by waves of increasing strength and height.

Lorian felt like he had been holding on for dear life forever. He was soaked, freezing, and without any strength. It seemed that the only reason he stayed on was that his hands had frozen into a tight grip around the speeder's controls.

He barely noticed the speeder hitting the bottom of shallow water in what seemed to be hours later. A final push from the lake sent the speeder over onto its side and flung Lorian into the water where the waves pushed his unconscious body to the shore.

There he lay until morning. In Menenyr he was immediately listed as missing and his speeder's locator was picked up at the edge of the lake.

A single patrol was sent out to look for him. It found his faint heat signal on the shore of the cold lake. The wild storm that had come out of seemingly nowhere had dissipated, returning into the nothingness it had been born from.

The craft set down on the grassy field where the patrol quickly found Lorian.

"He's barely alive," one of the soldiers said after feeling his skin.

"Let's get them back to medical. The other one is in the same way."

Lorian's unconscious body was taken aboard and immediately sent to medical, where he was slowly brought back to health.

By mid-morning, he had woken but did not realise where he was. A single medical droid was busy adjusting medication and checking vital signs.

"Good morning, Lieutenant Shane. I have reported your response to our ward doctor."

"Where am I?"

"Medical station for Menenyr. You gave your commanders quite a shock and I believe you may have to answer some serious questions."

"Oh?" Lorian was adjusting to his new surroundings.

"You and the other man were very lucky to have been picked up when you were."

"What other man?"

"There was another picked up from the shoreline, far on the other side of the lake. Initially, the crew of the scout thought it was you, but he is an old man. Do you know him?"

"No. Stupidly I went alone." Lorian cursed himself for his foolishness. His whole unit would probably be laughing at him and he couldn't tell them why he went. He would have to come up with an excuse, like he crashed on a late mission, or something like that.

"Am I able to go?"

"Your vital signs are improving and there is no damage to your body. I will notify the doctor of your request."

Lorian sat up and looked about his small room. He would have to come up with a real good reason why he was out so late and had more than likely written off a piece of military equipment. He was expecting hell to pay from his superiors.

A screen on the medical droid came alive and a female's face appeared.

"Good. You're awake and everything appears normal. How are you feeling?"

"Okay. I'll be feeling better as the day goes on."

"Not after your officers get hold of you, I imagine. You're free to leave when you want."

"Thank you."

The screen went blank and Lorian climbed out of bed and began putting on the torn and still wet clothes he had on last night.

Lorian was well gone and on his way back to his quarters when the man woke. For a moment, his eyes adjusted to his surroundings, and then he quickly sat up.

"Good morning. How are you feeling?" said the medical droid.

"Where is Lorian Shane?"

MINERAH

Thara stood tall over Karthukan. She looked up at him, his hands now laying gently on each cheek.

"Mother would not talk to me," she cried.

"It's alright child, we don't need her anymore."

He looked up at the expanse of the Minerah moon, homeworld of Ashlar, the Chieftain of the Ethereals. The fight on Kiam had weakened his body but not doused his ferocious spirit.

The Ethereals were capable of astro-projection, but Thara had the skill of actually transporting his body. The fight on Kiam had forced him to take a shuttle to the moon. Karthukan had piloted the craft, refusing to leave her father alone to face Ashlar. She had brought with them dozens of loyal Flame Trees, who now called themselves Gorgoth, along with ordinary soldiers. All turned to the darkside of Thara. She had hoped to use them as simple fodder to wear down or distract Ashlar, to give her father every chance at victory.

Without any further words, Thara moved off towards Ashlar's

fortress. Karthukan's troops were already moving forward. She had wanted to be part of it but Thara had forbade it. Nonetheless, she stayed and watched, knowing this would be the greatest of all battles.

Ashlar had gathered many of the loyal Flame Trees and members of the Order of Light on Minerah, all ready to strike against Thara on Kiam, but his brother and sister's quick deaths had shaken him. The news that Flames Trees had murdered more of his family had broken him. When he finally shook himself off a few days later, Thara had vanished. For hours he would sit, eyes closed but mind open, looking for his lost brother but finding nothing. Nothing until this morning.

It was an evil fleeting presence. He only felt it for a few moments before it was gone again. It reminded him of a living black hole which sucked in all light and threw out only hatred. In the moments he was connected, he felt his own soul burn like grabbing wildfire that snapped back. What it was, he couldn't answer. In peaceful times he would muse over it with some of his fellow Ethereals, like Elle and Lunith. Both were obsessed with the mysteries of the universe. Elle was safe in her own fortress of Wolven Moor, but how long would it be until Thara came for her? Lunith was on her way from Anueth and unlikely to arrive in time.

He was here. He knew that before Juli, the oldest of the Flame Trees on Minerah, told him. She was afraid.

"You can't face him on your own!"

"Get rid of these Gorgoth. They're only here to wear me out."

She hesitated.

"Whatever happens is meant to be, Juli. Go, do your part."

She wiped the tears from her eyes as she ran from the chamber.

Minerah was a small moon covered in trees, water, and gentle hills. Ashlar had chosen it as an oasis from Runamore. Once the secrets of interstellar travel were perfected, the Ethereals were able to move through the known galaxy taking with them pioneers and explorers to settle on new worlds. He loved this place. Now he was ready to defend it.

A great burst of thunder echoed across the coming night sky. Thara knew that Ashlar was strong and skilled. Across the small moon, battles erupted between Flame Trees as they clashed in the forests. Soon, great fires burst through the same forests sending giant columns of black smoke into the air.

Juli's troops appeared to have done their work as none of Thara's thralls made an appearance near Ashlar.

In the darkness of the forest, they closed in on each other, like blind lions sensing the other's presence, drawing closer to do battle.

Thara struck first. His replacement staff shot repeated blasts of power, forcing Ashlar to drop to the ground and use his own skills to deflect the bolts that slammed into the trees, ripping them in half.

Ashlar used the fallen trunks as weapons, throwing them at Thara and forcing him to blast them into pieces. The two Ethereal Lords continued their assaults on each other but were each unable to land a blow that would end the fight. The only thing destroyed was the forest. Soon it was afire, with great hulks of stumps and trunks strewn about.

Thara now rested on such a stump. Ashlar stood some metres

away, his chest heaving from both the fight and the stress of seeing his world ripped apart. He was well aware of the fate of Kiam, where the very land recoiled at the presence of Thara and his evil.

"I'm not here to lord over you, Ashlar, but to destroy you."

"I know."

"You would never submit. You have too much pride and defiance."

Ashlar scoffed at the idea. "You are the one with the pride and defiance. I always knew you were akin to trouble, but this misery you have unleashed on our world is far beyond your usual insolent pouting. There is something else at work here, another spirit's work."

The thought of him being a puppet enraged Thara and he rushed at Ashlar. Faster than the speed of sound, they crashed into each other, the boom resounding across the moon. Each produced a sword and with furious strikes the electro-steel produced sparks that produced small fires on the remaining trees and scrub.

Thara used his powers to shake and crack the ground, hoping to knock Ashlar from his feet. Vicious swings were aimed at the Ethereal Lord's head but he had speed and strength to deflect the blows, even taking the opportunity to open holes in the ground, hoping Thara would fall to his death and end it.

Each time Thara escaped until Ashlar made a larger void, plunging him down into the darkness. He was able to take a breath then and approached the lip, on guard for Thara's counterstrike. There was silence, but for the raging water that poured in from a ruptured lake near the edge.

The void wasn't deep, but it was dark, and he was wary of being visible against the night sky and fires while Thara remained concealed in the dark.

Water was filling the hole and he could see it rising to the top, but no sign of Thara.

"Yes, I'm still here," Thara's voice echoed from the darkness.

Ashlar looked about, frustrated that he could not see or sense him.

A bolt shot from out of the water striking Ashlar on the shoulder as he tried to evade it. Thara burst from the chasm and resumed his strikes with new fury. Though wounded, Ashlar held his ground and defended each strike. Whatever force was driving Thara was strong and it drove Ashlar back across the plain.

The lake had filled the voids and now, washing out towards them, quickly covered their feet. Ashlar didn't want to be caught in the water and mud. He needed time to think.

Again, he used his skill to create a wave that was taller than both of them. It came up behind Thara and crashed down on him, trapping him in the mud. While Thara could not move, he was far from defeated. Ashlar was struck by rocks and ice preventing him from advancing on his trapped brother. A final wall of flame, ignited from the very ground, forced Ashlar away.

Ashlar moved back to his own home. His moon was burning. He passed the body of Juli. She had done her duty and cut down all of Thara's Gorgoth thralls. In doing so, they had all lost their lives.

Lunith's craft had been intercepted and damaged, delaying her arrival. He resolved that Thara would not leave this moon, even if that meant he would die too.

"He's strong," Ashlar said to his surviving Ethereals.

"What will you do?" Elle asked him.

"I'll end it here."

He could hear Elle crying.

"It's ok. I'll always be near."

He closed his mind off from the universe and rested, knowing the task before him was great. There was no way to tell how long the mud and ice would hold Thara. He waited in his chambers. Thara had to come to finish it, there was no need to waste energy tracking him down.

It was sunrise when it started again. The whole castle shook with explosions and quakes as if being shaken by massive invisible hands.

The explosions ripped off the roof and tore the walls down. Ashlar got to his feet as his home was ripped apart around him. In that tornado of wreck and ruin, he remained calm, at peace. The plan would succeed.

As the last pieces of wreckage fell upon the moon's surface, Ashlar remained at the rear balcony, overlooking the scene, his senses tuned to locating Thara.

He appeared out of the dust, his eyes already pinned on where Ashlar stood above him. Sensing a trap, he slowed his steps. All the Flame Trees were dead. There was just the two Ethereal Lords left.

Thara began climbing the stairs, throwing away metal beams and embers until he was halfway. He did not intend to come closer to Ashlar. Killing him with rubble or a metal spike through the heart was his aim.

Ashlar knew it too. He had nothing but contempt for his

brother's cowardice and betrayal. Preferably, a single stroke to kill him would be ideal. It would require successful little strokes however, or something completely unexpected.

Thara used his power to break apart the staircase, which came crashing down in a thunder of rumbles and explosions. Ashlar had seen it just moments before. He expected it and had jumped clear. Landing in the ruined gardens, he began running towards a small hill. Devoid of any trees or structure, he had used it to study the stars and meditation. This morning, it would serve another purpose.

Ashlar was close to the summit and in no real hurry. He could sense Thara close behind him.

"Are we going to chase each other all day?" Thara called out.

"Well, here I am!" Ashlar yelled back at him as he continued to the summit.

The whole moon seemed on fire. Great plumes of smoke rose up all over the horizon creating a massive cloud of dark and grey. The wreckage of his home also smouldered.

Ashlar's heart was broken at the sight. His gazed shifted to Thara who was closing the distance.

"There's a thousand questions, brother," Ashlar said, his voice strained by deep emotions now barely contained.

"And you will never hear the answers. These are my secrets and you will die never knowing," Thara replied. He had deep respect for Ashlar, but his aspirations overrode any sentiment.

"Your tears will not put out these fires."

"That's a pity," Ashlar whispered, for those tears were for his brother.

Two Lords, each resolved to finish what had been started,

both determined, one wishing to subjugate, the other a sentinel. The battle could only be to the death.

Thara struck first. He had to. Each moment of waiting allowed his enemies time to regroup. Ashlar knew it and had maintained his composure while he waited.

Great flashes of lightning exploded around Ashlar. Their noise and brightness blocked his hearing and sight, allowing Thara to come close. But Ashlar was expecting it and the two were locked in punches and strikes.

Ashlar had wanted Thara to come in close. His magic and tricks were not going to defeat his enemy. He would have to use his own bare hands to end it.

While Thara threw punches and lightning, Ashlar had grabbed his arm. A great chain appeared from under his jacket. It was thrown around Thara's neck. Using all the weight of his body and his strength, Ashlar threw him to the ground, pinning his head to the ground and holding onto the chain, now tight around his neck.

Thara screamed and thrashed about. Again, lightning burst from Thara's fingers as he attempted to blow Ashlar apart. His grip was too tight and Thara's shots, though close enough to burn him, were not enough to kill him.

Ashlar thrust his left hand deep into the churned-up earth. His eyes focused on Grotfer.

Minerah moved. He could feel it shifting orbit. Thara's thrashing about made the task more difficult. If he had more Ethereals here, the task would have been simpler and quicker. He was alone here, however.

Each kilometre that Minerah moved towards Grotfer, the

hotter it became. The grass singed and then caught fire, the woods burned, the lakes boiled, and great walls of fire danced about like breaking waves on the shores of hell.

Thara now knew what Ashlar's plan was. It would only take a few more moments and Minerah would be caught in Grotfer's inner gravity and be held there until the moon burned up as it plunged into the great fire.

He thrashed about harder, his tongue, blackened by foul speak, rolled out. Panic had gripped him and he was determined to break free.

Finally, he got a hand free and grabbed onto Ashlar's lower leg. Ashlar cried out as the electricity exploded through his body. Digging deeper, he struggled to keep Thara pinned.

It was the heat and the constant bolts of electricity that Thara was running through his body that he couldn't stop.

Minerah was burning. Grotfer loomed closer. With a final effort, Thara managed to pull himself free and flung Ashlar back, breaking his hold. He pulled the chain from his neck and used it to thrash Ashlar over his head and body. Each strike frantically followed the other, each filled with hate and anger.

Ashlar's face was ripped and bleeding. The great magic that had kept him from burning up was fading now. His clothes ignited, his body broken, he remained still.

Thara stood above him, victorious, though he could not savour it. The moon was doomed but Thara was resolved not to be. He could do nothing more but try to get back to Karthukan, if she hadn't already been consumed by the fire.

Thara bounded from the hill, now just charred dirt, and back through the ruins of Ashlar's home.

Above him was a ship that came in low. He jumped for the open door, which then slammed shut behind him.

An attendant droid stood by. Karthukan moved the ship from the burning moon, which had now stopped its descent. Thara cried out in angst-ridden bellows. He could barely stand and slumped crumpled on the starship's floor.

Karthukan glanced uneasily at him. He again cried out, but she did not know if it was in grief or pain. It upset her. She decided to remain silent as she moved her father to safety.

In space, close to the burning moon, Lunith watched helplessly. Tears filled her eyes at the shocking sight and the realisation that Ashlar was gone. Her Flame Trees in the shuttle were equally overcome with grief.

Different plans stormed in her mind. She had wanted to fall to Minerah and burn up with her beloved, but would that achieve anything for the galaxy?

"Follow that ship!" she ordered her pilot.

Immediately he pushed the ship to its maximum speed to catch up with Thara's. Soon he was tailing it as both ships twisted in turns, one trying to escape, the other clinging to its exhaust fumes.

Karthukan was a good pilot and had special skills to pre-empt any move of the other pilot. Space, however, was vast. How could they keep running?

Thara seemed to regain some of his composure after the exhausting fight with Ashlar.

Bright flashes exploded around them as Lunith's ship opened fire.

"We're should we go?" Karthukan called out.

"For the moment, we go nowhere," Thara replied.

He stood up, came towards her seat, and pulled back on the power throttle.

Immediately the ship came to an abrupt halt. Moments later, Lunith's ship crashed into it.

After pulling herself back into the seat, Karthukan noticed Thara was gone.

Inside Lunith's ship, she and her guard were thrown about. Thara's tactic had been completely unexpected. Now both ships were stopped and damaged.

Lunith sensed him close. He was in the rear engine. Immediately she transported herself there and saw him using his remaining strength to ignite the power core. His hand was over it and it was vibrating and spitting out flames.

"Thara!"

He glanced at her, no emotion in his face or eyes, before vanishing. Then the ship exploded.

The Black Ash Prince loved darkness. Here on the wild moon of Minerah, darkness was a fleeting shadow passing over small hills or ruins of buildings. Though the small moon orbited quickly around Grotfer, as Minerah's own rotational orbit was slow, the days were long.

He knew this place had never looked like the barren wasteland it was now. This was once the domain of Ashlar, the most powerful of all Ethereals.

"Be careful of this one," Kaw had warned him prior to his arrival.

Cryacur was fascinated by Thara's struggle. He had taken on all the Ethereals virtually singlehanded. Finally defeated, worn out by his struggle, he had been imprisoned and his body frozen into a rock of ice and expelled out into the galaxy. What happened to him after that was only speculation for he was never heard from again.

Kaw believed Ashlar was dead too. Nothing had ever been heard from him again and none dared come here. He was last seen burning alive atop his hill. After scanning the moon's surface and using old maps from when there was life here, Kaw had found that hill.

His home was now a flat mass of broken stone. Melted metal lay in pools or dripping from its battlements like frozen tears.

Everything was covered in ash. *Plexus* had stirred up dust and ash that had lain settled for thousands of years.

Immediately upon exiting the shuttle, he was overcome by the oppressive heat and wind. The ash and dirt that had been stirred up slowly fell back to the ground, quickly covering his cloak. As he walked, his boots were soon covered in it.

As he approached the summit, he was wary and unsettled. A fool would dare call him afraid. Grotfer was a massive ball of burning fire that filled much of the skyline and sent waves of fire and radiation over the surface of the moon. Cryacur felt he would burst into flames at any moment. He liked it.

At the summit there was a chain and burned bones, nothing else. He kicked about the ash until a skull appeared.

This was indeed where Ashlar had chained Thara. While having only scorn for the Ethereals, he had to begrudgingly accept the power of Ashlar. He had been able to move the entire moon and almost succeeded in throwing it, himself, and Thara into the Grotfer.

He picked up the skull to look at it, but more so he could show his contempt by dropping it back into the ash.

There was nothing else here to see. No ghost appeared. His task was done.

"Shallee," a voice whispered to him.

Startled he stopped and carefully looked about. Nothing. Again, no ghosts appeared.

It was time for him to leave. Despite only being on the surface for a few minutes, his coat was singed, his boots cracked. The biting breeze that was full of radiation and solar winds had pushed the fine ash into every crease in his clothes and helmet.

A few long strides and he was back in *Plexus,* though he felt he would not be safe until he left this place entirely. As the shuttle moved away, he had a vantage view of Minerah. This was a dead world. There was still that uneasy feeling, and it wasn't just the climate and the conditions. He felt like he was being watched. Something he could sense but not see.

He smirked in contempt as the shuttle moved away from the surface, satisfied that Ashlar was indeed dead and his soul trapped on his ruined world. There it would burn up every day, a just reward for his defiance of Thara and his power. Yes, Ashlar, Lord of the Ethereals, was dead and his power was gone from the galaxy.

REDSEE

In Admiral Zuke's apartment within Redsee, he had a view across the city. Often, his aides would find him standing at the large window, arms behind his back, staring far into the distance.

Tonight, he held a meeting within the same room. The view from the window was bleak with all the cities lights off except for the dotted military complexes.

After his expulsion of Metora, he had settled down to work on his own feat of arms. The refusal of the Bond to assist the Nunearanor had been of sound strategic value as he had been one of the numbers to veto it. However, from a tactical and propaganda quarter, it also had great merit. Not only would it infuse the fleet with the rush of victory, but it would also bring the spotlight back to himself and show the people of the Bond he was a great Admiral who could beat Kaw.

"Can it be done?" he asked Vice-Admiral Dyndarumm, his chief tactical officer.

"Sure, with enough ships, but not a full invasion," was the sceptical reply.

"If I downsize the objective, then is it feasible? After all, it's a simple extraction. I'm not after new territory. This isn't Ophistar."

Dyndarumm looked up from the holo-board which held all the objectives and order of battle that Zuke had put together. He took a deep breath.

"Nothing is impossible. We smash our way in, link up, and then get the hell out of there. If we can do it quickly and achieve surprise, above all, then the chances are that much greater. Still, it's a huge risk, especially when you so publicly humiliated Prince Metora for doing virtually . . ."

"It is not the same," Zuke spoke bluntly over the Vice-Admiral.

"The same thing," Dyndarumm continued.

"This is different. This is a mission of mercy for our allies, Dyndarumm."

"And it's also a great publicity stunt for you," he wryly added.

Zuke flashed a smile. Lor Dyndarumm had come highly recommended as he rose through the ranks and always appeared loyal. In recent months, he had found him increasingly opinionated and, at times, at odds with his superior officer. It was those opinions that Zuke was becoming increasingly annoyed with, though he had found no solution. The Vice-Admiral had the support of many of Anueth's top politicians and military hierarchy. In addition, he was good at what he did. It was now apparent to Zuke that the Vice-Admiral most likely could not be trusted. As he was part of the command council, however, his opinion had to be sought. If only a new crisis would emerge that he could use to bring the Vice-Admiral down. That would be a blessing.

"Listen to me, Vice-Admiral. I am going to put right the neglect of Nunearanor. If that results in favourable public opinion, then so be it. That is only a natural by-product of victory. It's elementary that leaders who bring victories are popular. I shouldn't be chastised and stabbed in the back because of it."

Dyndarumm seemed to mull things over. "Alright, Admiral. You'll get your battle. Let's see what you can do."

Zuke turned about to look out of his window at the night sky. "You'll see what I can do, Vice-Admiral."

An aide entered the room with a written order and stood to attention next to the officers, waiting to be acknowledged.

Dyndarumm turned to the young woman. "What is it?"

"A message from the royal palace, Sir. King Leigh and Colonel Halkinbraun have been killed. Prince Metora has been injured."

"How?"

"Is he dead?" Zuke muttered.

Dyndarumm took the message, his face contorted in shock and horror. "Iminus Kaw? Are you sure?"

"We received it just moments ago, Sir."

"Impossible."

Zuke stepped away from the window and took the message himself.

"This changes everything," the Vice-Admiral said as the aide left the room.

"No, it doesn't. But yes, another impossible escape by Metora."

Dyndarumm shook his head at Zuke's attitude.

"It's been ten years and no one has seen or heard anything

from Kaw and now this. And you want to send our fleet out beyond Trinity?"

Zuke merely stared at him.

"This will crush many Anueth, and poor Halkinbraun. He was a good man. Can you imagine if Metora had been killed too? People are despondent enough without this," Dyndarumm mused.

"Pull yourself together. You're a Vice-Admiral."

Dyndarumm steamed but said nothing. It was pointless to argue with such a pigheaded attitude as Zuke seemed to possess.

"Begin operational readiness plans. We must strike quickly. We can't have any delays."

"What of that?" Dyndarumm nodded to the message still in Zuke's hand.

"Ignore it. Order all information about this to be suppressed."

"Word will get out."

"Now you understand how imperative this attack is. It must succeed."

"If it doesn't?"

"Give me three days, Vice-Admiral, and let's see what magic I come up with."

In the immediate hours after the attack, Metora had been through the medical facility and had his wound treated. *Another scar*, he thought. He had then left the palace with Oberon and returned to his home. He had said little to anyone and his eyes had seemed vacant and distant. All the staff and guards were in complete shock and a blanket of silence and fear had fallen through the palace. With it came orders from Imperial Command that no one was to say anything about what occurred, under penalty of imprisonment.

Oberon had said nothing to him but watched the young man sit in the shuttlecraft with his head resting on his hand, his thoughts a million light years away, deep in reverie or lost in an ocean of melancholy.

"I'm going north, Oberon, to the Blue Hills, to see Koree."

"I will go with you."

They didn't stay long at his house, just long enough to collect clothes and alert Bannade House that he was coming.

Bannade House was a small complex, deep in the Blue Hills, that the Jashir had built. While most of the more important Jashirn arts and culture that could be saved were kept in vaults within the Anueth royal palace, Bannade House was more of a separate place for new art to be made and for Jashirns to meet and relax.

There were art centres and libraries, places to eat and just sit and talk around large wood fires. It was also home to Metora's heir, Koree, and many other members of the Royal Family.

It had been months since he had seen her, and he missed her terribly. The many images he had been sent were no substitute for seeing her in person. He had told family looking after her to keep his visit a surprise.

The shuttle roared over the tall trees where years ago he had spent time exploring the tracks that wound through them for kilometres. He had not been there since his sister's death. The sight of them brought back all-too-real memories.

As the shuttle passed over the landing strip, there were a large number of people waving. On opening the door, he was struck by the chilling wind that was blowing in from the east. It was crisp, and fresh, and the further he walked from the shuttle, its tang of oil and fumes were left behind and fresh air filled his lungs.

Aunt Dannul met him. Her long, greying hair was tied back in a braid. She had an aura of sternness and command. Bannade House ran to her instructions and Metora was quite happy for it to do so as he had other matters that took up most of his time.

"You look tired, Metora."

No word had yet reached them of what had occurred that morning. He nodded as she embraced him.

"Oberon," she said, acknowledging the sentinel droid.

"After that show trial, I expected you sooner."

"Well, things changed and I needed to get out of the city."

"It will do you good. And Koree, of course, will be delighted you're here."

They made their way to the main building. It was multi-storey and made from stone and wood, all local products. The emblem of the Jashir Sun, made of shining gold, blazed above the doorway. All the verandahs and walkways hung with flowers while people cheered and called his name. Several children came up to him, their hands full of flowers.

"We'll put these in your room," Aunt Dannul stated.

There was a separate apartment complex that some of the Royal Family lived in. Many of them were cousins and descendants. Metora was the only survivor of the immediate heirs. Koree was in her room. It was normally her bedtime, but family had kept her awake, knowing that Metora was coming. She hadn't noticed him yet as she played with her toys. She looked like her mother with her long, wavy hair.

He was going to let her go to bed and see her in the morning, but he couldn't resist.

"Koree . . . Koree," he whispered.

She turned around, not expecting to see him there. Her eyes lit up and she began giggling.

"Uncle Metora!"

She jumped from the floor and ran towards him. He kneeled down and put her on his lap, trying to ignore the pain in his shoulder.

"Have you come to see me?"

"I have."

"Are you staying?"

"I'll be staying for a while, ready for playing and doing whatever you want."

"Did Ron come?"

He laughed at her continued mispronunciation of Oberon's name.

"He's here too. Now you'll have to go to bed. I'll see you in the morning."

He put her down and she ran to her cupboard and began looking through her clothes.

"I'm getting clothes for tomorrow."

He laughed as he came over to see what clothes she was pulling out, all ready for the morning.

"How about I put you to bed and we can decide what clothes in the morning?"

"Ok."

She almost skipped over to the bed and climbed in. Metora tucked her in.

"After breakfast, I have to do my hair, then get dressed, and then I'll see you in my playroom where you have to wait." She held up one of her little fingers.

He laughed at her seriousness.

"I'll be waiting."

Already he could feel the pressure and turbulence of the war fading away. There was nothing to trouble him here and he could rest for a short time, knowing the war would come looking for him soon enough.

Joviann had made her way through the underground levels of Dunmarra to the repair facilities hanger. The whole fortress had once been a simple open mine drilling for hyrax, the crucial element that was mixed with bauxite to create heavy armour for the capital warships.

Having no large resources available to the Palaniri after the years of war, they were unable to create a new fortress. Instead, a derelict enemy ship had its bow and stern section cut off and placed into the open mine. It was merged with new structures to create all that the Khoru needed. Finally, an armoured roof was built to cover the original open mine and then a layer of dirt to conceal it. Only the various communication towers, gun batteries, and secured shield doors gave any clue that there was anything there at all.

Despite the hour, there were mechanics working on various fighters and other equipment. Joviann knew that Mahalia would be here somewhere. And there she was, working on a small Journeyman Class of freighter. Normally a cargo or personnel carrier, it had been outfitted with extra armament and defences. Mahalia had been told the *Wanderlust* had belonged to her parents and had been stored in Dunmarra until she had the chance to repair it. That was something she had a hard time doing as it brought back memories she wasn't ready to deal with.

There was a male's voice besides that of Mahalia, and Joviann was concerned to come closer.

"Dad, that booster isn't going to kick in. It's going to put too much strain on the frame."

"Well, it never used to," came the reply.

Both of them appeared and spotted Joviann. She wasn't dressed in her usual diplomatic attire, just plain work clothes like all the other workers in Dunmarra.

Only Mahalia showed any surprise at seeing Joviann.

"Can we help you?" Dekra asked.

"I've come to see your daughter," Joviann replied.

"I got this, Dad."

Dekra nodded. "Alright, I'll get back to work."

He walked back behind the *Wanderlust* while Mahalia stepped towards Joviann.

"You look happy."

Mahalia smiled, "Well I never thought I would see him again. You don't look happy."

Joviann took a deep breath. "It seems the universe is spitting out many things, including Iminus Kaw who decided to come out of his fortress and then killed King Leigh in the palace apartments."

Mahalia was visibly shocked. "What? Is it true?"

"Very."

"Something must have happened. Do you think he knows?"

"I believe his mind is mulling over it."

"Then we're in for some dangerous times."

"These runs must be stressful," Joviann replied, looking over the ship behind them.

"Yeah, but I'm alright."

"Those runs to Palaniri are dangerous. We have other roads to travel too."

"I know. I just feel I need to help people get where they need to be," Mahalia replied sheepishly.

"I understand all too well. Stay safe. May light be on you."

"May light be on you," she replied as Joviann walked back out of the hanger.

Mahalia was glad to spend time with her father, but duty always called. She wasn't sure if he was ready to return to active duty. He hadn't mentioned anything. Anyway, it was far too early for the wounds of incarceration to heal.

Perreder had approved her plan to send more ships. Trying to hide the disappearance of so many people was becoming harder. He knew that soon, someone would start asking questions about where these phantom units and commands were. With the events at the palace, however, things would start to get more hectic and hopefully panic wouldn't break out.

NUNEARANOR

While winter was just beginning to settle over the Bond systems, Nunearanor had already been covered deep in its chill for months. It had been the coldest winter in a hundred years, which befitted the once vibrant planet, now lifeless and alone.

The lakes had frozen. In some parts to the north, even the rivers had become solid. The trees were bare, the fields were covered in a thick white blanket, and the wind at night was the proverbial thousand knives piercing the skin.

In such conditions, the people of Nunearanor could not operate as they once did. Before the Axis occupation, they had learned to live with winter and the wide orbital pull of Grotfer. They could prepare food, lodgings, and transport. Now, with the infrastructure gone, there was little food or shelter and the Axis forces on the planet cared little for the inhabitants' suffering.

The Nunearanor had fought hard for their planet and suffered for it. The planet had become a clone of the other systems that had seen battles. Whatever uniqueness Nunearanor landscapes, cities, or culture had were now ruins and her rubble was no different from that of other Bond systems.

The cities had burned, the forests were cleaved from the nestled soil, and the rivers were filled with wreckage and dead washed down by heavy rains. Everywhere, the land was wounded by the power of the Axis fleet's use of brute force to weed out the determined defenders.

Such firepower had blown apart the mountain of Rargarlith. A large military base was created deep within the mountain and then expanded over the years as the war showed no sign of coming to an end. At the time of its destruction, it held thousands of troops, equipment, and fighters. It had disappeared under a massive bombardment. The guns of the Axis fleets had literally erased the tallest mountain on the planet.

So great was the destruction and so deep did the guns penetrate that it caused the lava, dormant in its bowels, to ignite and come to the surface. It had turned Rargarlith into a live volcano that destroyed the last of the mountain and scarred the surrounding landscape. Its volcanic plume reached so high into the atmosphere that even the crews of the fleets, locked in combat, gaped in awe and dread.

Nunearanor was not part of the original six systems of the Ethereals. Instead, a mixture of pioneers from Anueth and Kiam, with the Ethereals Elle, Ashlar, and Lunith, settled it once starships were able to begin exploring the galaxy. They named her Nunearanor, the beautiful dawn, the first settlement outside of the Sangreal systems.

After the destruction of the Ethereals and the creation of the Sangreal, Nunearanor had seen a great influx of people. In only two hundred years she had caught up to her older sister planets in the fields of technology and culture. Her inhabitants were known to be fierce warriors who had a passion for life but were light-hearted, heavy workers and repetitive travellers.

The first King, Beoriliss, elected from the ranks of the Order of Light, had made sure the new planet would be self-sufficient, proud like the old systems, and an important member of the Sangreal's galaxy.

With the strikes by Kaw, Nunearanor had joined the fight. As the war turned against the Sangreal, the Nunearanor Parliament knew war would come to them. The Black Ash Prince had targeted the planet as his priority after the initiation of *Torm Dor*.

The Bond had fought hard for her little sister but, with the release of the Sons of Gorgoth to turn their manic bloodlust loose on the planet, there was no doubt the planet would fall.

With the Bond overstretched trying to win back Jashir after losing Oneum and Kiam while defending Anueth, Taranova, and Mahnarosa, Queen Zoe took a hard decision. She sent her daughter, Sumer, and her fleet away to join the Bond, along with as much equipment and stores that could be spared. The ships also carried away as many of the children, civilians, wounded, and Nunearanor's cultural treasures as they could. Then she headed underground to a new firebase, christened Akara, while leading a guerrilla campaign.

That decision, along with the fighting that had gone on since, had taken a hard toll on the Queen. Her hope had been that, with the planet secure, the Axis would move forces away from the planet, giving her people a chance. She also knew, however, that those Axis forces would then be used on other systems.

She had taken to wearing silver armour made for her from

cutlery from the royal palace. Her people had dubbed her the Lady Silver as she travelled around the planet as best she could, trying to install strength, courage, and hope in her depleted army.

The Queen had four children — Talia, Sumer, Isla and Aideon. Her Consort, Amian, had been killed years before while commanding a frigate during the initial invasion.

Talia and Sumer had married, had children of their own, and did not take part in the fighting any further. Sumer remained on Anueth in the Nunearanor stronghold of Anorfer, *Dawn of Fire,* as a figurehead to exiled Nunearanor forces. Only Isla remained true to the warriors cause while their little brother had disappeared with his company during last year's winter on a mission to the capital, Dharahlun, to collect intelligence on the Axis leadership.

The Lady Silver had waited anxiously in Akara, far in the northern mountains, as Isla made her mercy mission to the Bond. On her daughter's return with the devastating news, Zoe sort solace alone in her quarters. So much had been lost and now the final gasp was upon them.

Her capital was in ruins and empty of life and sounds. Though the Axis held the planet, they seemed content to let the cities lie in ruins and had not bothered to repair any of it. Most of the inhabitants had fled. Many of those who hadn't were either killed or enslaved. Those who refused to surrender had hid in the smaller towns and forests.

Soon, the massive factories began arriving. Dockyards, fortresses, and barracks had been built, scarring the land, and filling the blue skies with grey hulks of twisting metal as the Axis fervently assembled their machines for the making of war.

For years, the Nunearanor had been striking from hidden bases. They hit convoys, troop stations, and factories, attempting to disrupt and annoy the Axis forces. There had been small victories, but this singled them out for counter measures. Even the Black Ash Prince had returned in the guise of a black storm and descended on the planet in an effort to wipe out all the resistance cells once and for all.

The Lady Silver knew that the chance of victory was slowly being eaten away. The Axis poured in more troops, especially the Gunadar and Diamalords, and smothered the planet in arms. It had proved too costly for the Nunearanor to attack and so they hid. One by one, however, the resistance cells were located and destroyed.

Each week, pieces of her situation board showing her troops' locations were blacked out as her force's strength shrunk.

Now, with the refusal of the Bond to help, the Lady Silver sat alone in her room. On the wall, a digital painting of the great Waterfalls of Demphin, where she would holiday in her youth and where Amian had asked her to marry him, moved like a living picture.

It had inspired her over the long years of despair to find strength to have her world return to what it had once been. Now, she looked deep into the waters for more inspiration. She was lost in memories. It was a way to block out the long waiting. Isla was overdue from her expedition south. She had had to wait before and always it ended with loss. First her husband, and then her son, had all failed to return.

Was there any point in praying for Isla's return? Pray to whom? Who controlled their fate? Was there any point in continuing to fight what appeared to be an inevitable, brutal end?

She looked again at the data board with its message. Decisions needed to be made. Time was running out.

Isla, Princess of Nunearanor, was a long way from her normal world of banquets where she would wear beautifully-made dresses and jewellery while officers and gentlemen would vie for the affections of her older sisters, all the while eating fine food and wine. Then there was school, her friends, and the times she would sit out in the sun having lunch with them, far from the royal world.

Now, she shivered in the cold and ignored the snow that had built up around her body and blaster as she lay in the whiteness. The snow had quickly settled in every crevasse of her uniform and equipment in the hour she had waited for the scout group to return.

In her old life, she had loved winter. Her sisters would make special boards that they would ride down hills and snowballs which they would throw at their little brother.

Now, she hated it. It killed her soldiers and her people. It was impossible to hide in and impossible to hide the blood that she had seen spilled over it too many times. She would always remember snow as being red from now on. Nothing grew in the fields and forests as the planet seemed to die for the long months it moved away from Grotfer.

Initially, guerrilla warfare had not been her forté. She had trained since a child in combat and traditional warfare but, since the occupation, she and her troops had had to retrain themselves in the art of shadow war.

Above all, she was desperate to take on the Axis face-to-face and deal them a fatal blow. The small strikes the Nunearanor had made occasionally brought benefits, but never a strong, strategic reversal.

The Gunadar who now occupied the planet were cowards and easy targets, but the Axis had reinforced them with Diamalord troops, and even the feared Wrydluk. The chance of strategic reversal was slipping away and their enemy was winning.

The rumours of a Son of Gorgoth awakening had been enough to keep people fearful. It was known as *The Will*. In its own language, it called itself Gronmalest Kedkule, which translated as *Life Obeys my Master's Will*.

Its lair was unknown, despite it dwelling on Nunearanor for several years. It had torn a bloody path through the Bond's soldiers when it first appeared. Everyone prayed that it remained asleep.

She brushed the snow from her face and her blaster, taking a quick look behind her. Parked up and barely camouflaged was a convoy of captured shuttles carrying food, medical supplies, and other equipment. Hopefully, it would keep them through the rest of the winter, if she could get it through the Gunadar troops guarding Orden Pass, the last barrier before Akara. In the quiet, she tried not to think about the consequences if the convoy was lost. Even worse, if they were captured. Death would be a better solution.

Akara was a new installation. It was buried deep in the mountains to the north and was never on the original defence plans. Its secrecy had ensured that it had remained just that. It would only take a loose lip from a tortured mouth, however, to reveal its location, depth, and size.

Up ahead, two figures appeared moving stealthily towards them. Finally, the scouts had returned. She could breathe a bit more easily knowing they had not been spotted.

"They're dug in, right across the path. A few heavy blasters and missile batteries," one of the scouts reported while catching his breath.

Isla pressed her lips together as she formulated a battle plan.

"You destroyed its signals?"

The scout nodded.

"There's a further firewall behind this one though," the other scout added.

"Sounds like we'll have to blast our way through," said Sherri Hume, Isla's second in command. She was tough, with the scars on her face to prove it. She had been doing these runs for some time and knew the land well.

"But I don't want them to follow us to Akara," Isla replied.

Sherri smiled, "Then we'll have to wipe them all out."

Isla knew that having to fight their way through the pass was a high possibility. She would have rather moved through unseen, as they had done many times before. Last season, the Orden Pass was not manned by the Gunadar. It was too far north and too inhospitable for the sickly race.

The Gunadar preferred the warmth of their own bases and compounds. Obviously, the Diamalords had pushed them out of their comfort zones in the final crack-down on Nunearanor resistance. The Gunadar in the Orden Pass probably didn't want to be there as much as Isla didn't want them there.

"There's no way around, but it has to be quick."

"The Gunadar aren't fighters," Sherri retorted with contempt in her voice.

"Sherri and I will take the scout battle group and force a way through. Harmen, you take the convoy and go straight through. We'll form the rear-guard . . . and we can't leave survivors."

The command group nodded and went its separate ways. Harmen, the commander of the convoy, disappeared back towards the shuttles that were quickly being covered in the still-falling snow.

Isla, Sherri, and a small group of soldiers moved forward on foot while their heavy speeders armed with blasters followed. They sent a reconnaissance drone ahead that would relay the positions of the Gunadar. It was invisible to scanners and small enough to be hard to spot by the naked eye.

Once the drone had reported the positions it could see, Isla would release three battle droids that would be programmed with the drone's information. They would provide covering fire. While extremely useful, their lack of armament and numbers meant the Nunearanor still had to clear enemy positions the old fashion way — by blasters, explosives, and the fury of soldiers fighting for their homes.

It didn't take long for the fighting to begin as the first Gunadar position came under fire. Drawing her short sword, Isla silently approached the Gunadar position. The two troops in the small barricade built into the wall of the pass didn't see her as she jumped in. One was dispatched without a sound and the other only had a second to react before he too was run through. Each Gunadar wore a helmet and special winter uniforms with a mask to protect them from the cold.

The attack group surged forward to the next one, but here the Gunadar were alert and firing, even though somewhat inaccurately, at the battle droids. As a consequence, they failed to see the Nunearanor approaching through the snow until it was too late.

An explosion knocked Isla off her feet as a bomb went off close to her. She got to her feet quickly and charged at the Gunadar hiding behind their small wall. A Gunadar tried to impale her with a long lance. Isla avoided it and struck back, decapitating her enemy in a flash.

"Signal the convoy to move!" she called out to the reconnaissance drone, knowing it would relay her commands.

Her troops moved forward and were now joined by the heavy speeders that began firing on the remaining Gunadar positions.

"Keep moving!" she cried out as she led the way forward. One side of the pass was clear, now it was the turn of the other.

A friendly speeder closed, its crew firing effectively at a Gunadar heavy-weapon system.

"Go forward and clear a path for the convoy!" she told the driver.

The remaining positions were too far away for assaulting directly by foot. The heavy guns had to go in first and her troops would clear out the survivors.

Explosions tore through the pass among wild, muffled screams from the Gunadar.

Isla climbed aboard the speeder, joining other troops who rode it forward.

The Gunadar fire was thick and concentrated on Isla's

speeder. Sparks flew from its hull, but it still moved forward. Another blast hit close to Isla and she cried out as shrapnel tore her arm.

"Stop here," she told the driver through gritted teeth.

By the heavy fire, reinforced protection, and arrays of antennae, it was undoubtedly the Gunadar's command unit.

More Nunearanor heavy speeders and troops arrived to begin the final attack, just in time, as the Gunadar had switched some of their fire to the convoy which was slowly creeping up the pass.

Explosives were placed on the main door of the small complex and then ignited. Bits of metal, rock, and snow were thrown into the air in the ensuing explosion. Isla and her troops rushed in, blasters firing.

Immediately, they spotted the Splint Cannon, the heaviest weapon in the Gunadar arsenal and capable of destroying the heavy speeders and the convoy.

The gun crew were busy firing out into the pass, believing other troops would be protecting them. Isla and a number of other troops went straight for it. As they came closer, she realised the five-man crew were a mixture of Gunadar and the hated Wrydluk. There was no turning back now so she pressed on, quickly crossing the complex ground and opening fire on the crew.

The Wrydluk wore special armour and helmets similar to those that the Gunadar wore against the cold. Despite that extra protection, two Wrydluk crew fell after being hit by dozens of bolts. One of the Gunadar also fell. The final Wrydluk got a shot off that hit Isla's blaster, flinging it from her hand.

Quickly, she grabbed a discarded enemy weapon while the

other soldiers killed the final Wrydluk, forcing the last Gunadar to fall to his knees.

"Please! I surrender."

Isla stopped, her weapon trained on him, her chest rising heavily as she caught her breath.

"Would you give me the same mercy?"

The humanoid struggled for an answer. His face was covered with a metal mask to allow him to breathe the cold air.

"If I let you live and I turn my back, would you shoot me in the back?"

"No. No. I'm a soldier," the Gunadar answered desperately.

There was a moment of silence between them. Isla was seriously considering taking him prisoner. She could only feel pity for him. He seemed frail, far from his homeworld, despite its desolation, and afraid. Maybe this place was a better place for him to die.

Troops picked up the Gunadar and began searching him.

Sherri came up behind her, her gaze on the Gunadar. She would probably have killed him. "The convoy is getting through."

"Take their weapons and destroy anything left," she whispered.

The complex was soon cleared and the final Gunadar eliminated. The Nunearanor carried away as many weapons and as much ammunition as they could carry.

Out in the pass, Isla watched the last shuttle of the convoy pass by. The heavy speeders waited to make up the rear-guard.

Harmen gave her a quick rundown on the situation.

"No losses. We picked up some of the Gunadar weapons and a few prisoners. Some of our troops didn't have the heart to kill those who had genuinely surrendered."

Isla nodded. She accepted that decision and said nothing about it. They had standard orders that prisoners were to be left behind as there weren't the resources to keep them. The few prisoners they had were kept in a prison facility deep in the lower levels of Akara. Most of them turned out to be quite content to be away from military life.

"Let's get out of here before Gunadar patrols turn up."

Akara, once a simple research base before being expanded into the rock, lay at the end of a long crevasse that was filled with snow and ice in winter. A solid tunnel which had been bored through the snow hid the entrance.

It was the last known centre of organised resistance on Nunearanor. Command had lost contact with many of the other bases around the planet. If they were still fighting, they had no information to confirm it. Some stragglers had found their way to Akara. Resistance forces would do wide sweeps looking for recruits and often brought back ex-soldiers or security forces that had been driven from their own cells.

Now they all huddled together waiting for the time when the Axis would find them. All knew it was just a matter of time. The sweeps for recruits had ended as there was a fear they would not return and would be captured, giving up the location of Akara under torture. Or Axis agents would be recruited and unintentionally inform their masters of Akara.

Few patrols went out at all. Isla's was a last desperate strike, organised quickly at news of the convoy headed north bringing equipment and supplies for the Gunadar. It would undoubtedly attract more interest in the northern regions of the planet, and more Axis troops. The noose was tightening.

Isla followed the convoy into Akara without incident. When the giant doors closed, the troops and her knew it would probably be some time before they would see daylight again.

She stood in a large, vaulted room, filled with gun emplacements and security details. To the sides of the vault were four lifts, two on each side. These led down several kilometres where there were workshops, power supplies, living quarters, and a host of rooms with other uses.

At the end was another large door that led through a long tunnel and ended in a fighter and starship hanger.

The stolen convoy and the combat patrol went through this door. The long corridor ended in darkness. Its purpose was for the larger starships to enter and exit. Many of the fighters also used it for quicker, emergency flights. Just inside was another lift that took them down to the flight hangers.

Within the giant hanger, there were work crews who had been waiting nervously for the convoy to arrive. Now, with it safely inside, they could begin unloading it.

"Isla," a female voice called out from within the sudden bustle. It was Talia, Isla's sister. Tall, slender and with short, dark hair pulled into a tail but still with a fringe that framed her blue eyes, she walked the short distance to her sister with her arms already out to hug her. Her two-year-old daughter, Eden, was in her other arm, smiling excitedly at the sight of her aunty.

"Hey," they embraced.

"Glad you're safe. Looks like you pulled off another miracle," Talia said while looking at the work being done on the convoy.

"It wasn't easy."

Talia then noticed Isla's torn jacket. "You got hit?"

Isla looked surprised, "I didn't even notice. Just a nick."

"Mum won't be happy about that. I'd get cleaned up first."

Isla took Eden in her arms and ran her hand through the little girl's hair, "Mum's used to seeing us wounded. It goes with the shit we're in."

"Well, she wanted to see you when you got back. Apparently, some big news has just come in."

"What is it?"

"It's top secret. Even I don't know what it is. But you're about to find out. She wanted me to get you as soon as you got in. So here I am."

The three walked from the hanger in silence, Isla's focus on her niece as she tickled and kissed her.

Isla cleaned herself up for her mother. She patched up the ripped skin on her arm. It was just a nick but enough to bleed heavily and it required a bandage. She put on another jacket to hide the tear and blood stain.

The Queen was waiting for her in her spartan apartment. She was reading from a data board and seemed so fixated on that she didn't realise Isla was there. There were a few lounges and mats. Children's toys were neatly kept in a corner. Often her grandchildren would spend time in here which the Queen enjoyed.

"Mum?"

The Lady Silver jumped slightly.

"Oh, Isla," she exclaimed as she smiled and stood up.

They embraced.

"It's quite a haul you've brought back. It should keep us for a while. Casualties were very light too, which I am thankful for."

"The Gunadar were guarding the Orden Pass. It won't be long before they track us here. There were a few Wrdlyuk with them too."

The Queen remained tight-lipped. "Come and sit down."

There was just a table and comfortable couches in the room. Pictures of all her children, her husband, and her grandchildren were on the table and walls.

"You followed the usual security measures?"

Isla nodded. "We covered our tracks, destroyed the tracking devices, and left no survivors at the pass."

"Such missions are getting too dangerous. Axis surveillance in orbit is tracking all their convoys. One that suddenly disappears into a mountain will create serious problems for us."

"What else can we do?"

"Nothing. Trying to beat technology that is far greater than us is impossible."

"Talia said you wanted to see me about a transmission?"

"Yes. The Bond has contacted us. We're leaving Nunearanor."

Isla's eyes widened in shock at the news.

"What? How?"

"The details are yet to be organised, but they have heard our calls for help. The Bond under the command of Prince Metora has retaken Ophistar in an attack and put the Black Ash Prince to flight."

"So, they can liberate us?" Isla asked anxiously as she tried to take in the exciting news and figure out the practicalities of a resurgent Bond of Seven Kings attack on her planet.

"No," the Queen said bluntly. "That is the part I need you to remain tight-lipped about. The Axis is too strong here. It's time to leave and join our friends in Anueth and add our strength to the Bond."

Isla was bitterly disappointed but not surprised at this turn of events. The prospect of the Bond launching an all-out attack to retake the planet was ridiculous.

"But Metora was able to retake Ophistar? Why not here? They turned us down to my face, Mum."

"The Axis are too strong and entrenched. They would be slaughtered."

"But to abandon our planet and all those people. We can't do that."

The Queen took her daughter's hand. "I know. It's been the hardest decision of my life, but if we stay here, we will be discovered and destroyed. If we leave, we may still have a chance. Better to flee a Kandrol dragon than have him eat you. Right?"

"Is there no other way?" Isla implored.

"I have spent weeks playing this over in my mind. You're wise enough to know time is against us."

Isla was almost in tears and her mother embraced her.

"This isn't a defeat. It's about survival. If Akara is all we have left of our world, I can't sit here waiting to die when there is a chance for us to live on. What else would you have me do?"

Isla looked at her mother, "Alright."

"Good. General Jan has been placed at the head of a taskforce. I want you to assist him. We have to take everyone and as much equipment as we can."

"Is Metora planning this?" Isla asked hopefully.

"I can only assume he is a part of the planning staff as he always has been."

Isla smiled, "Then I will give it my best."

"They're coming for us. We haven't been forgotten."

In the Menenyr hospital ward, medical droid M200 was doing the rounds. There had been the usual casualties from the week's exercises — broken bones, burns, and other ailments that accompanied training.

As he entered the room where the older man found on the shore of the Lake of Souls rested, his scanners showed the room was empty. Further scans revealed the same and his downloads showed that the patient had not been released. They did not even know his name and he had not offered it, asking instead for the whereabouts of another young pilot who was also found on the shoreline.

He checked the visual security of the ward and it showed the man did not exit the room. The droid watched as the man stood from his bed and simply vanished. Could people do this? There was nothing in his datafiles that showed that humans could dissipate in their present form. He reported the matter to his superior, as he had been programmed to, and exited the room, noting that he no longer had to check on Room 13C.

SETTING THE PIECES

"The mission to save the Nunearanor is on," Zuke proudly announced to a packed audience of the various commanders of the Bond's forces in the war room of Imperial Command, deep within Redsee Tower.

The commanders of the Taranova, Anueth, and Mahnarosa forces were there. Admiral Dreer, the new commander of the Jashirn forces, in her first conference, sat quietly. The other systems of the Bond — Kiam, Oneum, Palaniri, Chene, Ophistar, and Nunearanor — had no sizeable navy and generally were aligned to whatever system was providing the naval support for a particular mission.

"You may now open the sealed documents sent to you." He waited while computers came online and a massive hologram appeared on the table so that all could see it.

"As you can see, it is a simple operation but with high rewards. We are striking towards Nunearanor. The forces of the Lady Silver are at the end of their resistance. We will aid their rescue by striking here at the moon cluster of Wolven Moor."

The centre of the hologram became magnified and showed the moon called Wolven Moor orbiting Nunearanor.

"Wolven Moor is uninhabited except for a military garrison that controls a large battery of guns and defences. It is the hub of the command system around Nunearanor."

The magnification centred on the main fortress at the northern pole of the moon. A long tear that stretched for hundreds of kilometres was the most striking feature of the moon's surface. It was as deep as it was long. In some places, light could not reach and there were strong winds and heavy mist which prevented anyone reaching the bottom.

An old monastery, now converted to military use, with large radar installations, communication towers, and gun batteries, sat on the edge of this chasm. It was surrounded by a further three large gun stations that were all linked by a monorail. Dotted about were large hangers that held Striketroopers, fighters, and the large battledroids.

"Using radiation missiles, we will blast a hole through the minefields and maintain a fleet for planetary bombardment while we land an assault force on the surface to finish off the gun emplacements and command buildings. Knocking out the guns and communication channels will allow the other fleets to strike deep into Axis space through a thinly defended corridor and contact the Nunearanor fleet coming to meet us. It will then form a protective shield and rear-guard, guiding the fleets back through Wolven Moor. There we will retrace our steps, pick up the assault force, and fall back to Trinity. This is not liberation but a rescue."

There was a moment of discerning quiet among the high ranks as they each flicked each other worried looks.

"You want us to go through Wolven Moor? Why not breach the defences elsewhere?" Admiral Dreer queried.

"It is quite simple, Admiral. As I said, it is the least defended. Once we are through, the fleets shouldn't have a problem. They only need to contact the Nunearanor and guide it back. The rest of the fleet will counter any Axis forces while Wolven Moor is neutralised."

Zuke's response still didn't infuse the ranks with confidence.

"Do we even have enough forces for this?" Vice-Admiral Croner from Mahnarosa asked.

"Of course we do," Zuke snapped. "Metora assures me that this plan is airtight. There's nothing complicated about this, nothing at all."

Metora's name had the required effect with the ranks suddenly becoming more relaxed, except for Dreer, who appeared perplexed at the information. It also annoyed Zuke, knowing that his own plan met with silence but the mere mention of the Jashirn name made the questions stop.

"We are on a tight schedule. The fleet is ready to march. The Bond is ready to strike back!"

There was polite applause for the Admiral, though too much hesitation and doubt to satisfy his ego.

With the conference finished, most of the officers left to begin preparations, except for the Taranovian command staff. Their commander, Admiral Wistrall, a moustached, older man who had commanded their navy for years, made straight for Zuke.

"Grand Admiral, a moment," Wistrall asked.

Zuke nodded, not wanting to really hear from the old man.

"We won't be part of this. It's a suicide mission."

Zuke was appalled and didn't hide his contempt with any diplomatic mask.

"Why? Are you afraid?"

"No, this is just sending our troops to their deaths. Call it off." Wistrall was blunt.

"This has to happen. I know it's dangerous but to leave the Nunearanor there is criminal."

"You didn't want to help them when Princess Isla asked you to. You denied it to that poor girl's face, and now this." Wistrall wasn't going to be intimidated and pressed his argument.

It took all Zuke's strength not to physically attack the old man. He took a deep breath.

"This attack will go ahead. I have issued my orders to you. If you ignore them, you will suffer the consequences."

Wistrall nodded. "I will inform our headquarters."

The Admiral walked away and joined his delegation, then they all left the room. Zuke watched them go. The belligerence that seemed to be infecting Imperial Command was beginning to grate on him. He blamed Metora.

The old man had gone to bed and Quisto was finally able to continue his clandestine activities. Documents had arrived from his sources. They were classified as most secret and bore the insignia of the Commander-in-Chief of the Bond, Admiral Zuke himself.

As he began reading them, he couldn't wipe the smile from his face. Here, literally in his hands, was a prime chance to destroy the very heart of the Bond's fleet. They would be powerless to resist any offensive that the Axis initiated. It would be impossible for the Bond to reconstruct a new fleet in a short time. The Dark Lord would then have his victory over the Sangreal.

He sat back on his chair, pondering his next move. His predecessor would normally send an encrypted message back to an Axis intelligence agency, but he had new orders to pass on all information to this Nash Beren. It was in his nature to be distrustful. He could not have survived for so long if he had not been. Nonetheless, he would follow orders.

It was night in Anueth City. Nash Beren and Quisto walked along the promenade that wound its way around a large lake that sat in the eastern part of the city. It was dark and few people were around. Quisto was still anxious about seeing her out in public but she brushed off his fears.

"I still would prefer some caution."

"It's dark, no light, no people, the occasional patrol. I really don't care."

Quisto was a master in subversion and believed himself an intricate part of the Dark Lord's plan. Had he not slain a Chief of the Merenmere and been instrumental in starting the civil war? Surely the end would come when he would no longer be chained to an old man?

"So, you have urgent information?" she asked.

He was unsure of her purpose. Her sudden appearance in the city perplexed him and there were times he thought perhaps she was a double agent attempting to expose him.

"I received instructions to pass on all highly classified information through you. Even though I do not know you, I will do as I am ordered."

He passed her a data file. "The Bond are attacking. Nunearanor is the new target. The Dark Lord must receive this information urgently."

She laughed. Her eyes gleamed in the dim light. "This is excellent news, Quisto."

"I'm sure it will be put to good use."

"Soon all will fall into place. The amount of bickering and ineptitude among the Bond is atrocious but makes being devious all the easier."

Quisto was not a socialiser. He didn't really know what to do next. He certainly wasn't going to ask her for a drink. Beren seemed professional, even cold. Then again, so was he. Knowing how close she was in the inner circle of Kaw's world made him jealous. He had done great things and was babysitting an old man.

"I will return to the tower and await developments and, of course, pass on what I know."

She nodded and he left the area, glad to return to his hideaway. Even as he walked, he felt he was being watched. The amount of surveillance in the city was significant and he was aware that in this area there was little. Still, he wanted to be cautious. The last thing he wanted was to expose his operation. He would have a double deathmark then, from the Bond and the Axis. It was something he lived with, as he had orders to kill Beren if she failed. No doubt, she had the same with regard to him.

Lorian's punishment was to spend three days cleaning up in the mechanical workshops. Merenmere petty punishment wasn't designed to humiliate, that was reserved for worse crimes, but to educate, and he found being covered in grease and grit to be satisfying. It reminded him of being back home. Of course, his mind drifted to what his brother was doing. It still pained him about their last parting. Dez had changed while enduring the siege, no doubt brought on by the suffering and stress of the situation. He could only hope that he was able to find some peace.

Word of his failed sortie out to the Lake of Souls had not spread through the fortress, of which he was glad. His superior officers had stated it would remain classified and he would also be held to the same standard. Meaning, they would say nothing if he said nothing. He felt like an idiot and was able to laugh to himself at the repetition of his failure to cross the Adwene.

"My arms are killing me," complained Chips. He was another in the punishment house. His crime was to overstay his leave by two days. Getting lost in Anueth City wasn't a good enough excuse. So the two had spent three days taking apart damaged fighters which were ready for repair.

"Lieutenant."

Lorian looked up to see their supervisor, Sergeant Durran, approaching.

"Your time's up. A message for you." He handed Lorian a data file that could be put into the small telecommunication device all soldiers carried.

"What about me?" Chips asked.

"You're done too until we meet again."

"Not going to happen."

"Sure," Durran replied sceptically before leaving.

Chips extended his hand to Lorian, which he shook.

"It's been a pleasure. Let's meet somewhere better next time." Chips laughed before he walked away too, leaving Lorian to wander to the messroom, opening the message as he went.

It was from Kuring-gai.

"Lorian. I'm heading to Menenyr at 1600 hours to collect you and then we are going to see Metora. It's an urgent matter and I have cleared it with your commander. You can tell me how you ended up in the penal company on the way."

The message ended and Lorian looked at his watch.

"What's all this about?" he whispered to himself as he looked at the time. He'd have an hour to get ready.

Right on time, Kuring-gai was waiting in a smaller hanger.

"What's the urgency?" Lorian asked.

"We'll talk on the way, after you explain yourself."

"I smashed a speeder."

"Fair enough. Let's go."

They climbed aboard and took off, heading north at great speed.

"Where are we going?"

"Bannade House. It's a Jashirn complex in the mountains. Invitation only."

"So, he managed to get away."

Kuring-gai grunted his approval and continued concentrating on piloting the shuttle. Lorian sat back and enjoyed the view. He had never been this far north. Most of his training missions had been to the east and south.

These mountains were not like the bare and rocky Mountains of Peril on Ophistar. As far as he could see there were tall trees of green and blue, while the tallest peaks were covered in soft snow. There must have been a high wind as he could see the snow being blown from the tips to form clouds of snow that was then spreading over the trees.

Bannade House came into view. It didn't look like a military complex and he reasoned that this would have been what Anueth and many other planets were like before so many of the installations were militarised or destroyed.

There was a crisp wind blowing across the platform as they walked quickly into shelter. Kuring-gai led the way. He seemed to know the place and where to find Metora.

There were a number of Jashir Grenadiers dressed in deep blue standing guard in the doorways. They did not flinch on seeing Kuring-gai. Many of the walls were filled with paintings and artworks. It was warm and inviting and felt more like a home than a fortress.

At a great wooden door that carried the Royal Seal stood two Grenadiers. One of them opened the door to allow them in.

It was a large room warmed by a fireplace. There were plenty of couches and seats to sit on which were occupied by many men and women. They were all watching some children playing on the floor and chatting among themselves.

Metora's chamberlain, Gregor, approached. "Gentlemen, welcome, the Prince is expecting you."

Gregor led the way, but Metora had spotted them. He was sitting in a big chair close by the fire, a little girl curled up in his lap. He was in conversation with several younger girls.

"So, what was he really like?" one of them asked.

"Does your skin burn?" another quizzed.

Metora breathed in deep.

"Girls, Metora doesn't want to tell war stories. He came here to relax." Aunt Dannul came out of another room after finding out there were guests.

"Aunty, we were just asking. We don't want to be rude," one replied.

"It's alright. I thought you'd be sick of hearing solider stories?"

"This is different."

The right-hand man of Kaw clearly had the effect of fear and fascination for many people. The thought that this monster could kill them so easily seemed incredible. Maybe they wanted to know whether he really was so fearsome.

The glamour of war was gone. It had died a long time ago. Once he enjoyed telling and listening to these stories, but not anymore. One last time he would tell them as it was.

"I felt my skin wither and I thought if I looked into his face any longer then my blood would boil. There is no soul there, just a deep dark pit where all life ends."

The girls remained silent. Kuring-gai and Lorian stood waiting close by. Lorian was reminded of that encounter on Elsenmere Ridge. The very thought of the Black Ash Prince chilled him and he subconsciously began rubbing his hands together to keep them warm.

"Why do you want to know about that creature?" Kuring-gai bluntly asked them.

"We were just curious." They seemed embarrassed and moved away to talk with other relatives.

"You have something important to tell me?" Metora asked.

"In private."

Metora stood up, Koree still in his arms, her eyes on Kuring-gai.

She reached her left hand out towards him and he took it and kissed it, which made her laugh.

"This is Lorian, from Ophistar, the planet I was telling you about."

"Hello," she whispered.

The three moved to the window that looked over the valley.

"It's Nunearanor. Have you heard anything?" Kuring-gai began.

Metora shook his head. "I'm doing what I'm told to do. I haven't even been looking at any reports."

"Then you've missed the big news. Zuke seems to have been inspired by our handiwork and is going on the attack."

"Nunearanor? Idiot," Metora replied.

Lorian was just as surprised, as he had heard nothing since coming back to Menenyr. Being confined to the workshop didn't help either.

Kuring-gai produced a small hologram which showed the images of the plan.

"What does he plan to do?" Metora asked while looking at the hologram.

"I don't know the full operation, only that my command is part of another assault group which is to land on Wolven Moor and take out the defences there. Are you sure you have nothing to do with this?"

"I've heard nothing."

Kuring-gai looked aghast and let out a deep breath.

"Zuke is telling the commanders that you had input into this."

Metora scoffed. "Bit late to honour the plea of the Lady Silver now. I guess I'm to be left behind."

Kuring-gai shook his head, "You're in the tip of the spear, my friend. You're the commander of the assault group."

Metora's eyes widened, "Is that so?"

He looked to Lorian, "You heard anything?"

"There's been an increase in the number of older fighters being refurbished but I didn't think anything of it. Now I think they're trying to find any bit of material they can get their hands on."

"Your fighter unit hasn't received any instructions?" Metora asked.

Lorian shook his head, "I've been in the penal company, so I haven't heard anything."

Metora raised an eyebrow. "For what?"

Lorian looked to Kuring-gai. "It's a little more than crashing a speeder. I smashed it trying to get to Runamore."

Now it was Kuring-gai's turned to be astounded.

"Really? Did you get there?"

"No. A huge storm came up and swept me back to the shore. I almost drowned out there."

"No one returns from the mist. You were lucky," said Metora.

"I won't be doing it again."

"I wouldn't be sure of that," Kuring-gai responded.

Lorian looked to floor and caught the gaze of Koree who was staring up at him with a smile on her face. He smiled back.

"You haven't heard anything else?" Metora asked seriously.

"No. I received this yesterday and spent all night looking at it. I wanted your opinion, brother. What else is there to hear?"

"Nothing about King Leigh? Halkinbraun?"

"No. What is it?"

Metora breathed deeply and seemed to choose his words carefully.

"I knew there would be a blanket ban on any word getting out. We had a visit in the afternoon, three days ago, in the mirror room. We saw him."

"Who?" Kuring-gai pressed.

"Kaw."

"No," Kuring-gai exclaimed.

"It's true," came the voice of Oberon, seemingly appearing out of nowhere.

"In the palace?" Kuring-gai asked.

"Out of nowhere. Suddenly, he just was there, smashing the mirrors on the wall. He killed the King and the Colonel, right in front of us. Kaw said he'd been threatened and branded. He demanded that a person be given up. I don't know what he was talking about."

"Do you know?" Kuring-gai asked Oberon.

"No. However, something happened on that battlefield after the death of Laylana. I cannot explain it. That is why no one has seen him since."

"Some people thought he wasn't dead, only wounded," said Lorian.

"You know something?" Metora asked.

"Just been reading the report of the battle from General Lex. Laylana was killed and her body dumped at the foot of Kaw. He took her crown and put it on his head. Then, suddenly, there was a loud boom and a great wind blew up that shrouded a chilling cry of pain. Then he was gone."

"That is true. I remember that cry," said Oberon sadly.

They all went quiet for a moment before Metora spoke.

"If this battle fails then it could be the end of the Bond."

"Especially if Kaw is able to strike so easily. This is the first time he has been seen in years, right?"

Metora nodded.

"I know the King was an uncle to you and your sister. And poor Halkinbraun. More misery and death," Kuring-gai lamented as he looked up at the ceiling, his eyes closed and his chest heavy with breath.

"I've been told to say nothing, but you know how these things get out," said Metora, still hiding the fact that he had been wounded. His treatment was working and the little pain he had he was able to hide. He was used to carrying on with wounds, both physical and mental.

"And now Wolven Moor," Lorian added.

"And now Wolven Moor," Metora repeated bitterly.

"What do you want us to do?" Kuring-gai asked.

"I'll ask Admiral Dreer for more information. If I'm being sent out on a suicide mission, I at least want to know where I'm being sent to die."

"How many days did you get off?" Kuring-gai laughed.

"Three," Metora replied sharply, clearly not impressed with being dragged back into the fray.

Kuring-gai looked to Lorian. It was time to leave.

"We'll head back. I'll let you know if we hear more."

Metora nodded.

"Bye, cheeky girl." Kuring-gai tickled Koree's belly and she laughed.

They both turned then and left the room, followed by Oberon, leaving Metora with Koree.

"You don't want to go?"

Metora looked down at his little niece.

"No, I don't," he replied sadly.

Oberon watched the shuttle leave Bannade House, this time piloted by Lorian. Kuring-gai had slumped in the co-pilot's seat and seemed to fall asleep.

Recalling Laylana's name had brought back many memories for him. The battle outside the Jashir palace was the worst of his existence. It was the only day he ever had to face the Sons of Gorgoth, and they had decimated the Bond forces and killed three Sangrillions as well as the last Sangreal herself. He could hear her screams still. He had never been programmed to be able to completely delete memories unless he had his mind wiped, which he would not do. His empathy made him more connected with the soldiers he fought with, but there were days he wished he could delete them. Perhaps he would be destroyed? Then his memories would vanish. But there would be no swimming the oceans for him. It would be just like turning off a light.

He would walk these woods, allowing his mind to bury these memories deeper. It would also allow him time to consider all he had learned today — the return of Kaw, the Nunearanor offensive, and the revelation that Lorian had somehow been drawn to try to get to Runamore.

Akara base had been a hive of activity for days now. Food, equipment, and other supplies had been carefully rationed, even more than the standard of the past few years. Anything useless had been destroyed.

Patrols outside of the base's limits had been curtailed. The Axis was drawing nearer, like a blind man grasping in the dark, and the Nunearanor had been backed into a corner. Kaw's minions only had to reach out a little more and their fingertips would be close enough to expose Akara.

Enemy fighter patrols over the Orden Pass had become more frequent. They would find no sign of their missing convoy, only the remnants of the destroyed outpost now slowly being buried beneath the snow.

Some communications had been restored to other cells around the planet. These cells had been ordered not to reveal themselves or come to Akara. Too much traffic would make the Axis more suspicious. When the time came, they could leave their hiding places, muster off planet, and link up with the main fleet. Hopefully.

These final days would be the hardest. All personnel hid their tension by keeping busy planning.

In her private quarters, the Lady Silver listened while her command staff read out their progress and assumptions for the coming departure.

"All our reserve food has been stored away. We have enough left to last us until we leave," General Jan reported.

"The whole thing worries me," the Lady Silver interjected. "Getting off the planet will be the easy part. Getting through the enemy will make or break us."

"It will only take a number of lucky shots and we're doomed," replied General Jan.

"We should remain positive," she said with purpose in her voice. "All our energy should be put into getting as much as we can off-planet. We can only deal with the enemy fleets once we are in space. Do we have any further information on them?"

"None, My Lady. The information we have is old and incomplete. Imperial Command has not forwarded any updates and we are limiting our signals responses. Recon, of course, is not an option. We have enough cargo space to take all personnel, but a lot of the equipment will have to be left behind."

"I don't want anyone left behind. If we get out of here with nothing but our clothes on, so be it."

"We won't be much use to the Bond if we arrive with no weapons."

The Lady Silver shrugged. "True, but I wouldn't like to be thrown off a transport so a heavy auxiliary whatever can be put aboard. Much of it can be broken down into pieces, yes?"

"Yes, My Lady, of course."

"I leave it to you. We haven't got much to take with us anyway. I'm more concerned with taking our people. Any more reports from our cells?"

"None today, just yesterday's three cells from the western escarpment. They have managed to merge themselves without detection and have enough cruisers to make the move with us, but they are staying low and keeping their communications to a minimum."

She smiled, satisfied that everything was in good hands. Over the years she had grown close to many of these people, the soldiers, their families, and new families. Most of the personnel were military except for some scientists and engineers.

It had been a new world to her having been raised in the royal palace since she was a child. She had always meant to be Queen and the Nunearanor royals were probably the most martial of all the Bond's sovereigns, after the Merenmere. They were not aggressively warlike, however, though they were still fully trained in military matters. She was in command of a regiment of grenadiers by the time she was nineteen before taking the throne at twenty-one.

The invasion of her homeworld brought about the decision to bring many of her forces fighting in other areas of the galaxy back to Nunearanor to defend their homes. That decision had met with brutal verbal attacks from Imperial Command, ranging from cowardice to selfishness. How could her army fight on Jashir knowing their homeworld was under attack?

It had been the hardest of fights and the Nunearanor had made the Axis pay for every piece of ground won or city captured. Soon other systems from all the Sangrillion worlds joined in the fight. In the end, it wasn't enough.

The dreaded Striketroopers could be replaced easily but the Nunearanor couldn't just make new soldiers in a factory. With the Bond powerless to defend everywhere around systems, the planet was lost. The Lady Silver took her survivors underground to wait liberation.

"This whole enterprise scares me to death," she whispered. Her thoughts were on the memory of the day Rargarlith vanished under the guns of the Axis fleets and the ground rumbled in its own fear and revulsion at the destruction of the tallest mountain on the planet.

"Death is all around us, whether we stay or leave. Our chance is that this course of action will totally surprise the Axis. Only in those precious moments of shock before reaction kicks in will we know our fate."

"True," she whispered. Years ago, she thought she would die in bed surrounded by her grandchildren. She still had wanted that, but now matters were pressing.

She breathed in deeply. She sensed a migraine forming again. They were frequent, almost daily now, and they interrupted her decision-making. Many of the little things she now had her daughters complete.

While the decision to go had been made, there was another more personal decision she had to make.

"It's madness," Wolfcastle exclaimed through the monitor. He was still located in Myr Edele, putting the pieces of a fractured world back together.

Tiber, his second in command chuckled wearily to himself. Tiber had been doing his own part in keeping the peace between Zuke and the Merenmere forces in the Bond. It was a task made easier by the fact Zuke had all but ignored the Merenmere. Tiber had only found out about the attack when Jashir Command passed it on. He found it amusing that Zuke's spite had extended to the fact that the Merenmere were hardly involved, just their fighter units.

"When is it ever normal?"

"How are preparations? I noted that these orders came down from the Jashir. I'm betting he's regretful that his naval forces aren't powerful enough that he can afford not to invite us."

Tiber laughed. He hated Zuke as much as Wolfcastle did.

"I'm scrapping the bottom of the barrel with equipment trying to meet his quota. We've spent this time to rebuild our units and now they are going to be thrown away," Tiber complained bitterly.

"We're doing it for the Nunearanor, not Zuke."

"That is the only reason we're doing it, no one wants to leave them behind."

"Good. I've got another transport unit ready to send but Axis incursions are making it a difficult time. So, we must be careful when we run the gauntlet. I'm not sending you any more raw recruits. We're training them here."

"As long as they get here eventually. The troops I have are veterans and have the attitude that comes with it. It would be good to do a rotation back home."

This time it was the turn of Wolfcastle to chuckle.

"Many of them are soldiers with no place to go. Their families are dead and their homes destroyed. They've got nothing to lose. That means trouble for us but also danger to our enemies."

"Is it true that the senior veterans have refused to fight anymore?"

Wolfcastle took a breath. "It is true, but don't judge these soldiers too harshly. They have fought for years, some for two decades, and now they want to enjoy the remaining years with family. They have done their duty."

"We will do ours for the Nunearanor. Zuke says you're too scared to come back."

"That scrum-licker. I hope this grand plan works, for their sake and Zuke's. Because if it fails, then I'll kill him myself."

Lorian and Kuring-gai had said little on their way back to Menenyr. He seemed tired and had slept all the way, only waking when Lorian had landed on the platform.

"Good luck," he called out as Lorian left.

Back in his quarters he had orders waiting for him to return to his squadron, which he was surprised to see was back in Menenyr. While he was doing his punishment, he often wondered what they were doing and if they were still on Ophistar.

In the morning, he made his way to the squadron hall, which was a huge recreation centre for pilots of the fleet. There were lounges, food centres, and places where the pilots could relax.

There were quite a few people about, some in civilian clothes, others in fatigues. He recognised Kandrol Squadron's patch and a few others, proof of the military build-up in Menenyr.

As he made his way through, he could instantly hear Imogen's laughter. They didn't notice him at first as Trix, Imogen, and Kahil sat about laughing. He was surprised to see Kahil still in the unit. He had thought he might have been transferred already.

"Oh, look, it's our glorious commander!" Imogen shrieked.

She rushed into his arms and gave him a big hug. Trix followed soon after.

"Look who's the popular one," Kahil dryly replied.

Lorian sat down with everyone.

"Where have you been? With Prince Metora?" Imogen asked eagerly.

"I have seen him."

"Did he ask about me?"

"No," he replied bluntly but with a smile.

"Awww, not fair." She was disappointed.

"I'm sure he's got a lot to deal with," said Trix.

"Well, maybe he needs a woman's touch." She and Trix traded a knowing stare that made them both burst into giggles.

"You know, you're probably right," Lorian replied.

"Well, put in a good word."

"So, are you back with us, or still hanging out with Metora?" Trix asked.

"No, I'm back."

"Where's your droid, getting your lunch?" Kahil joked, but Lorian knew it was just a mask hiding his misplaced resentment.

"Still on her missions. What have you been up to?"

"Stayed with our parents in Star Mun, helped clean up, that sort of stuff," replied Imogen.

"How bad is it?"

"It's getting better. Myr Edele is looking good. Winter wasn't too bad. Things are getting organised now that the Chief is running things. A few old politicians have popped their heads up wanting their old jobs back," added Kahil.

"How's your wound?" he asked Trix.

"Healed, cleared for flying."

"Did Metora touch this jacket?" Imogen leaned in close, her hand on Lorian's shoulder.

Lorian just laughed.

"Imogen, stop it." Trix laughed too.

"I was just asking."

"No, he didn't touch the jacket."

"Are you sure?" She looked at him deeply.

"Very."

"Ok, I lose." She put her arms around his shoulders.

"It's good to have you back."

"There are rules against fraternisation you know," Lorian replied.

"Oh," she said, lifting her head up to look at him. "Maybe I just can't help myself."

Lorian didn't know what to do. She was gorgeous with her bright eyes and playful personality.

"The boy just got back, Imogen. Leave him be," Trix called out between laughing spurts.

"Ok, I'll be good." Imogen sat back with her hands on her lap and a little distance between herself and Lorian.

"Have you heard what's going on?" Kahil asked.

"Yeah, we're going somewhere again. Your handsome friend tell you?" Imogen asked.

"No," he lied.

Lorian was conscious to keep the information sharing secret. If it was found out that a lowly Lieutenant had read the entire operational plan, heads would roll, especially Metora's. He was just as surprised as Metora to see his name as part author and battlegroup commander. The commando detachment had been given an almost suicide mission of taking the fortress at Wolven Moor. Everyone who had read the history of the old wars knew that was where Thara had finally been defeated. In the years since Elle, the last Ethereal, had flung herself into the crevasse, the place had become even more important to the Order of Light. Many members and even some average people would travel there to walk among the chilly ramparts below the fortress walls, reliving that fateful day.

It was ransacked by the Gorgoth during Kaw's extermination of the Order, the bodies of the dead thrown out into the cold. No one hoped for any survivors.

Zuke had organised the attack right down to the last minute and detail. Fleets and groups all had a time limit to reach their assignments. Lorian quickly found out that the Merenmere fighter groups would be part of the contact group that had to punch the deepest into Axis space and guide the Nunearanor back to the Trinity. He wanted to believe it was because they were the more experienced pilots, but the pessimist in him believed it was punishment for Ophistar.

"I've got a hunch," another pilot nearby who had heard the conversation leaned over.

"Yeah?" Imogen raised an eyebrow.

"Nunearanor," he whispered and put his finger to his lips.

"Oh, heaven. We're all gunna die," Imogen said. The light that had filled her face moments before was gone. Lorian was visibly shocked. Not because he wanted to fake his knowledge, but because someone else had either guessed it or had their own informants.

"And do what there? Liberate them like we did at home?" Kahil exclaimed.

"I don't know." The pilot wouldn't say any more as the mood had turned sullen and he began to really worry about talking about things he shouldn't be.

"Sins of the fathers. Who knows what they have got in store for us?" Kahil fell back onto the couch, his eyes looking up at the ceiling.

Lorian looked at Trix. "So you've grown your hair."

She nodded. "Yeah, while I was in bandages, I let it grow."

"At least he noticed. Kahil never said a word," Imogen laughed.

Kahil remained impassive, his thoughts seemingly far away.

"Well, I'm sorry to have ruined the party. It's just a hunch. I might be wrong," the pilot said as he walked off.

"You wish you were wrong," Imogen called back.

"I think he's right." Kahil had come out of his staring at the ceiling. "Is he right?" He looked at Lorian who let out a full lung of air he hadn't realised he was holding in.

"'Cause, you know things," Kahil waved a finger at him.

Lorian did know things and he realised that he needed to be careful to keep them to himself in the future, but he felt guilty in not sharing this information with people that depended on them. These were the people who were closest to him. How could he not share it? Guilt was something he didn't want to live with.

An alarm sounded three shrieks before a red light began flashing. It was the alarm for pilots to report to their flight stations.

"Another exercise?" Lorian asked.

Imogen shrugged. "Maybe. It's been almost daily and some flights have been engaging Axis recons outside the wall."

"Kandrol Squadron alarm. Kandrol Squadron alarm. All pilots report to your stations."

"That's us," Imogen smiled.

Many of the other pilots yelled out calls of support and waved as the pilots of Kandrol hurried out of the hall and to the elevators.

Lorian walked with his unit to the elevator that would take them to the flight deck. Obviously, there was going to be little resting.

Trix took his arm. She looked at him and Lorian felt she was able to read all his secrets.

"Kahil's right. It's ok, I understand. We'll get through this together."

"Thanks, Trix."

They reached the flight deck and went for their fighters. Lorian ran to their flight commander, Major Tauchmann, who was waiting for all wing commanders to report.

"An Axis fleet has appeared near Trinity sector Gamma. A number of fighters have been hitting a shield complex. Our orders are to drive away their fighters. Orders and coordinates have been downloaded."

Lorian looked at his data panel and saw the full report, even footage of the fleet. It was a full-strength fleet that sat threatening and unmoving.

"They know we won't touch it," Lorian said to himself.

"We don't know what it's doing," Tauchmann said.

He clapped his hands. "Alright, to your fighters."

Lorian ran to his fighter. It was still scorched from the combat on Ophistar. The paint was already coming off in parts and there were patches of repair.

His mechanic, who had already fired up the engines, handed over his helmet and patted him on the shoulder.

Inside the cockpit, he put the target information into the data panel, allowing his pilots to see.

"Where we going?" Kahil asked.

"We are going outside Trinity to beat off Axis fighters hitting an outpost," Lorian said while checking his systems.

"Easy," Kahil replied.

"Yeah, that's the easy part. The Axis fleet that appeared today might leave you thinking again."

"Are you serious?" Imogen exclaimed.

Lorian's flight lifted from the flight deck to join the other fighters all forming up to fly out into the void of space.

The fighters twisted in a long column through the planet's lines of defences. At times, it was hard to make out what were stars and what were defences. There was always work going on, repairs and improvements, more guns, more mines, as many as the stretched resources of the Bond could build.

It took some time to navigate the endless channels through the defences and out towards Taranova.

Taranovians weren't the most militaristic of all the former systems of the Bond. Being shielded by the more powerful systems of Jashir, Oneum, and Kiam, that were attacked first by Kaw's Axis, saved her from annihilation. Strong counter moves and the fierce battles for Jashir made her occupation a lesser concern for Kaw.

Not that the war situation made the Taranovians change. They bitterly resented being dragged into the war and there were grumbles from Imperial Command that Kaw could have them and see how he treats their whingeing or, better still, see how Taranova would have felt if they had been conquered instead of Oneum or Kiam.

Slowly, they changed. They knew that for the sake of the former Sangrillion worlds they had to. Many left the planet, not wanting to fight, believing it was just punishment for the decline of the Sangreal. Where they went, no one knows. Soon, no one cared and no one wanted them back if the war was won.

Taranova soon disappeared behind her veil of ubiquitous defences. Her population mobilised for total war and they would win so they could return to a life of peace.

The Merenmere fighter group was joined by a Taranovian squadron and together they exited a gate through the outer defences, quickly coming into clean space.

The first thing Lorian saw was the mass of ships in the distance. They just hung there, not moving and not firing, intimidating in their mass and potential.

Ahead, there were Taranovian fighters engaged with Axis fighters attacking a number of firebases manned along Trinity.

Lorian thought it a strange thing for this Axis move. It seemed more of a test than anything serious. Zuke probably wanted a show of force to prove the Bond wouldn't be intimidated. Somehow, he believed that just wouldn't be the case.

"Kandrol Squadron to the left flank," ordered Major Tauchmann.

The flight pushed across the face of Trinity, many of its guns firing wildly at the distant fighters. Though Lorian saw burning and debris coming from some of them, it seemed a mere flea bite.

Other pilots' voices were coming over his earpiece indicating they were now engaged with the enemy, though he saw nothing.

"So, where are these fighters?" Kahil asked.

"No idea," he replied.

His flight did a few more circles around the damaged part of the wall, not seeing any of the enemy. Other fighters were engaged in dog fights, but nothing for them to be concerned about.

"Bit of a waste," whispered Trix.

"True," whispered Lorian.

"Kandrol Squadron, return to base. It's all over."

"When did it begin?" an anonymous pilots asked.

"Alright! Time to bitch when we get back," came Tauchmann's reply.

Lorian breathed out a few times. This was going to be his life over the next few days, countless alerts, pointless scrambles for pointless missions that achieved nothing but give their enemy an advantage. They were watching.

Metora's thoughts were far away, torn between distant hearts across the galaxy. Their fate was constantly uppermost in his musing. He wanted something to fight for. There had to be something or there was no purpose anymore.

He often joked about death, as any person who is surrounded by it does. It was a strange trait of many veterans, more of a coping method because of the dehumanising effect war had on people.

Still bleary-eyed, he continued to look through the battleplan secretly provided by Kuring-gai. It was ambitious and highly structured. Fleets and squadrons all had to be at certain locations and accomplish their mission by certain times. Every minute movement had been timed to detail. It would only take one problem to upset the whole timetable. It made his stomach twitch with trepidation. There was no flexibility or initiative to allow a good commander the space to react if a plan didn't go to its author's intent. In fact, there was no single commander who would be there. Zuke, who would remain safe on Anueth and not join the crews he was sending out to their possible deaths, was commanding the whole enterprise from afar. It was a recipe for disaster.

Of all the objectives, Metora's assault group made up of various troops from all corners of the Bond were to seize Wolven Moor. There was little information about this detail. He was kept out of the loop and he believed that Zuke was deliberately keeping it secret just so that Metora couldn't complain or change it.

If Metora was truly honest to himself, he was horrified and, worse, his name had been mentioned in its planning — a scapegoat ready to be offered up.

All morning he had been receiving messages from Jashir command staff requiring confirmation of his involvement and pleading for changes to be made to the plan. After more of them arrived from other command sections he had sent out an unofficial retort that he had nothing to do with the planning.

This had started a whole tirade of more messages that he eventually just stopped replying to.

He had orders to report to the Jashir flagship, *Aquila*, by nightfall. For hours he had delayed it, preferring to spend time with Koree. For someone so young, she was fully aware of what was going on.

"If Uncle Metora dies, then it's my job to protect people," she once announced to Aunt Dannul.

She was the only reason he wanted to come back.

The time had come. He could delay it no more. The wound to his shoulder had still not healed fully, making use of his arm difficult. A few days more and it would have been fine, but now he wouldn't be given that chance.

Koree had fallen asleep and Aunt Dannul had come to take her. Metora couldn't do it. It was best if he just left.

"Look after yourself," Aunt Dannul whispered, her hand on his cheek.

He could only nod, shielding his broken heart. Earlier, many of his family had come to say goodbye. It had been emotional and there was no way he could do that at this moment. Aunt Dannul knew that and had organised it all. She was the head of Bannade House. Her husband, Fein, had been seriously injured and resided here. She counted both lucky. She knew how hard it was for a soldier to say goodbye.

Nepta was waiting for him at the shuttle.

"Everything will be alright Sir."

He could only manage a half smile.

The shuttle wasn't taking them straight to the Jashir station in orbit but back to the palace. Princess Serimay had requested he come.

He and Nepta went back to his quarters. It was empty now. The confrontation with Kaw was still fresh. All the glass from the shattered mirrors had been removed and curtains now covered the empty panes.

"We're not sure what to do with it now," Serimay said from a doorway.

She was in her late thirties, tall and slender, dressed in simple clothes, and held a cup of wine.

"I'm not concerned. Maybe you should lock it down."

"Well, this was always your place."

"Have you decided what to do?"

From the way her shoulders seemed to hang, the decision on her father's burial had been heavy on her. Serimay was a qualified doctor and had been stationed in the large military hospital in Anueth. Now she had to decide what to do about that too.

"Admiral Zuke is still ordering a blackout, especially now. I haven't been informed formally about what is happening. Can't even give him the dignity of a formal burial. Morale may suffer, you see." She seemed to be repeating words spoken to her.

"It isn't fair," Metora lamented.

She sat down on a seat that hadn't been taken away.

"I wanted to see you before you go. I'm worried about you."

Metora looked at her, one eyebrow raised in surprise.

"Really?"

"Of course. After all that has happened in the past few months — Ophistar, the trial, and now this — I know the Elector is pressing you."

He looked at her with mock suspicion. She looked at Nepta.

"You know I have my sources, Sir. You forget about my psychological programmes," stated Nepta.

"Oh, I'm losing my mind. That's no secret to me."

Serimay took her time looking at him, almost scanning him for problems.

"I wanted to pass on to you personally some information that I received. There is a faction building within all the Bond systems that could tear us apart. I haven't got identities, but there are those wanting to overthrow the Elector. Some want to sue for a separate peace, others want power for themselves. I have no doubt that the outcome of Zuke's plan will reveal what road these groups will put us on."

Metora sighed heavily. "There have always been splinter groups and those targeted for assassination, like me. How big is the grumbling?"

"Nepta," Serimay indicated for the droid to speak.

"Oberon has been tracking several transmissions from Axis spy sources about serious plans for a coup. There appears to be a number of groups made up of various dissidents."

"Blaster to our faces, knives to our backs," Metora replied. "I've been reading reports on this for a while but it looks like the rumbling is getting louder."

"I'm not sure what to do about it. This thing isn't really my expertise."

"Too many things to think about."

"I'm sorry to dump that on you know. If you win, you gain time, but if you fail, I don't know what sort of Bond you will come back to."

There was a moment of silence between them. She took a moment to finish her wine before getting up to embrace him.

"Alright, just come back safe."

He began to walk away when Serimay called out.

"Look after him Nepta."

"I will, My Lady."

Metora was silent as they walked through the corridors headed towards the hangers.

Nepta had wanted to say something, but it seemed the Prince was lost in his own world, taking in the information just given to him.

"Sire, Imperial Intelligence has a number of files on certain agitators like Ishil, Tyn, Marra, and Lonna Darn."

"I know. Ishil isn't stupid, he knows how Kaw works. Lonna, well she isn't far from the rule, 'the end justifies the means'. But I really don't know what to do about them." He was rubbing his temple with his fingers.

"Migraine, Sire?"

"Yeah, more frequent now."

"I would say to rest, but that is mute considering the Imperial Command's contradiction on your status. I understand you would rather stay in Bannade House or your own home. I can only offer my sympathies."

They entered a lift and Metora put the back of his head against the steel wall. It was cold and it soothed the pain in his head.

"Where would you like to end up, Nepta?"

She seemed surprised by the question and took a moment to process it.

"My favourite of times was being on Ophistar with Lorian and his family."

Metora smiled. "That's a good wish."

The lift stopped and the door opened into a hanger. It was cold. A chilly wind was sweeping across the platform embracing the drizzle that now covered the palace.

They made their way to the shuttle. The autopilot had it set for the Jashir Station.

As the shuttle left the hanger and headed into the rain, Metora looked out over the grounds of the palace and the city.

"You know, Nepta, of all the combat missions I've done, this is the one that makes me truly think maybe I'm not coming back."

"I hope that it is not true, Sir. Have you prepared for this eventuality?"

He laughed to himself at the cold logic of droids.

"I have." He sat back and breathed out deeply.

"Sir, I have received a green code. We are to report to the command group on the *Aquila* immediately,"

"Here we go again."

The *Aquila* was a new Dynastic Class battleship with dozens of heavy guns, three squadrons of fighters and bombers, heavy armour, and shields. It was the new flagship of the fleet with a multi-system crew from all over the Bond.

They were powerful but expensive ships. The shipyards had managed to build only three, with a fourth currently under construction. If more had been available, they would cause the Axis problems, but it seemed time was running out.

The fleets had to carry on with the older Caraver Class. While strong for their day, they were dated as new technology came into being and each side put more guns and more armour on their ships.

Jashir Station was a huge floating battlestation, lying just out of orbit. All the fleets were stationed here, safe within the massive gun towers and shields. Here they would be restocked and their crews rested. Ships with more serious problems were returned to Anueth for major repairs.

Much of the station had been recovered after the fall of Jashir itself. Knowing that the Navy would need resources, Admiral Rayker had ordered as much saved as possible. Most of it was put back together with new defences, hangers, and quarters added over the years.

In the docking bay of the *Aquila*, Metora was pleasantly surprised to see there was a large number of Jashir officers. Captain Journ stepped forward. He was only in his early forties and found himself in command of the newest ship in the fleet. He was a man of average height with several scars across his face, caused by flying shrapnel during his long years of naval combat.

"Sire, we're glad to have you with us."

"I hope I can be of use to you. I don't bring any answers about what this is all about."

"Well, we haven't heard much either. Is it Nunearanor?"

Metora nodded. "More than that I can't tell until the full briefing when all will be revealed."

Journ seemed to be conflicted. "I feel like a man going to his execution."

Metora smiled. "I'm glad I'm not the only one."

They made their way to the briefing room and he was once again pleasantly surprised to see Perreder waiting among the officer group.

The Old Father of the Khoru put his arm on Metora's shoulder and squeezed his cheek with the other hand.

"Ready to die?"

"Doesn't anyone have faith in our Grand Admiral's vision?" Metora mockingly asked the assembled group.

There was quiet laughter from the assemblage.

"There's a whole bucket of talk and theories going around this one. I knew this this one did not have your spirit, am I right?

Metora's jovial mood was gone, replaced with worry and anger.

"I had no input into this insanity, none at all."

"True? Then I really am filled with fear."

"Where's Kuring-gai and your combat team?"

"Saying their prayers."

"Oberon isn't here." Nemarluk appeared at Perreder's side carrying data discs. "I'm thinking he's the smart one and decided to hell with this and stay at home pulling his carb cord."

"That's not Oberon's style," replied Metora.

"True. How are you, Metora? I haven't seen you since that terror on Chene."

"I try not to think about it. I've been staying in the Blue Hills with family."

Perreder's face lit up. "Good, I'm glad to hear it. How is that little one?"

"Happy."

"Good. I see your eyes come alive when you speak of her. Nemarluk has become a father again but it hasn't stopped him offering his opinion." He looked at his son with a tight smile.

"I see a krick pile, I say a krick pile."

"I wish I was there to see Zuke turn pale when he saw you in the Admiral's room."

"It's one of my favourite memories I will take north with me. He knows I'd slit his throat," he said with a smile.

"What is your child's name?"

"You will find out before embarking. We're having a naming ceremony before we leave. Old Father insisted because he thinks none of us are coming back," Nemarluk said with a touch of aggression that Metora picked up on.

"Gentlemen, let's head to the bridge," Journ offered.

"We're in Hanger Seven fitting out the last of our stuff. We'll see you there," Nemarluk nodded.

Metora, Perreder, and Journ headed towards the bridge.

"You haven't seen Oberon?" Metora asked Journ.

"No, I'm sure he'll get here when he's ready."

"Have you heard from our fearless leader?"

Journ chuckled to himself. "He's bunkered down in Redsee. Admiral Taurus is in command of this battlefleet."

"I was hoping he would change his mind and join us, so we at least had a unified command. Taurus used to be a Commodore?"

Journ looked at him with a knowing chuckle. "Some of us are moving up in the galaxy. He's on the Admiral's bridge sorting out last minute problems."

"Problems?"

They had reached the entrance to the bridge which was guarded by two guards dressed in white uniforms and armed with large blasters.

Journ took a deep breath. "Let's talk in my quarters."

The Captain's quarters were behind the bridge. It was a large comfortable room with paintings and, significantly, a portrait of Laylana, the last Sangreal.

"Taurus hasn't been on a mission for years. Few of the crew have. There are equipment shortages, spare parts are critical, even ammunition has been rationed. Then there are problems with the fleet."

"This is news to me," Metora replied.

"We're used to having to scrounge and improvise when it comes to equipment," said Perreder.

Journ began to pace about. Now they were behind closed

doors his cool demeanour was gone.

"It's been inactive for way too long and some of the boosters don't work, electrical problems of all sorts, you name it. We had to leave behind almost two dozen ships because the engines wouldn't start. We aren't prepared for this. It's all too soon and hurried."

"Morale?"

Journ nodded his approval. "That's the only good news. Have you seen the battleplan?"

Metora nodded. "It came my way."

Perreder had a quick chuckle.

"It's complex. Zuke thinks he can just reach in and grab the Nunearanor and escape. With more ships and troops, it could probably be done, in time and with effort. But what he is throwing at it is not enough."

A buzzer sounded, interrupting their conversation.

"Enter," Journ called out.

The door opened to reveal a young officer. By the narrowing of his eyes and slight twist in his mouth he seemed a little put off on sighting Metora. Metora knew why.

"Captain, the briefing is about to begin."

Journ nodded.

Metora felt like saying something, but the officer turned about and left just as quickly as he entered.

"Was that Zayn Taurus?" Perreder asked.

"Correct," Journ sighed.

"I wondered what happened to him."

"As you can tell, there are men loyal to Zuke here. The Ethereals only know why, but blood and promotion would be the reason. They will be watching you."

"He could have let me stay at home."

Perreder laughed, "And miss the chance of a hero's death?"

"Or a scapegoat," added Journ as he grabbed his officer's cap.

They all left the Captain's quarters and made their way to a nearby lift that would take them a few floors higher. Inside was Taurus, an average height male, older, with balding hair cropped short. He was looking out the viewscreen at the assembled ships. His white uniform was pressed and pristine, the medals on his chest freshly polished. He had an air of arrogance and confidence. None of the assembled officers made any effort to go near him, except his son, who appeared at his side and whispered in his ear. Taurus turned to face Metora and Perreder. He nodded but said nothing, instead going back to looking out of the window.

"Officers!" he suddenly called out. The room went silent. He made his way to the middle of a large screen and stood beside it.

"Briefing has now started. All take their seats," Taurus ordered. Many of the officers were already seated. Perreder decided to take a seat while Metora and Journ stood on the opposite side of Taurus.

On the screen, Admiral Zuke's face appeared.

"Officers of the Bond, our hour has come. With lightning speed, we will crash through the Axis defences, rescue our Nunearanor allies, and guide them back to Trinity. We expect surprise to be complete. I expect all soldiers to do their duty and fight hard for the Bond. Good luck."

The transmission ended leaving many bewildered faces. The more cynical simply shook their heads. Metora looked about at the officers whispering to each other. Many gave quick glances his way, looking for reassurance or answers.

The whispering stopped when Taurus moved to the centre of the screen. "Questions?"

"How much time before the Axis react?" An officer asked.

"That can't be determined. We strike, we relieve, we shield. That is our mission."

Taurus' answer didn't seem to satisfy the officers who all still looked concerned.

"There is nothing in these reports that mention Axis strength," another officer stated.

"There are four fleets in the system."

Mouths dropped. Even Metora's stomach twitched. He knew there were sizeable Axis forces in the Nunearanor system. Having it confirmed made him sick.

"Prince Metora's battlegroup will take care of Wolven Moor, allowing passage through. We're not liberating the planet, merely allowing the Nunearanor a chance to escape. Surprise will be our asset. Drive hard, gain your objectives while the other fleets gain theirs, and then fall back together. It really is that simple," Taurus stated bluntly.

He then checked his watch, ignoring the faces of those who wanted to ask more questions.

"The time has come. Back to your ships."

The officers stood up and began to file out. Metora joined their group. Many of them were angry and confused.

"What do you think of this, Sire?" an officer asked.

Metora was aware of both the Tauruses looking at him with steely eyes. The men's faces showed worry and fear. He had to bury his own concerns deep, for their sakes. He would pick himself up and fight for them.

"If we stay together, we can survive." He turned to Journ. "Just keep the fleet together. We'll knock out Wolven Moor as quick as we can and make sure they get the Nunearanor. Don't piss about fighting when it turns to krick piles, which it will. We'll need to get out as fast as we can."

"It won't be pretty."

"No, but let's look after each other, like we always do. Good luck."

Lorian wasn't part of any higher command briefing. He and his other pilots had finished their own. They had their mission, and that was what he knew. A mixed fleet would delve deepest into Nunearanor space, contact their fleet, and escort it back. Information regarding the defences of the system wasn't given to them but Lorian had done his own homework by asking Nepta. He was aware of just how strong the system's defences were. None of them had any illusions about surviving the battle. Only the lucky ones would come back.

He had wandered down to the *Gemini's* flight deck. As its shield door was open, he could look out into space. Many Bond ships were stationed nearby. Even the large shields and minefields could be seen in the distance. Beyond that, more battlestations and, finally, Trinity itself.

He needed these quiet moments, and he knew others were the same. No more of his strange dreams had come to him but he was perplexed by a name — River'eah. It had come to him in a dream but he had no idea who or what it was.

"Lorian Shane," came the booming voice of Oberon walking towards him.

He cast his shadow over Lorian.

"I thought you would be on the flagship."

"I will go there next, but I want to ask you about Runamore."

Lorian was puzzled. He hadn't even seen anything of the mythical fortress.

"Why did you try to get there?"

"I don't know. It felt like I had to, but I didn't get there. A storm took care of that and I almost drowned. You lived there once?"

"I did. It was my home until the tears boiled on the lake and hid her."

"Why?"

"The Order of Light and the Ethereals belong to a different spiritual world that many people don't understand."

"What happened on Jashir when Kaw disappeared?"

"I saw my Sangreal cut down and the Dark Lord cry out when he put the crown on his head, and then he fled."

"Do you know why?"

"No."

"Do you know the name River'eah?"

It took only a second for the droid to scan his memory for the name.

"I know of him. He lived five hundred and eighty years ago and was one of the greatest of the Order, but he fell into wickedness attempting to murder a Sangreal before repenting before his death. Why do you mention his name?"

Lorian knew this, as he had also run the name through the library. Indeed, this River'eah had stabbed his wife, the Sangreal Lynstrall, over jealousy. He had been a great and wise man but his emotions had boiled over in him. He spent the rest of his life incarcerated in Runamore.

"I dreamed it. I'm tired of these dreams of a woman who appears out of the water and calls to me. I don't know what she wants. It's beginning to frustrate me."

Oberon's head quickly turned to look down at the boy.

"What woman?"

"She comes out of the water, which is like an underground lake. I've seen her die and rot away."

"The Ethereals were born out of a lake hidden in a mountain."

"Why is she coming to me?"

"I don't know but I believe she is an Ethereal."

"She should be talking to you."

"I don't dream."

"I think you do." Lorian looked up at the droid.

Oberon remained silent.

"Are you joining the Khoru?"

"Wolven Moor is my target. Without its destruction the fleet with find themselves in deep trouble."

Lorian looked out at space. Oberon stood over him.

"I truly believe this woman is an Ethereal. She calls from her grave to her children that all is not lost."

Oberon turned and left him. Lorian hoped this was true. He wanted to believe it too, but it was hard to be optimistic in such troubled, pessimistic times, especially when death was waiting for you in the coldness of space.

After Oneum was overrun during Kaw's first offensive, she remained in the darkness. All that was known was that the planet was handed over to the species called the Wrydluk.

No one knows where in the Dark Worlds this species came from. They were unknown to the Sangreal and their appearance in the Axis army was a frightful shock.

Their physical appearance did not match any known humanoid and they were not the result of failed nuclear experiments like the Gunadar were. None of the remarks about them were complimentary. They were feared and loathed, and not just in Bond circles. The Diamalords avoided them unless ordering them into battle. The Gunadar feared them as much as the Bond but saw them as a necessary, brutal fighting force. Just how many more savage creatures like these existed beyond the known galaxy? And were they too in league with the Dark Lord?

What was known about the Wrydluk was that they loved to kill. They would eat the enemy dead on the battlefield in wild celebrations. It sickened the soldiers of the Bond and it was a fate all were keen to avoid. No one wanted to be left behind on a battlefield, whether wounded or dead.

It had been the inglorious fate of the last Sangreal. Her guards were unable to retrieve her body during the defeat outside Jasmin. They and the survivors were forced to witness the desecration and were filled with impotent hate at the spectacle.

Here on Oneum, the Dark Lord had given the Wrydluk a forward base, much to the horror of the population. There had been wild looting and murder after the planet's fall. Then there was no further information coming from Oneum. No strength reports, no resistance cells, and it was years before the trickle of survivors managed to reach Bond lines and reveal the great horror.

The Wrydluk had immediately begun dismantling and pillaging the infrastructure of the planet, including the fuel and precious minerals, and returning it to their own world. The Diamalords had put a stop to the plundering as the resources were necessary for the war effort. This had even led to small firefights between so-called allies as the Wrydluk sought to keep their booty until orders from the Dark Lord himself forced them to obey. While the worlds of the Sangreal feared the Wrydluk, it seemed the Wrydluk feared the power of Iminus Kaw.

Axis commanders had seen that the habits of their new allies had paid high dividends and had begun moving units from Oneum to other planets in an attempt to crush resistance. They had been earmarked for Nunearanor, but the Gunadar insisted they could do the job themselves.

The Wrydluk were not plentiful and, much to their frustration, they were kept in reserve waiting for the final offensive. They wanted to be in on the kill but hated waiting for it. There were things to set right first, however.

By the Great Middle Ocean, now polluted with oil and the debris of war and manufacture, stood a figure cloaked in black. The Wrydluk were loyal to the Black Ash Prince as his viciousness and cruelty matched their own. It was an honour for the Wrydluk for him to visit their new world, whatever business or orders he would bring.

His gaze was directed out to the ocean where dozens of probe droids buzzed about in the fading light. They would come out of the water and then re-enter to sink to the bottom of the ocean again.

"Probe seven has found its mark, my Lord," a computerised voice spoke as it translated the Wrydluk commander's unpronounceable language.

Cryacur merely nodded and continued to wait. Another planet and another grave of an Ethereal for him to find. This one was at the bottom of the sea, deep beneath the ocean.

While the graves of the most powerful Ethereals had been located, it was the others that had disappeared from the galaxy which now concerned Kaw. The panic had passed and Cryacur was sure the dead Ethereals were no longer a threat. His Master was no fool and understood that overlooking the smallest detail could undo all that he had built. This was the last of the Ethereals killed by the hand of Thara.

Jharoneum was shy and slender. She detested violence, preferring to remain in the forests and oceans of this world. The population hardly saw her but she would always be there in times of crisis, especially childbirth. For years she had maintained her habit of being there for every newborn child. She delighted in holding new life.

All the Ethereals had their own unique attractiveness. Jharoneum had red hair and bright green eyes and many men on Oneum would go out looking for her, inevitably failing to catch her eye.

Once, she loved Thara, before his demeanour changed. She had born him three Flame Trees but had withdrawn from the universe for reasons that the other Ethereals never knew, and which she kept secret.

It was sunset when Thara came out of the woods near the Great Middle Ocean. Jharoneum was spending time deep at the bottom of the ocean, her mind closed to the voices to the other Ethereals. But it was Elle who finally broke through her wall and warned her.

She had already spent weeks under the ocean and it was time for her to return to the surface.

As she emerged from the cooling water, her red hair falling at her back, she was taken completely by surprise by Thara.

His grip was around her throat before she could even open her mouth to take a breath.

Her green eyes were like emeralds in the dying light. They bore into his own before he closed them out of shame. Her fingertips brushed his cheek, spreading the tear that had fallen from his eye.

Finally, her body went limp. In reaction to the emotions burning inside him he flung her far back into the ocean she had just come from.

He refused to look back as he began to trudge through the woods where his shuttle waited.

Behind him, the ocean began to roar, and he could feel its chill as the spray dampened his clothes. He finally stopped and looked. A mighty whirlpool erupted from where Jharoneum's body had disappeared. Then she rose from the angry water, her eyes alight with fire as she stared at him.

"You will gain all your dark heart desires, oh mighty Master of Sorrow. Alas, you will not keep it, as that is the folly of all evil souls."

Then she slowly sank below the waves and the sea was calm

once more.

Thara merely grunted his contempt and left the planet, never to return to it. Jharoneum's words, however, would haunt him.

From that time on, this sea was a haunted place. The Oneum rarely ventured across this cove. Underwater craft would report strange lights and strong currents that became whirlpools and could whip craft about almost tearing them apart.

Even the Wrydluk avoided this place.

"It is reporting no finds, my Lord."

"Nothing?"

"Only rocks and mud."

Cryacur nodded his approval. Soon the probes broke the surface and returned to their mothercraft which was hovering close by.

"Any further orders, my Lord?"

"No, there is nothing here."

The Black Ash Prince could do no more. No burial site or body was found but he could not shake that familiar feeling again that a presence was close by, watching him.

In Oneum's orbit, a massive battlecruiser appeared. It was larger than any other ship in the fleet. The *Warloch* was the new flagship of the Axis fleet, fresh from the shipyards in the Dark Worlds.

Cryacur strode back to the *Plexus*. Striketroopers stood guard. Inside his quarters, a hologram turned itself on.

It was Kaw.

"I did not expect anything to be found here. Are you ready for greater glory?"

"Yes, my Master."

"The *Warloch* has arrived in Oneum. Take it to Nunearanor. Destroy them all."

Cryacur nodded as the hologram turned itself off just as quickly as it had come on.

THE BATTLE OF WOLVEN MOOR

A special hanger had been prepared for Metora's assault team in the forward part of the *Aquila*. Eight large, armoured shuttles had ground crews giving them a final check. The final ammunition and equipment had already been loaded and secured.

Their crews and troops, both Khoru and Jashirn, stood about in large groups, laughing, and cheering. He could hear them before he even entered the hanger, the loudest being Nemarluk.

"Into our last battle!" he cried out.

Nepta was the only one to notice Metora approaching.

"Sire, all preparations have been completed. We're waiting for the final word and celebrating."

"Celebrating death and rebirth!" Nemarluk called out again.

The men cheered and one raised the cup and drank from it.

"Here he is," Kuring-gai exclaimed while reaching out an arm to grab Metora's shoulder.

"Everyone's ready?" Metora asked.

"As ever, brother."

Metora examined the cup and saw it contained the brown water that the Khoru would often drink before battle, supposedly to give courage. It tasted and smelled awful.

"Can't you add some flavour to it?"

Kuring-gai shook his head. "Drink it."

Metora did and had a tough time keeping it down. "That's still awful."

The Khoru laughed at him. They knew that it was like drinking sewer water.

"I don't know who he was, but I think the legend that before a final battle one fellow poured all the water and drink he had into one bowl and drank it, 'cause that's all they had, is true. Because no sane man would make this. I wish we were drinking that Julamun wine from Kiam. Now that's a nice drop," Kuring-gai said.

Metora looked over to the assembled soldiers. The Jashirn men had lined faces that framed ashen features and the beards and hair of many were streaked with grey. They stared back at the prince without menace but with determination. This was their last mission. Glory was coming and there was no need to make it known.

Kuring-gai broke the silence.

"We were just about to return to the olden times and celebrate a birth."

"Overdue, you joining us, Prince Metora," Nemarluk said.

"Lead the way," he answered.

The Khoru led a small group of family and soldiers towards a rear door where Anook stood. She led them to an adjacent room, darkened but for several candles. There was a low table with a black orb on it in the middle of the room. Perreder was there and he showed them where to sit. Most of the soldiers stood and lined the back wall. A woman sat on a large cushion along with a child that made small noises to announce he was there.

The Khoru sat around it with Metora at the back.

They all closed their eyes and began to hum, each going into a personal place of peace, a moment of reflection before battle.

The black orb had turned bright, like Grotfer, and gave off enough heat that Metora could feel it on his skin. He tried to rest his mind but couldn't relax.

Perreder was the only one who spoke. "Old Father, we bring our child before you and name him Woonara, after his father's father."

"Command Group to bridge," came a voice over the ship's communication system, breaking Metora out of his attempts at relaxing.

He could see the orb now as a tiny sun giving off light and heat. Then he heard voices which he thought were coming from the men about him. But then he also heard female voices and children's mixed in.

"You need to relax," Kuring-gai whispered under his breath.

"I can't."

"Try."

Metora closed his eyes, exhaled, and tried to relax.

"Sealing all docks aft," the same voice blared over the system warning the crew that the ship was going through its preparation phase before moving out.

"It's a little hard."

"Block it out."

He tried again.

"All personnel, Command request battlestations, battlestations."

One of the troopers managed to turn off the audio to the room, leaving them in peace.

Kuring-gai remained with his eyes shut and his consciousness seemingly far from this room.

Metora refocused himself. The noises died away, though he could still feel the heat on his skin. There was a voice, his father's voice. His heart skipped its beat. Mahren! Jai! He saw his brother as he now was, his emaciated body covered by the ruins of his clothes and a simple shroud. His cracked lips were moving but Metora could hear no words. Where Jai was, he could not tell. There were rumours he now slept beneath the royal palace, deep within its dungeons.

He found himself calling out to his brother. His parents and sister were all dead. Most of his family were dead. He saw a flash of Jai on that day, his eyes white and bleeding as he strangled and brutalised everyone he came across.

Metora had found an abandoned blaster. His whole body had filled with incapacitating fear, but when he saw one of the guards strangled, Metora fired several shots, hitting his brother's arm. It had wounded him but had allowed the soldier to flee. Jai picked up his brother and threw him through a glass window where he ended up in a garden.

He could hear the screams. Again, he called out his brother's name.

Suddenly there was a hand on his shoulder. It should have been the guard that he had just saved from death, but it was Isla.

Why was she here?

"Metora," came a voice, but it was a man's and not Isla. She had vanished and there again was Jai, dragging the bodies of his parents through the mud and throwing them at the feet of the Dark Lord himself.

"I miss you," came the voice of Isobel.

Finally, Metora's eyes burst open. For a moment, he did not know where he was. Was he calling out for real? Was he crying?

It was Kuring-gai who had held his shoulder.

"It's okay. You were calling your brother's name, and hers," he said gently.

Metora was in tears. He was shaking. All the loss and misery that he had burdened himself with over the years, all of it, had been buried deep. As his soul seemed to crack with that heavy load, there was nowhere else for it to go. It came back in waves of heartbreak and emotion.

"It's alright, it's alright," Kuring-gai repeated.

Metora took a few moments to pull himself together, knowing that the room was full of soldiers and families.

"The dead call to you, but it's the living that will answer your call," Perreder said.

Metora looked at him, his breath still heavy, his cheeks wet. Yes, they were all dead.

"Today we'll find out if I'm joining them."

"This will be a great victory," Quisto boasted to the Elector on a balcony on Redsee as they watched the fleet prepare.

"Yes. It's a sight I haven't seen in a long time,"

And never will again. It will be Axis ships next time, Quisto thought to himself.

There were plenty of officials, politicians, and military officers, all watching the preparations in quiet awe and excitement.

"Good luck to it," Crowcraw whispered.

The flagship moved out to Trinity first, closely followed by her defending escorts. Other squadrons had their own route to clean space through the mass of mines and defences.

Great hulks that had sat idle for months around quays or workshops began to fill the emptiness around the planets with their bulk.

To watching civilian eyes, it seemed the fleet was on its way to manoeuvres but to more devious visions the real purpose was hidden by sly smiles.

Metora had spent a few moments alone calming down and telling Nepta what he had seen.

"The Khoru's mysticism is also related to the Order of Light. They could speak with the dead but also have the dead manifest itself in our reality."

"If I was alone waking up in the morning, I could explain it as a dream, but this wasn't. This was not memories or a subconscious desire. It was a connection to another plane."

"I didn't know you believed such things?"

"I do. I've read enough and seen enough over the years to know that it existed and still does. We've just lost the way to listen."

"Fascinating isn't it, Sire?" Nepta replied with genuine

excitement.

"Where do droids go, I wonder?"

"If I was destroyed, Sire, do you think you would hear my voice in that same darkness?"

Metora smiled. "So many people get emotionally attached to our droid companions. I've seen people in tears mourning a friend just like they were one of the family. It would be a wonderful thing to hear your voice, Nepta."

"Master Lorian would think so too."

"Oh, I know he would."

"His flight group are ready for deployment."

"Good. I'll see you in the hanger. Can you please upload the latest scan results for Wolven Moor and keep scanning? I'll head to the bridge and see if I can get anything useful."

"Yes, Sire. I'll do my best to get what you need."

Metora made his way to the bridge of the *Aquila* as it moved through the Trinity defences. It was quiet but for the heavy breathing of Captain Journ standing next to him.

In minutes, the great flagship was clear.

"Put us on course for Nunearanor," he ordered.

Metora now had a horrible realisation. While the *Aquila* waited for the rest of the fleets to clear the lanes through Trinity, every Axis surveillance system would be alerted.

"We shouldn't have taken up lightspeed positions so quickly," he told Journ. "I'm sure they've already tracked our trajectory."

"I'm just following orders. We go as soon as the bulk of the *Semirath* fleet is clear," Journ replied sourly.

"Captain, scanner has picked up Axis recon signals, ascension 35, third quarter."

Journ swore under his breath. He knew fully what was at stake, but he was under orders.

"We should go now, Captain," Metora said leaning in close to his ear. "Give the troops a chance."

"How long until the fighters are deployed?" Journ asked his bridge flight officer.

"Last fighters are launching now Captain," came the reply.

Journ looked intently at Metora. "It's seven minutes and fifteen seconds to Nunearanor."

"Ample time for us to deploy," Metora replied before moving towards the lift doors.

"Good luck," Journ called out as Metora entered the lift.

"We'll both need it," he replied before they shut.

Journ turned back to face his bridge crew. "Take us into the abyss helmsman."

With that, the *Aquila* and her strike force disappeared into lightspeed, much to the shock of the other fleets.

Admiral Taurus came storming out of his cabin at the back of the bridge. He had only moments before been in conversation with Zuke, telling the Admiral how all had worked out. He had just adjusted his jacket ready to watch the moment of lightspeed when the starlines prematurely filled the view screen. His moment of triumph had been snatched away.

"What the hell are you doing? You'll give us away you fool!"

Journ looked at the old man with disdain. "The Axis already know we're coming."

When the mass of the fleet had finally exited the wall and

began disappearing into lightspeed, alarm bells were rung high in many parts of the Axis high command.

Indeed, they had worked out the trajectory of the fleet and it pointed to Nunearanor. For what purpose, the average ranking soldier in the Axis army didn't know. For those crews, pilots, and ranks manning the fleets and on Nunearanor itself, it had now become apparent why they had been put on red alert. The Bond were coming. In seven minutes and ten seconds.

The light reflecting off the crown was artificial. It was dull and did not give the aura of radiance that the occasion demanded.

Talia sat upon a simple cushioned seat, the Arcuralie, the crown of the Nunearanor, upon her head. She was Queen now. Her mother's silver armour did not fit her taller stature, but the other vestments of royalty did. Around her neck was a woollen cloak with a woven map of the planet and bordered with many of the animals and vegetation that were native to Nunearanor.

In her right hand, she held a staff with a solid gold disc at its top, beaten and decorated from a single bar of gold, created by Olivess, and symbolising the union between the Ethereals, the land, and the Nunearanor. Arcuralie had also been fashioned by the first King. At her feet was a long sword once owned by Ashlar.

For hundreds of years, they had been used in the coronations. They had been saved from the royal castle before its destruction, along with many of the other pieces of art and literature from all over the city. They were destined to head to the mountain and were delayed, which saved them. They had remained in Akara, deep in the vaults, until this morning.

It was a small bare room that had been used to store food. All of that had been moved to the ships leaving a convenient space for the ceremony.

The small royal family, generals, and political positions were the only ones in attendance. Zoe had kept her abdication quiet and in her usual style had arranged everything so it would be done quickly. There were protests, but she was adamant. She would not leave this place.

Talia stood and the priest behind her made the announcement.

"Talia, Queen of the Nunearanor, may the Ethereals shine, may Grotfer shine, may the union shine."

"May she shine," the small crowd said as one.

Talia looked at her mother and her husband Lukas, who held their daughter, Eden, while Isla held her son, Vindon. They were holding hands and overcome with emotion. Talia's coronation was not meant to be this rushed and bare. She deserved better.

Zoe nodded to Talia and the priest that she could now sit, and the crown and investments could be removed.

Attendants carefully returned the crown and investments to their purposely built boxes. Zoe and Isla stepped towards Talia and they all embraced.

"It's too late now to change anything," Zoe said.

Lukas embraced his wife while Eden received a kiss from her mother.

Isla was tired. She had spent the days organising the evacuation. It had become almost a muscle-memory to check her datapad. She found herself doing it again while the generals and staff all congratulated Talia. It had been an emotional and exhausting few days. Her mother's decision had been a calculated one. There could be no chance of objection or delay as this was the day of evacuation.

The remains of the Nunearanor fleet were scattered across the planet. Fighters and smaller craft were either hidden in underground hangers in the cities or camouflaged in the woods. Many of the remaining, larger corvettes and cruisers were gathering dust in Akara. This was all that remained of one of the largest fleets of the old Sangrillion world. Most of the survivors were sent to Anueth. It was too dangerous for most ships to reveal themselves as they would instantly be shot down. Isla's mission to Anueth took weeks of planning with the consular ship being moved around and then hidden in the ruins of the city of Lora. It was taken apart and in a massive effort returned to Akara where engineers were still putting it back together.

Small commando groups and survivors had remained camouflaged in the forests and even in the deep seas, all of them too afraid to make their presence known for fear of destruction. Many had been hunted down and destroyed.

The first orders about the evacuation sparked arguments about whether they should follow them or disobey their Queen. They were afraid, as they should be, but it was the only chance to survive and continue fighting. Some individuals indeed left their hideouts and ventured alone further into the forests. Many elderly people refused to leave, believing some Nunearanor needed to remain.

Those willing to go were waiting and preparing for the call to run the gauntlet. They had their orders to remain hidden, gather their people, and wait.

Inside Akara, ships had been filled with personnel and equipment. Even the Gunadar prisoners wanted to come. What couldn't be taken was wrecked. Everyone had been kept busy and there was no time for resting.

Isla had been working hard sifting through what equipment should and shouldn't be taken. Every time she made up a list, she had to cross out equipment that there was no room to take. Small arms, power generators, spare parts, and other major military equipment filled up the storage holds of the cruisers. The crews worked through the nights to load it all.

It was hard to tell if it was daylight or night in Akara. The lights were always bright and the hum of the air filters never ceased. Soon, all would fall silent.

Zoe and Talia, who now held Vindon and Eden as Lukas had to return to work, excused themselves from the ceremony to return to the Queen's private quarters to have some final, private time together. The ceremony was all but over anyway. There would be no extended coronation celebrations here. There was still work to be done.

The royal investments were now boxed up. The crown, the cloak, the staff were to remain in Akara, while the sword would come to Anueth.

Isla, her cousin Bree, and a small group of soldiers carrying the boxes, travelled in the lift to an underground armoury.

Bree had spent her time going through the library where the history of their people had been kept. Books, manuscripts, art, and objects filled the storage area. Over the years, most of it had trickled in from all over the planet. In the rush of the evacuation years before, many things were lost or left behind. The collection was digitised over time. There was no room for any of the originals on the ships. It was all taken out and placed into the now empty armoury. It was one of the strongest vaults in the depths of Akara and there it would be sealed in, buried for future generations. The royal investments would also remain. It was Talia's decision. It would give them something to fight for. Besides, Talia would have preferred to have flowers in her hair then a metal crown.

A number of library staff and soldiers were overseeing the last of the library's treasures be placed inside. Many of these were letters and personal items from soldiers and staff. Their voices were just as important as any piece of art.

Bree checked with them that all was ready, then came to Isla who was taking one last look at the aisles of boxes and items that were covered. It was impossible to see what was in them.

"Are you finished?" she asked.

She nodded. Bree loved books and art. She was heartbroken to leave it all behind.

"I hope it survives."

"It will."

"Then I hope someone lives to come and claim it."

Isla looked around for the last time. "Let's go."

She led the way out when troops turned off the power, plunging the armoury into darkness. The door was sealed and the group went to the elevator taking them back to the main hanger.

The hanger was now busy with engineers setting up the final charges.

"I wish I could have seen the ocean one last time," Bree mused.

"Me too." Isla had almost forgotten what it was like to swim in the warm water, or sit in the sun, or wander the streets of the cities. It would have been good to savour one last time in her homeland, but the time had now come to say goodbye to her world.

"Princess Isla, the last ships have boarded." Commander Krull, Akara station's commander, approached her.

"Is there anything else you can think of Commander?"

He shook his head. "The rear-guard have finished their final sweeps. The order to evacuate has been sent to the surviving cells. The command bridge and all its computers and files has been destroyed."

A deep heavy boom thundered through the base, making small pieces of rock fall from the ceiling, and filling the air with the burning scent of metal and fried electronics.

"That would be the turbines and storage areas," Krull said.

The group walked out into the hanger towards the *Tanami*, a small Astro Class destroyer. The *Tanami* had been fitted out with much of Akara's computer system and her guns and shields had been increased. She still would be no match for any Axis capital ship, but she was fast, and that's what counted.

Pieces of wreckage and rock were scattered about the hanger floor. It was quiet, the quietest it had ever been. Usually there was the sound of engines, tools, wheeled vehicles, and chatter from the troops. Now all the ships stood silent, waiting for the word to break out.

The Queen and General Jan waited at the bottom of the ladder of the destroyer.

"There's no one else here and all the demolitions have been

done," Isla reported.

"The final charges have been laid and are ready, Majesty," Krull added.

"It's time to go then. We need to rendezvous with the other ships." Isla looked at her watch, it had been given to her by her father.

Both Queens were waiting with locked arms at the *Tanami's* gangway. Talia seemed to be in a state of shock, her eyes fixed as she held on to her mother's arm, afraid to let go but knowing she must.

Isla and Bree joined the final embrace.

Queen Zoe breathed in deeply. "It was never meant to be like this. I just wanted to live out our days without a worry in the world. Never could I imagine leaving my home for an uncertain future. I hope we are doing the right thing and that our children forgive us."

"There's no going back now Mum," Talia said.

"I know."

Talia's eyes were on the *Serene*, a smaller cruiser. Its gunnery officer was Lukas. Eden was safely aboard the *Serene*, Vindon on the *Tanami*, and Bree would join them soon. It had been decided to split up the royal family as a safety precaution.

Both queens had already said their goodbyes to them, but Talia could not shake her worry.

"They'll be alright," Zoe reassured her anxious daughter.

She let go her embrace and stepped back. Around her now were a few older soldiers, many horribly wounded or ill. They were going to stay behind with their Queen. General Jan held Zoe tight and kissed her forehead. Isla always knew they were close and now they would remain entombed together.

A final group of soldiers came out of the darkness of the far hanger — the last demolition crews. One of them, a woman in her fifties, was in tears as she embraced her Queen one last time. The other soldiers also embraced before they boarded their ships.

The Queen had spent the previous days visiting all stations of the fortress, saying her goodbyes. There were many tears and pledges to stay with her. This group around her had kept their pledge.

"There aren't any more words to say. We'll be here, waiting for your children to come find us. Now go . . . go." She was barely holding back her tears now.

Bree ran to the *Serene*. Talia was last to board the *Tanami*. The final sight of her mother was in an embrace with the final guard, many of them friends and family who had pledged to stay with her until the end.

One by one, the fighters and capital ships fired up their boosters to file out of the exit from Akara. The exit tunnel was curved with three main doors that led out the side of the mountain. It was a tight fit as many ships closed together for protection. Axis scanners would no doubt pick up the ships as they exited.

As the last ships left the hanger, their departure was saluted by the final explosions that erupted bringing the great cavern down on itself.

Isla took her place on the bridge. Putting her mind on the job now before them helped her forget her grief.

Krull had already sent the order to all cells around the planet and in Akara.

She had secretly wanted to see a final glimpse of her world but by the time she arrived on the bridge the *Tanami* was far into the atmosphere as all of the ships raced to clear the planet.

"Are the other ships able to meet us," she asked the bridge commander, Captain Colion.

"They're heading our way. A few fighter patrols have locked onto us," she replied.

She was relieved to hear the good news, but anxious about the fighters.

"Most of the planet's defences face outwards and won't be looking for us," Isla added.

"Axis fighters have locked on," announced Colion as she looked over the shoulder of a soldier manning a radar array.

"How many?" Isla asked, just as the whispers of cloud vanished only to be replaced by the blackness of space.

Colion looked over, dread in her face.

"How many?" Isla asked again.

"Over a thousand."

"Alert the gunnery crews," Isla ordered.

She looked behind at Talia, who had come to see developments and was wide-eyed with shock, then back at the grey mass descending onto the little fleet.

It was almost like a mechanical snake, slithering through space towards the Nunearanor fleet. Isla had never been in a space battle before. Her diplomatic flight managed to avoid any Axis contacts on the way in but had needed to dodge a few fighters and suffered heavy damage. But not like this. This was overwhelming in numbers, and she knew exactly what the old pilots would talk about. She would do her duty as she had always done. She prepared for death.

Lorian's Kandrol Squadron deployed while still within the safety of Trinity and he was unaware of the *Aquila's* pre-emptive blast into lightspeed on its own.

They took up their position with the rest of their battlegroup within the fleet. After seeing that all his fighters were in position, he was given the order to go into lightspeed.

He wasn't nervous until now, he had been distracted by preparing his fighter and his pilots. Now he was alone. With the bright pulse of light, his mind raced. His usual excitement about his role was absent. It was replaced with a sense of foreboding and distance which he couldn't explain. As the seconds ticked on, he dared not ponder it any further. He wanted to focus on the coming tasks. The thought of that now brought fear into his system.

His fighter's control began beeping, announcing the countdown to coming out of lightspeed. He breathed deeply, trying to contain the fear of what he would find in Wolven Moor.

When the starlines ended, he saw the *Aquila's* guns blazing against the mass of fighters swarming around her. Beyond the Jashir flagship, Wolven Moor hung like a huge shining orb, her surface completely covered by ice and snow.

"Strike team, follow me. Let's break through and find the Nunearanor," came the voice of Major Tauchmann. Kandrol Squadron would join the dozens of other starfighter squadrons tasked with fighting their way through to the Nunearanor.

The onrush of Axis Griffen fighters and unmanned DFS

drone ships broke him out of his stupor. A group of DFS rushed past him. They were small robotic fighters with a large cannon and a small flight control. They were difficult to destroy as they were small, fast, and manoeuvrable.

He ignored them and increased his speed.

"You with me, Flight?" he asked his flight group.

"Here," Imogen replied.

"Same," Trix added.

"Yeah, right here," Kahil replied.

"Number one is in the lead. We're going in full speed. Everyone watches each other's backs."

Lorian pushed his fighter faster. There was no time to think of Metora and the *Aquila*.

Information flashed on his heads-up display. The lead ships had reached the outer defences and had managed to blow a hole in the large minefields.

"A group of fighters has broken off and is tailing us," Imogen reported.

Kandrol Squadron was close to the rear-guard, with Lorian's flight at the rear. He could see about a dozen fighters closing fast.

"There's another mass attempting an intercept. Three Flight, swing round and clear out those tailers. Don't get left behind," came their commander's orders.

"Copy."

Lorian turned his fighter about, as did the rest of his flight. It was a short dog fight. The Axis pilots and DFS drones had been so intent on the chase that when the Bond fighters suddenly wheeled about to take them on, they hesitated for a few seconds, which cost them their advantage.

Lorian was able to destroy two DFS, while the others bagged one each and Kahil damaged a third Griffen.

"These ones don't want to play," Trix said as the other Axis fighters simply roared past them, continuing hunting down the rest of the squadrons.

"We'll chase them down," Lorian replied.

The Axis fighters had managed to catch up to the main bulk of Bond fighters but in doing so had come up against ATAK bombers whose rear gunners began firing accurate laser fire, forcing them to take evasive manoeuvres.

Then Kandrol Squadron pounced. The Axis fighters found themselves between the hammer and anvil and were quickly destroyed or driven off.

"Good work. Heads up, we've got another welcoming committee ahead," Tauchmann warned.

Lorian could see on his monitor more large masses of fighters pressing to intercept them. He took another deep breath to calm himself. They were making good distance through Axis space.

"How you doing, Trix?"

"I'm good," came the quick reply.

"Imogen?"

"My right engine is playing up, but other than that she's holding together."

"Just worried about the girls, huh?" came Kahil's sarcastic remark.

"No. I was about to check up on you."

"Kahil, really? Shut up," Imogen spat.

Lorian shook his head. He really didn't understand Kahil's aggression. Secretly, he thought it best if Kahil did go to another squadron. It would be something to think about later. If they got back. Now wasn't the time or place to bring up rubbish like this.

Another deep breath. Axis fighters were roaring in. He tightened his grip on his controls. Another deep breath.

Metora was horrified by what he saw. A mass of Axis fighters and a whole fleet moved to intercept the Bond fleet. Then the guns of Wolven Moor opened up, rocking the *Aquila* with accurate fire. It was as he feared. The Axis was waiting for them.

The bridge crew went about their work quietly. Orders were issued and status reports passed along. They had been the first and only ship to arrive in Nunearanor space and it would have been a comical surprise for the Axis to expect a massive invasion fleet and then to be confronted with only the *Aquila.*

The flagship had borne the brunt of the attacks for a few minutes before her escort ships arrived and joined in the bombardment of the Wolven Moor fortress. It would be a good ten minutes after that before the rest of the fleet appeared to share the load.

"Would it be cowardly to order a retreat now?" Journ mockingly asked.

"Well, that's not everyone's style."

"No, but I wouldn't blame anyone for thinking it."

Admiral Taurus had spent most of the time while in lightspeed verbally blasting Metora for his actions.

"Giving the game away", "Upsetting the schedule", "Another court martial might be in order," were just some of the threats and accusations thrown his way in full view of the bridge crew.

Metora gave as good as he got, throwing back onto the Admiral the futility and suicidal nature of the mission.

Kuring-gai had actually stood next to the Admiral, staring at him intently, not saying a word. It was enough for Taurus to retreat to his quarters, no doubt informing Zuke what had happened.

"Maybe it was stupid to go early," Metora mused.

He was doubting himself again.

Journ shook his head. "We never had surprise on our side but now your assault team is behind schedule. If you still think it's worth going?"

"Well, I guess there's nothing for it but to get into it and follow our orders."

"As always," Kuring-gai smiled.

The bridge commander, Warrant Officer Rewann, came up to them. "Sir, all ships have arrived. We've detected another fleet moving port side."

"They are a lot closer than we believed. Are they on an attack run?"

Rewann shook her head, "It doesn't look like it."

"They'll be trying to cut us off," Metora stated.

They went to a computer display.

"I think you're right. That or they'll drive up our backsides," Journ said.

"There's another one," Rewann called.

Indeed, there was another Axis fleet that had appeared to starboard and it was coming out from behind Wolven Moor.

Both men let out the air they had been holding in. They were now in the middle of two pincers that were slowing moving forward and threatening to cut them off.

"That's a kick in the guts," Kuring-gai said.

"Have all ships been committed?" Journ asked Rewann.

"No, there were a few smaller squadrons that have just turned up."

"Could we leave the ships back and try to delay their fleets? That's our escape route," said Metora.

"We'd lose planetary bombardment ships. It's going to be tight."

Metora knew the implications, but what else could he do with such a flawed plan and an impossible situation? His assault team would have to go in and do what the fleet now couldn't do. It was shaping up to be one of the most brutal and stressful battles he had ever been in.

"Sire, we're receiving a message from the enemy. I'll put it on screen," Rewann announced.

The large screen suddenly filled with the snarl of the Black Ash Prince.

"Dear Metora, you're a rat that just will not be killed."

Metora was disappointed to see that the creature still lived. By Kuring-gai's snarl, he felt it too.

"What do you want? Come to gloat?"

"No. I have come to accept your surrender."

"Impossible."

"You have fallen into a trap. Don't think you can escape again."

"Since when do you want your enemy to surrender, Cryacur? You should know that we don't surrender. We won't live in chains. So, stop trying to win us over the easy way, or are you afraid to fight us?"

The smugness of the Black Ash Prince vanished in an instant, replaced by viciousness and hatred.

"I fear nothing, *you should know that*. I don't care about your fleet. It will be destroyed. I wanted your surrender. I merely wanted to entreat, one prince to another."

"Well entreat this," Metora cancelled the transmission.

"That will piss him off," Kuring-gai chuckled.

"Get your ships into position," Metora told Journ.

"We'll do our duty for King and Sangreal."

Metora was losing most of his planetary bombardment ships to take out Wolven Moor. They were needed elsewhere now, meaning there was no prospect of neutralising the entire moon's defences, but they could still take out some of it and give the Nunearanor a chance.

Zuke's plan was abandoned. The situation had changed desperately.

"What is the situation?" Taurus had entered the bridge.

"Well, Admiral, you've got two Axis fleets moving on our flanks for an intercept and to cut off our escape path," answered Journ.

"Then we'll keep our battle plan to bombard Wolven Moor's defences while extracting the Nunearanor."

"That's not going to happen," Metora replied.

"Yes it is," Taurus replied menacingly.

"I haven't got time for this, Captain. The assault group will head to Wolven Moor with a small protection fleet. We'll take out the north pole fortress. Keep those fleets from intercepting."

"You cannot just throw out the Admiral's plan."

"Nepta, can you give the Admiral a read out on the Axis fleets."

Nepta had returned to the bridge after Metora had failed to show.

"The fleets are at full strength with five hundred ships, a thousand fighters, approaching at maximum speed which should intercept us in approximately 92 minutes."

"That's what is waiting for us."

"Where are the Nunearanor forces?"

"They have formed up but are being attacked by strong fighter defence. At this rate, they'll take several hours to reach Wolven Moor. Our pathfinders have breached the outer minefields and will shortly link up with them."

"So, everything is going according to plan. Our defences are holding up," Taurus smiled confidently.

"Not at all. The guns are not destroyed, because you'll need those ships to fight off these two fleets coming at us. We've already got one engaged. We can't beat three," Metora said frustratingly.

"It's a mess, Admiral."

To add to the stress, the ship was continually being rocked by fire from Wolven Moor.

"If we can knock out the old monastery, we should give them some protection. Damn trying to take them all out," Kuring-gai added.

"If we put the *Aquila* close to the moon, it will attract their fire, hopefully allowing our ships to rush past," offered Journ.

"You want to use us as a shield?" Taurus exclaimed.

"We can't spare any of the ships for planetary bombardment

anymore. They need to be attacking Axis capital ships," said Metora.

"The guns will wipe out anything less protected than the *Aquila* and the way the moon is orbiting we will have the moon on one side and the Axis fleets behind us. Stuck between the anvil and hammer, Sir," Nepta added.

Taurus remained quiet. "I'll seek confirmation from headquarters."

He turned and left the bridge, leaving everyone else frustrated and bewildered. Zayn Taurus stood there watching, almost guarding the Admiral's quarters, probably expecting Metora to burst into the room and begin ordering Taurus about.

Instead, Metora turned to Journ.

"It may well be the case you'll have to scatter the fleet. Ships will have to make their own way back."

Journ nodded his understanding.

"We're going, Nepta. I'll need you with us."

"Yes Sir,"

"Good luck," Journ said quietly.

"Shuttles ready to go," Kuring-gai said.

It was Metora's turn to nod. The three left the bridge, Zuke junior eyeing them intently.

They quickly made their way to the hanger. The shuttles were ready, their troops boarded and their engines humming. Once on board the command shuttle, it led the others from the hanger, several fighters escorting them towards Wolven Moor.

"Close defence, blast your way through. Don't stop to engage, just get through," ordered his commander.

Of course, words were easier than deeds. Lorian was twisting his fighter about erratically trying to avoid enemy fire and not to collide with any of his own squadron. Added to the stress was a small space station that was firing accurately, causing casualties, and making a nuisance of itself.

"Someone get rid of that bloody station!" came a call over the radio.

Kandrol Squadron were diverted towards its destruction. Lorian's wing and one other roared in firing concussion missiles that blew the station apart.

"Done," Lorian reported.

"Good work. Now watch those flanks. Enemy are on our backs."

The three fighters roared through the debris followed by the rest of the squadron.

It was all, but for a moment when Axis fighters regrouped and tried to block their path, forcing the Bond fighters to again open fire.

Ahead, a massive explosion seemed to fill up space itself. It was enough to momentarily blind every pilot, both enemy and ally.

"Pathfinders are pushing through," exclaimed their commander.

"The minefields have triggered," Trix said.

"We're almost there, groups. Keep our defence tight," voiced the commander.

The last barrier for the mission was the great minefield outside Nunearanor, one of many that ringed the system. There was no way to go around it, and certainly not through it. It would be impossible to wipe it out completely, but at least some of it was erased, making passage easier.

Lorian's group had moved close to the point of the attack and now he could see parts of the Nunearanor fleet ahead.

Many of the ships were damaged but still firing all they had at the swarms of Axis fighters bussing about them.

"Signal fleet that attack force has made contact. Create a perimeter. Get rid of those fighters!" voiced the commander.

Seasoned pilots were already doing just that. Axis fighters exploded as they were taken unawares by the sudden Bond attack. With their attention having been solely on the Nunearanor, they now had to face Bond fighters.

Very quickly, the enemy fighters were driven away, though they remained close by, apparently waiting for new orders.

For the first time since the attack began, Lorian was able to take a few moments to let his heart return to normal beats.

He could see that the Nunearanor fleet was a jumble of different types, all of them battered and worn. There was no sign of the emissary ship that had taken Isla home but he knew that she would be out there somewhere.

"Kandrol Group move to point." The commander's voice woke him from his meandering.

"Blue follow leader," he ordered his own wing.

The small force moved ahead of the battered fleet. They were halfway there. They had smashed their way through the Axis defence with heavy losses and now they had to turn around and do it all again. As before, their enemy waited, angry, wounded, and waiting for their prey.

Taurus looked over the computer simulations showing Bond and Axis ships. Bond fighters had penetrated deep into Axis space, extending like an arm reaching out to take the Nunearanor, just as Zuke wanted it. Reports were coming in that they had made contact. Already the *Mara*, *Semirath*, and *Inigo* fleets were moving deeper through the tunnel forged by the fighter squadrons. There they would form a shield to hold back the Axis and protect the vulnerable Nunearanor ships.

Elsewhere, the Axis fleet had pushed forward trying to engage Bond capital ships. It was almost impossible to maintain control as each ship strove to save itself. Some had combined in small groups, giving each other mutual defence. There was such a mass of Axis red, it seemed the machine was bleeding.

"Have us move closer to the centre here. Have a small squadron as defence."

Journ was really biting his lip to stop himself speaking his mind in an aggressive manner that would only get him dismissed.

"We're the only ship protecting the assault team. We can't just leave them with no cover."

"Our mission is almost done, Captain. Contact has been made. Now we need to extract ourselves."

The *Aquila* was rocked by heavy fire again as Wolven Moor cannons continued to target her.

"Plus, that is beginning to grate me. I cannot maintain control while we are being slowly destroyed."

"Parts of Admiral Runke's fleet are attacking both enemy pincers, but we don't have enough ships to slow them down."

"Everything is going to be okay, Captain," said Taurus.

Journ wanted to believe him and had the bridge commander pass on the orders. The situation was becoming more dangerous with each passing minute as the Bond were slowly encircled. He doubted the Admiral could lead them out of this and he was ready to take control if need be. The fact that that outcome was almost a certainty pulled the knot in his gut much tighter.

The *Aquila* was rocked again as it moved away, the image of Wolven Moor disappearing in the view screen, replaced by the mass of grey of ships all around them.

The assault group's small escort of fighters and heavy bombers roared ahead. They blasted apart the small minefields surrounding the moon and in doing so attracted nearly every enemy weapon.

Its resulting explosion was the brightest orb of light Metora had ever seen.

"The new spark bombs are working out," Kuring-gai said.

The point bomber was destroyed after delivering the payload which cleared a path for the remainder of the small force.

The survivors forged ahead. The surface of Wolven Moor was now open to them.

"We might actually be able to pull this off."

"I hope so, because none of us will be leaving this place," replied Nemarluk.

"You're so full of optimism," Metora smiled sarcastically.

"Well, I like to be realistic."

"Fifteen seconds," Nepta reported.

"Have the bombers taken out the batteries?"

"Unknown, Sire. They still appear to be operational."

"What about the *Aquila*?"

"Moving away."

Metora grimaced. "Thanks Taurus."

"He's now on my list," Nemarluk stated.

"Shuttles are on target." Nepta reported the movement of the other shuttles in the battlegroup as they manoeuvred to their targets.

The pilot had the shuttle skimming across the frozen plains of Wolven Moor. Most of its surface was ice but for large areas of rocky surface at the northern pole and equator.

The northern pole held a monastery with wild gardens that was a sacred place to the Nunearanor. Only the bravest were allowed to come here to rest after wars.

Of course, the Axis had usurped the monastery, converting it to a military outpost that controlled the defences and convoy lanes into Nunearanor. Its cannons were the most powerful in the system and could destroy anything in range.

The rocky, frozen outcrops began appearing under the shuttle as it raced across the endless wasteland.

Explosions rocked its path as the defences locked on and began firing. In response, Bond fighters and bombers roared ahead to provide a protective screen. They could keep the Axis fighters away, but little could be done to knock out the cannon fire. Nonetheless, the bombers pressed home their strikes and soon pillars of smoke and fire could be seen on the horizon, signals of the destruction of military installations close to the batteries.

"Five seconds," called the pilot.

The mix of Bond troopers checked their weapons for the last time and prepared to disembark. Oberon stood by the main door. He was still and silent. Metora was so intent on his mission that he hadn't even noticed the Sangrillion droid and Oberon had said nothing.

As they closed on the north battery, the damage caused by the *Aquila* became visible. Buildings were on fire and the landscape was scarred and burned. Small points of damage could be seen on the fortress walls where missiles had impacted but caused no damage or delay to the powerful cannon fire that continued to roar out into space, targeting the Bond fleet.

The firing was murderous as the shuttles closed in, their own weaponry firing back at the smaller gun emplacements that were designed to protect the larger battery.

Friendly fighters seemed to have disappeared as they scrambled across the sky desperately holding back their Axis counterparts. Their intensity was so great that the fighting around them seemed forgotten as they concentrated on killing each other.

Surrounded by explosions and fire, Metora's shuttle touched down as close to the former monastery as the pilots dared. The other shuttles did the same. The main door opened. Oberon was the first to jump out, followed by Kuring-gai, Nemarluk, and troopers.

Immediately they drew fire as Striketroopers and defence emplacements targeted them. The great guns of Wolven Moor roared again as they fired into the darkness of space. The small team of troops, led by Nemarluk, advanced through the smoke-filled, broken terrain which hid the blaster fire that would flash in the embers and bury itself in rock and flesh.

Metora cursed under his breath at the sight of the cannons firing. Each shot could mean the destruction of a ship and the death of its entire crew.

Kuring-gai looked back at the shuttle. "I'll see you soon!"

Metora was about to disembark. "Sire, the Axis have pushed away our cover ships!" called Nepta.

"Sins of the fathers!" Kuring-gai muttered, "It seems I will be one of those who has no grave, lost in the oceans of the universe."

Metora stood on the precipice of the shuttle's door. Nepta was by his side. Only moments before he had held a candle of hope in his heart that his force might just get out of this alive. Now that candle was extinguished.

"Time is against us, Sire," said Nepta.

"Let's get into it, Kuring-gai," Metora replied.

He jumped onto the frozen surface of the moon. It was cold and the wind was picking up, drawn to the war now besetting its once peaceful world, already burned and splashed with blood as it was.

As the *Aquila* moved away, the guns of Wolven Moor continually targeted her. At least they weren't shooting at the rest of the fleet.

Journ feared that, with the threat gone, the Axis would start targeting the rest of the fleet. They could do little against the planetary guns now. His gut wrenched for having to abandon the assault group but he reluctantly obeyed orders and tried to do what he could to save his ship.

As they moved back, he could see the damaged Bond ships also pulling back, hoping the flagship would protect them. The communication consoles on the bridge were working overtime trying to deal with all the frantic messages coming in from other ships.

There were at least a dozen ships with guns destroyed, weakened shields, and shell-shocked crews, that had grouped themselves together.

"Sir, these ships should be withdrawn. They're no good to us now."

"Any reports on whether we're *causing* any damage, Captain?" asked Taurus.

"Some," grimaced Journ.

"If these ships retreat then it may cause the others to abandon their position. True?"

Journ breathed in deeply. "Not necessarily. What do you want me to tell them?"

While the Admiral thought it over, Journ's heart sank as he saw the bright stab of red lights flashing from the surface of the moon and striking ships in the fleet. His fear that the Axis would turn their attention away from the *Aquila* was being realised.

He was still waiting for the Admiral's reply. Before he could say anything more, Rewann stood up from her battlestation,

"Captain, enemy ships have broken through!"

As he turned, the bridge came under fierce fire which knocked everyone standing off their feet. Sparks and fires broke out, the lights flashed, and the bridge crew yelled out orders and information to anyone listening.

Taurus had been thrown onto the ground and was barely able to move.

"Father!" Taurus junior called out. Horrified, he rushed to his fallen father.

Journ got to his feet just as another blast hit the bridge and the ship began to roll, throwing everyone to one side. Crews fell from their seats and droids, unable to steady themselves, were thrown against terminals and walls.

Three Axis, Claymore Class cruisers breaking through weak points in the Bond gun-line had pounced on the *Aquila*. Her few fighters, left behind as protection, were unable to hold them back. Other Bond ships turned to intercept and began firing at the Axis ships. Instead of spreading their fire, they concentrated on a single ship. When it was deemed damaged enough and moved away, they turned to the next one. The Axis ships were so intent on destroying the *Aquila* they didn't notice or care they were being taken out one by one.

The final one put up a fight. Each Axis ship had refused to turn their guns to defend themselves, instead using the last of their strength on the flagship. Finally, when all three were damaged, they began to retreat. Only one remained left behind, its engines damaged and its guns ruined. It sat there, surrounded by debris cast off from its own hull, mixed with debris from other ships. It was no longer a threat.

The *Aquila's* crew managed to right their ship, but the bridge room was a mess. It was eerily quiet but for unanswered queries from other ships. Some of the crew managed to get back to their positions. Rewann found Journ badly wounded and barely able to speak.

"Get us back."

"Most of our communications are down."

"Just get us back."

"Strike force, centre around Kandrol One," came the order from Tauchmann.

The situation had not eased since linking up with the Nunearanor. Masses of Axis fighters continued to swarm about them, the guns of the Bond ships barely keeping them at arm's length.

"How's everyone doing?" Lorian asked his group.

"We've got a few holes. A big problem is my port engine. She's coughing a bit from a hit," replied Trix.

"Yeah, I'm still here," Kahil said

"Same, nothing to report," Imogen replied curtly.

"Good, cause it ain't over. We're heading to Wolven Moor."

He led his flight, along with the remains of his squadron, away from the rest of the fleet in the direction of the moons.

On his scanner, he could see the mass of Axis ships waiting for them and the great pincers drawing closer to the Bond fleet on the other side of the moons. In his mind, he was preparing for the coming fight. He was sweating, despite the coolness of the cockpit, and his heart didn't seem to have stopped its erratic beating.

"Let's keep it close, troops. We're almost there," the commander said.

Suddenly great red streaks of light flashed from the moon and roared over his fighter, destroying one of his colleague's ships. Immediately, more streaks impacted on other fighters before anyone could react.

"Those guns have targeted us!"

"Fighters above us!"

"Evasive manoeuvres!" Lorian ordered.

His flight pushed their fighters to the limits as they desperately avoided the moon's fire as well as the fighters that were now plunging down on them from above.

"I can't keep up!" Trix screamed in panic.

Lorian saw her fighter suddenly pull out of line, trailing smoke.

"Trix, pull left so we can cover you," Imogen said.

"I can't get to her!" Lorian said as he tried to move around to protect her fighter. There was too much pressure from his enemy, however.

Trix's fighter was hit again then and seemed to stop dead in space.

"Oh no," came her last words.

Two Axis fighters swarmed in, fired, and Trix's fighter exploded in a flash of fire and metal.

Lorian's ears were filled with Imogen's distraught cry. He was stunned and for a moment the war around him seemed far away. Trix was gone.

"Blue One, Blue One . . . Lorian!" came his commander's voice.

"Copy Leader," Lorian mumbled.

"Peel off and attack those batteries! Take the rest of Blue and Red flights!"

"Copy," he again mumbled, barely registering what he had

been ordered to do and how to do it.

The rumble of the blaster fire, the voices in his earpiece, and the shake of his fighter brought him back to the situation he was in. Trix was gone and he was determined that the rest of his friends would live.

He couldn't console his friends. He knew Imogen would be in tears and her brother angry. As for himself, he couldn't even wipe the tears from his eyes because of his helmet.

He switched his radio over so he could talk to Imogen.

"Imogen, you okay?"

"No, I'm not okay!"

"We're going to finish this."

"Okay, okay."

He turned the radio back to the right frequency. Around him half a dozen heavy bombers had joined his small group as it headed towards the surface of the moon.

Isla was listening in on the Bond radio traffic. There was a lot of confusion, even panic, as voices yelled commands. Voices would be cut off in mid-sentence as their communications were severed or, more likely, their ship destroyed. Listening to it was heart breaking.

"We're not getting any reply from the *Aquila*. Other reports put her disabled and her bridge probably destroyed," Colion stated.

Isla was rubbing her face as frustration and fear boiled away inside her.

"The Wolven Moor guns are slicing right through them."

"Why aren't they down?" she asked no one.

"When does anything go right in war," said Talia as she appeared behind her.

"How long to the junction?" Colion asked an officer.

"An hour," came the reply.

"We'll be shot to pieces before then," Isla stated.

"What happened to the strike force?" Talia asked.

"Only some shuttles have been launched with a few ships to back them up. That's all we can get."

"We could take some troops and help them."

The Queen remained stone-faced. She knew it was highly dangerous with a very low likelihood of her sister returning safely.

To add to the tension, another explosion lit up the bridge as a frigate to the port bow was hit by fire from Axis capital ships. It fell out of line as its crew struggled to maintain its position. It was hit again then, forcing it further away as other Nunearanor ships moved to protect it.

Before they could complete their work, the frigate suddenly exploded throwing white metal all over the flagship where it again exploded in sparks as the debris hit the shield.

"We will have to do what needs to be done. Please come back." Talia embraced her sister.

Isla then sprinted from the bridge, making her way to the hanger where the last rear-guard and the engineers were stationed. When she approached them, they were already going through their equipment and weapons. Their commander, Major Dathurst, along with his daughter Sherri, were checking their equipment.

"The bridge notified us. I can take a guess we're going to the moon."

Isla nodded. "This is a volunteer mission."

Dathurst smiled. "We've already volunteered. We don't have much in the way of heavy weapons, just what we can carry."

"That'll do."

The soldiers began filing towards a small shuttle while Dathurst and Isla held a council of war.

"Do we know where on the moon we should be?"

"Most of the fleet never got a chance to deploy properly. The *Aquila's* out of action, but we know that there is a Bond unit near the north monastery."

Dathurst listened carefully. "Why doesn't the fleet blast it away?"

Isla shook her head. "I don't know. Considering the damage, they probably can't get close enough. It's doing what it's built to do, Major."

"The monastery's got most of the targeting systems and commands. It's also got the biggest cannons."

"That's where we should go."

"Agreed," Dathurst replied.

They turned to climb the rear ramp. Isla turned to see her sister standing there with her youngest child, Vindon, both waving with crying faces. Isla blew them a kiss and quickly went in and sat down. She was shaking, and there were tears which she covered by burying her head in her hands. Her heart was breaking but there was duty to be done.

She pulled herself together and wiped away her tears. She reached out for a communication terminal.

"Captain, have the Bond send as many fighters as they can

spare to cover us."

"I don't like your chances but will pass it on," came the reply.

She sat back down and breathed in deeply. Her heart just wanted to burst in tears and let it flow out, but she held it back. Not because of any embarrassment. She knew these soldiers and there had never been any hiding of emotions in the Nunearanor army. She held together as they were about to go into battle. She had to remain focused. Each of these soldiers were the same, their emotions buried deep, shunted aside by the need to remain focused on the job at hand. Their lives and those of others depended on it.

It took all Lorian's skill to dodge and weave his way towards the moon. At first, most of the defences were firing at the fleet. Now they were closer to the surface, the second line of Axis defences began to fire on the small battle group as it dived towards the northern pole and its fortress, which continued to fire out at the fleet.

"Let's do this quickly and get out of here," Lorian ordered.

"I'm in range," said the pilot of the bombers.

"Open fire."

The bomber's missiles roared towards the former monastery complex which was clearly visible against the white surface of the moon.

The fighters engaged in evasive manoeuvres to steer clear of the counter-fire that was becoming heavier and more accurate.

The missiles landed home and there was a great flash of red and orange as they detonated against the armour of the one of the cannon housings, which in turn exploded in shards of metal and fire.

Lorian's fighter roared over the battlefield in an arc, ready for another run.

"Let's go again," came the voice of another pilot.

A barrage of fire suddenly hit his fighter as Axis gunners locked on. Frantically, he tried to keep it in the air, but his fighter had lost all power.

"Lorian!" came Imogen's voice before his earpiece went quiet.

With great strength and his heart beating faster than it ever had, he levelled it out to an almost flat plane. He was too low, however, and the frozen surface of Wolven Moor came up quickly in his cockpit glass.

The impact jolted him about, forcing his instrument panel to shatter in electric explosions. The grinding of the metal on the ice mixed with exploding panels until the fighter came to a rest almost on its side.

Spurred on by rising panic, he forced open the canopy, unbuckled his belt, and almost fell onto the ice. The grinding of metal signalled that the fighter hadn't quite finished moving.

He scrambled away from the slippery ice as the remains of the fighter's forward fuselage rolled onto its side crushing the open canopy under its weight.

His chest heaving and the panic still not subsiding, Lorian looked about to see where he was.

The smoking fortress complex, which wasn't far away, was still firing sporadically out into space. Fighters flew about. He saw Imogen and her brother flying past, no doubt checking to see it he was still alive.

There was no way he could stay where he was. The smoke from his fighter marked the spot clearly enough.

Getting to his feet, he had the urge to get away and hide. There were few places to do so, however. His only chance was to find Metora and join his group. There he would feel safer.

Metora and Kuring-gai had sought shelter beside a burning substation while the bombers had come in for their attack. Oberon was out front doing a reconnaissance on the cannon to see if the bomber strike had damaged it.

Axis fire was intense and, in this battle, time was a luxury they could not afford to lose. Being pinned down made the process agonisingly slow. Striketroopers were firing from defensive emplacements that were hard to destroy without the help of the fleet. Frustrations were building.

A console appeared beside them after running the gauntlet of fire.

"Sire, we've got a partial message that there is a Nunearanor strike team on its way to help."

"How long?" Metora asked.

"We couldn't get that. Axis are blocking most of the transmissions."

"Then it should be soon. Surely that will give us the numbers?" said Kuring-gai.

Metora merely nodded. "We can't wait too long for a ship that might have been destroyed."

"Oberon's coming back," stated Kuring-gai.

The tall bulk of Oberon appeared above them. He was

scorched by blaster fire and dropped his broken cannon to the ground.

"Their strength is increasing. Battle droids have been deployed around the monastery and not all the guns have been destroyed."

Right on cue, the fortress erupted as its cannons fired out into space.

"That's not good. We're going to have to get in there to destroy it," said Kuring-gai.

"That will take time," Oberon added.

"If we close on the monastery and destroy the communication array, that should be enough. It's pointless trying anything else," Kuring-gai stated.

"Have you picked up any signals from the Nunearanor?" asked Metora.

Oberon looked up to the sky. "Yes, to the west, a single transport. It should be here in minutes."

"Good. Let's get this done and get the hell out of here." Metora's spirits had lifted with a solid plan and the possible means to achieve it.

"There is more, Sire. The Black Ash Prince has arrived on the moon with more Striketrooper regiments."

"Sins of the fathers," Kuring-gai mumbled to himself. The short-lived euphoria was gone. Their difficult situation had just become that much harder.

Metora turned to the console. "Send a signal to the Nunearanor. Get them to follow our attack. All effort on the cannon."

He then turned to the Sangrillion. "Lead the way, Oberon."

With that, they dashed from out of their cover and into the

shadow of the fortress, away from its flashes of light and fire, praying their job could be done before it was too late.

Lorian tried to remain buried in the snow as the Striketroopers closed in on his downed fighter. His heart was beating fast and he could see the snow melting under his breath as he tried to remain calm. A small recon droid was hovering around the wreckage, transmitting information back to the squad. It circled about looking for heat patterns and he was sure he would be found.

It was coming closer. He had his blaster ready as it hovered close and followed the footprints leading to his body heat. Lorian didn't give it a chance as he fired point blank, blowing the little machine to pieces.

With that done, he wasted no time in changing position, trying to hide from any more droids. He had hoped the enemy garrison would be too busy defending the fortress to send out a droid looking for a single pilot. That didn't appear to be the case.

He ran through snow drifts that had built up around rocky outcrops, stopping every few metres to listen for the enemy.

"About time."

Lorian spun around, his blaster millimetres from firing. An older man stood close by, his face thin and ragged under a cloak that hid the rest of his features.

"Who are you?" Lorian asked, though he felt the voice was strangely familiar.

River'eah sat down upon an ice-covered boulder.

"What are you doing here?" Lorian asked, confused and wary.

"Doing what I promised to do. Don't be afraid of me, Lorian," he replied as he pulled back the cloak to show his grey hair. His sideburns covered half his cheek but left his chin smooth.

"How did you get here?"

"I can go wherever I want to. It's a free universe, right? Well, some of it."

"Well, I have to go before I get shot."

River'eah suddenly stood up and raised his arms out, creating a wall of snow which engulfed two Striketroopers.

Lorian saw their black armour appearing and reappearing in the white mist as it enveloped them, forcing them back.

The droids' instinctive reaction was to fire and a blast exploded close to Lorian's leg. River'eah strengthened his hand and the two droids were flung metres backward, coming to rest on their backs among chunks of ice and snow.

Lorian held his leg and then realised that he was also bleeding from the other one, as well as his arm, though neither was serious.

"What do you think of that?" River'eah smiled.

"A neat skill."

River'eah kneeled down to inspect the wounds.

The Dark Lord would give his black soul to have this blood.

"So how did you really get here?" Lorian asked

"I live between worlds."

"What worlds?"

"This one and death."

While confused by the man's sudden appearance, Lorian felt no fear in his presence. If he wasn't fighting for his life, he would be able to ponder the nagging feeling that he knew River'eah from some other time.

"I believe your friends have arrived," River'eah whispered.

Lorian looked over and saw a line of Nunearanor troops using the cover of the snow drifts to edge their way forward towards the fortress and battlefield.

Lorian and River'eah made their way towards them until they were challenged by the troops.

"I'm Lieutenant Shane, Kandrol Squadron."

One of the figures took off a helmet, revealing long dark hair.

"Isla?" Lorian gasped.

"Was that your fighter?" she asked.

"Yeah."

Lorian couldn't believe his stars. Here she was, tired, but still beautiful. "Are you okay?"

"Well, we're in the middle of a battle, but I'm okay. You?"

"Not really."

She then noticed his blood.

"Why didn't you say so." She immediately opened a first aid kit and applied guri juice to the wound, cooling it instantly.

"We're moving to meet Metora's team," Dathurst said to her.

"We should press on. Time is short," River'eah finally made himself known.

"You are one of the priests?" Isla suspiciously asked.

"I'm afraid not Princess, not on Wolven Moor."

"Then we can trust you?"

"Of course. I am now a servant of the Sangreal."

"Then you can look after Lorian?"

"Where are you going?" Lorian asked, put out by seemingly being pushed aside.

"Over there," she said, pointing to the battle still raging about the fortress.

"We'll go to together," commanded River'eah, who then began leading the way.

As they walked, Isla took Lorian by the arm. She wiped the snow that had covered her eyes and hid her tears. "So many people have died today, all for us and all for nothing."

"I know." Lorian was reminded of Trix. He was still in shock over her death. The continued pressures of more danger just made him want to burst into anguish and cry out to the sky.

"That is not true, my young friend," River'eah called over his shoulder. "Good always comes out of a bad situation. Trix knows this."

Lorian stared at him, not saying anything. He had thousands of questions, but it was Isla who spoke up.

"Who *are* you? You speak like a wise man but you're out here in the middle of a battlefield." Isla's voice was raised.

When he didn't reply, she continued questioning him. "Do you have a transport here? *Who* are you?" she demanded.

He stopped. "No," he replied, answering only the first question.

"Then you must have escaped from an asylum."

"Oh, you are a fire of the universe, Princess Isla."

"You know me? What is your name?"

"I am River'eah, emissary of Runamore. I am here to guide you."

Isla looked to Lorian. "We need to get to Metora."

"Indeed, Cryacur has arrived and this battle is heading towards its crescendo."

The three stood looking at each other, Isla certainly the more suspicious.

"Come, young ones, follow this old bastard into battle." With that, he began running.

Isla and Lorian looked at each other. "Where did he come from?" she asked.

"He just appeared out of nowhere, but I have an idea who he is. I'll tell you when we get home."

"If."

"When," he replied.

She then began to run too, following in the tracks of River'eah. Despite his wounds, Lorian followed suit.

Progress was slow for Metora's team. The intense enemy fire and the uphill climb were burning up time. If it hadn't been for Oberon clearing a path forward, they would still have been stuck at the foot of the fortress. It seemed the Diamalordian troops were unwilling to approach the Sangrillion droid, preferring to send in the Striketroopers and tall battle droids to continue the fight.

Kuring-gai kept pace with Oberon, finishing off Axis troops that had hidden and Striketroopers that had been damaged but were still operational. They worked as a pair and, without realising it, had pulled far ahead of the other troops.

To Kuring-gai's surprise, though the secured entrance to the fortress was now in sight, Oberon began moving in the other direction.

"What are you doing?" he cried out

"My mission overrides the destruction of the gun."

"What mission?"

"To protect Lorian Shane."

"Lorian? Why?"

"He is the last Flame Tree."

Kuring-gai didn't have an answer for him. His mouth hung open in shock.

"Are you sure?" he finally said.

"Have I ever been wrong?"

Kuring-gai looked back at the fortress rising high above him and with it the noise and fumes of battle.

"We have to finish this, otherwise we all die!"

"It is urgent."

Kuring-gai pointed to the massive cannon as it blasted another shot out into space.

"No one will get off this moon, Oberon, you know that, unless we blast it into a million pieces! We'll share a grave together!"

"What's happening?" Metora called out as he arrived with more troops.

"Oberon has a place to be," Kuring-gai bluntly replied. "And so do I."

"The time to save Lorian Shane is short," stated Oberon.

"He's here?" replied Metora incredulously.

"There isn't time, Sire. Your nemesis is lurking about here somewhere looking for you," Oberon replied.

"He's here too?" Metora's skin had gone cold.

"You finish this while we get Lorian," offered Kuring-gai impatiently as blaster fire continued to target them.

Metora knew full well that in war the individual counted less when there were many to save. In this situation, that was brutally clear.

"We'll explain later, brother," Kuring-gai added softly while placing a reassuring hand on Metora's shoulder.

"Alright, we'll do what we can. We'll meet back at the transport."

Kuring-gai nodded and they parted ways.

"Form up!" Metora called his troops and then led the way towards the main entrance of the fortress.

A tremendous screech pierced through the gunfire from the great fortress. It was the cry of the Black Ash Prince. He was in his element as he threw back Bond troops with a swipe of his hand. Each time, he laughed like a drunken madman at the power he had over mortals.

Nemarluk kneeled in the mush of snow and mud, completely lost as to what to do. His troops exchanged confused looks between themselves. Their blaster fire seemed to have no effect.

Prior to the Black Ash Prince arriving, Nemarluk's troops had reached one of the main doors leading into the fortress. Demolition charges were placed on the door when suddenly the troops were thrown back into the slush.

Now they crouched behind whatever cover they could find as they tried to come up with a new plan.

"This is impossible!" cried out Sergeant Donnerman, one of the unit commanders.

"I know, I know!" Nemarluk yelled back in frustration.

Huge explosions flashed around them as more of the massive battle droids appeared to the east. All eyes shifted to the sight of the tall mechanical monsters crunching their way over the ice, blasting anything that resembled their enemy.

There was nothing more they could do here. Nemarluk knew it and the thought brought an uncomfortable lump to his throat. He did not like to lose or admit defeat. If he kept his troops here, however, they would all die for nothing. The only course of action was to regroup further back where there was better cover and then try to protect the other attack groups as they tried to get into the fortress.

"Pull back!" he called out.

Under heavy fire, his troops quickly laid mines and other traps for the enemy before moving back to better positions.

"We can't get in here. We're digging in on your flank," Nemarluk spoke into a communicator attached to his glove.

"Understood," came the reply.

After taking one last look at Cryacur guarding the door with a wide smirk on his twisted mouth, Nemarluk began joining his troops. Defiantly, he lined him up and fired a few shots. Cryacur blocked them all.

"Scrum-licker," Nemarluk muttered before moving off.

Cryacur was immensely pleased with the defiance shown by the Bond troops. It energised him and filled him with bloodlust. He could only pity them now. They would never get into his fortress. Metora's troops had come up against a steel wall and could go no further.

Soon he would launch his counterstrike and wipe them out. Metora would have nowhere to go and would finally be brought to his knees. Cryacur could almost feel it as the Bond's prince grovelled at his feet, begging for mercy. It would be a moment he would savour.

Somewhere out there he knew his nemesis was getting frustrated. The battle was going against him and his fear would be rising as panic set in. There would be no escape.

Through the smoke and fire, he saw the Sangrillion droid move away from the fighting. Earlier reports told him Nunearanor troops had landed on the other side of the fortress, but they had not been deemed a threat. Perhaps they were planning something. He knew that wherever Oberon went there would be action. He would follow them and bring the last of these droids to battle.

"Did you see that?" A Khoru officer said to Metora as they took cover behind a ruined wall that held the command section with its communication devices all manned by droids and troops.

Metora had watched through his magnifier as the Black Ash Prince disappeared from the battlefield and headed into the fortress itself.

"He's going for the Nunearanor."

The Nunearanor troops were on the other side of the fortress attempting to get into the rear entrance.

"Are you sure?"

"Do your best to wreck this place, then get back to the shuttle. Take off if you're under pressure. That's an order."

"Yes Sir."

Metora ran from the rubble as blasters fired at him and missed. Sparks and bolts of light exploded around him as he made his way to where Oberon had moved to.

The Nunearanor had fought their way through the fortress' northern defences and reached the rocky plateau that the former monastery sat on. Though the Axis focus had been on Metora's troops and the appearance of the Nunearanor troops had not been expected, that was quickly changing. More Striketroopers and battle droids were being moved to liquidate the Nunearanor attack.

Isla's command group huddled in a destroyed guard complex which held firing stations that protected the lower reaches of the fortress complex. Dead Striketroopers lay about, mixed with a number of Nunearanor guardsmen.

"This is tough going, Princess," Dathurst said between heavy breaths after slumping down next to her. He had just returned from the point squad that was moving forward.

"We'll be out of ammunition before we get any closer. Is there somewhere we can get in?"

"There's a doorway further up. I've sent a squad to check it out. Other than that, it looks sealed. I couldn't imagine the Axis allowing too many doors into their prized fortress."

"True," she replied tiredly.

Lorian had managed to sit down and hold in his obvious pain. Isla helped him get comfortable.

"I'll head up to have a better look, but I think this might be as far as we go," Dathurst said.

"We may have to link up with Metora's troops. Send some scouts to make contact."

Dathurst nodded before leaving to head back into the fight.

While Isla thought things through, she caught the image of River'eah seated on a pillar. He was looking around at the ruins of Wolven Moor.

"How are your wounds?" he said without looking at them.

"Fine. It's not the first time," Lorian replied.

River'eah smiled. He knew this too. He breathed in heavily. He could no longer contain the great thought in his mind which he had kept hidden until now.

"I have a task for you Lorian," he said, finally turning to face the two young ones. Isla continued to check Lorian's wound, with her eyes darting up to the old man then back again.

"Now?" Lorian asked, his tone reflecting the difficult and obvious nature of the situation they were in.

"The Dark Lord has had his greatest stooge searching the galaxy for the graves of the Ethereals."

"Really?" he exclaimed.

"Rumours have reached his ears of a descendant. You have heard of the Flames Trees?"

Lorian searched his memory of his childhood teachings. "They served the Ethereals."

"They were the children of the Ethereals," Isla corrected him.

"Yes. The apprentice of the first Dark Lord, Thara, hunted them down long ago, a beast by the name of Karthukan who herself was a Flame Tree but turned on her brothers and sisters. She was brought to the throne of the Ethereals after her capture and was almost sent out in an ice prison, just like her Master. But Karthukan's mother felt pity for her, as a mother would, and she was allowed to live in exile, far from the light of the world."

River'eah looked down at Isla and Lorian, "It was she, Lorian, it was she who Iminus Kaw found after his flight from Anueth all those years ago. It was Karthukan who taught Kaw all she knew. Then, when it was done, Kaw cut her down and ended her misery.

The surviving Flame Trees disappeared into time and were never heard of again. Their blood was diluted with that of mortals and darkness no longer feared them."

River'eah kneeled in front of them, his hands slowly rubbing together as he gathered his words, his eyes always on Lorian.

"Something magical has happened, Lorian. The last of the Ethereals came together and bore one more child, a true-blooded Flame Tree, a child of power, filled with the goodness of the world to counter the hatred that now encompasses it."

"How? They all died thousands of years ago?" Isla pointed out.

"That is what troubles the Dark Lord and why Cryacur has been sent to find their graves, to count them off. Because only an Ethereal can give birth to a Flame Tree. If he finds all the graves, then the rumours must be false, but he must have proof. That has made him dwell on it. For there is some mystery there that even he cannot explain. He doesn't understand everything in the universe yet."

Lorian remained silent, taking in the words despite his tiredness and sore body.

"It's you Lorian," River'eah whispered, placing his hands on Lorian's. "You are the last Flame Tree."

Lorian's mouth had opened and all the pain in his body disappeared for a moment as he sat stunned.

"I . . . I can't be. That can't be true," he protested.

River'eah's heartfelt smile widened. "Of course, you had to be hidden. A spell was cast around you, hiding your more . . . spiritual side. Otherwise, a child with such power would have been detected and killed years ago. A very necessary veil was placed around you as protection. But now the Dark Lord is only moments away from discovering who you are."

"But how? This is all incredible," Isla exclaimed, speaking for Lorian who sat silently stunned.

River'eah stood up. "I have tasked the last Sangrillion droid to protect you with all his soul. The Dark Lord is coming Lorian. He is coming for you and we have to get you out of here."

Lorian couldn't speak. The revelation seemed a great weight that had suddenly materialised out of nothing and now sat, unmoving and silent, on his shoulders. He tried to delve back into his memories, but there was nothing that gave him any clue or hint that any of this was true.

Oberon appeared above them. "My Lord, I have come."

"Just in time. You know what you must do, my loyal friend. Are you ready to do your duty one more time and with all your heart guard Lorian against all evil?"

"I will do so," the droid replied.

Isla held Lorian close. Her eyes looked up at the tall droid. She knew that this simple war had now become much more complex than she had ever thought possible.

Loud explosions rocked the outside of the complex where they had been hiding. They could also hear the screams of wounded men along with calls of command from officers.

"My troops!" Isla cried, getting to her feet and heading for the exit.

"He's here," River'eah whispered to Oberon.

The air seemed to grow colder and a stiff wind blew in bringing with it dust and snow.

Oberon reached down and grabbed Lorian's arm, helping him to his feet. "We have to go."

Isla led them out, followed by Oberon and Lorian. Many of her soldiers were falling back, firing into a dark cloud of smoke and fire as they retreated.

Kuring-gai appeared behind her.

"Fall back to the shuttles!" he called out.

She looked about to see who had survived and where her troops were. The figure of River'eah standing in the middle of the road caught her eye. The cloud mass had disappeared and there stood a cloaked, black form. She knew instantly who it was.

Cryacur had beaten back the Nunearanor and now they ran. He scanned the group that huddled around the Sangrillion droid. By her uniform, the girl was a Nunearanor. One of the men was a Khoru. The older man who stood defiantly in the road seemed unhuman, however, like a spirit who did not belong in this world. He immediately feared him. And there was a boy who he recognised as the friend of Metora. He had been imprisoned at Anarc and had fought him at the Elsenmere Ridge. Then it all made sense.

"It's you!" he cried out. Now he could clearly see and he tensed as he prepared to strike.

"So, my Master was correct. The Ethereals have schemed to bring back their withered old ways," he called out to the old man.

"You have no place in this universe, you who are born of ash and selfish dreams. Menace is all you are. Find your place in the abyss where all soulless beings suffer," River'eah called out in reply.

The Black Ash Prince had come closer towards the group as it was backing away step by step, all but the old man who continued to stand his ground.

"I should say the same for you. You and your kind are no more. Their days are long over. I now see the last warrior of your dreams of hope. Is he ready to die, old man?"

"The light of this world can only be dimmed, never blackened. It is you who will fall. You, and your Master too. Long overdue it is, too."

Cryacur laughed menacingly. He seemed to enjoy the taunting, as if all these thoughts had been in his mind and now he could finally spill them out.

Without warning, he unleashed a string of flames and lightning from his hands that was directed at Lorian, half hidden behind Oberon.

River'eah reacted instantly and the fireballs became water. The lightning was deflected back towards the Black Ash Prince.

"Run!" Kuring-gai cried out.

Oberon took the moment to open fire with his blaster, immediately joined by Kuring-gai. They covered the retreat as Isla took Lorian's hand, the two running from a fight they could not master.

"Get back to the shuttle!" she called out to Dathurst. He was pressed up against the rock wall with Sherri and a number of survivors.

"We can fight him, Princess," he replied, still determined despite his bloody face and torn uniform.

"No! Just get back to the shuttle!"

Dathurst did as ordered and began helping the wounded back towards the Bond's shuttle. Their own shuttle was too far away now.

"Keep running," Oberon said behind them, his blaster still aimed back where they had come from.

"I'll get them back," said Kuring-gai, "You just keep him away."

The three continued to run after the soldiers. She was surprised to suddenly see Metora appear on the road running towards them.

"Get back to the shuttle!" he called as he ran past, not even stopping. Isla stopped and looked back.

"Where are you going!?" she cried out, but he did not reply.

Kuring-gai stopped too and watched the prince run towards the fight. His own blaster was hot in his sweaty hands and his heart beat fast. Isla looked at him for a moment with pleading eyes. Though he was torn, he knew there was much more at stake. He didn't want to, but without a second glance he urged Isla and Lorian to keep going. Oberon would have the rear-guard.

River'eah saw that more time was needed for his charges to make their escape. Seemingly with his bare hands he brought up a snowstorm that engulfed the Black Ash Prince who immediately countered with a great explosion of fire which melted the snow and broke the wind.

Great lightning bolts flashed from both Cryacur and River'eah, colliding as they arced towards each other creating explosions of light and electricity that sparked in long lines of brilliance.

River'eah used the delay to fall back. The Black Ash Prince was just as quick, however. He leaped from the ground like a wild, black animal and landed right behind the old man, ready to make his final pounce.

"Metora, no!" River'eah cried out as he saw what was about to happen.

Metora's blade glittered in the dying electric bolts that still danced about. Cryacur did not see it coming.

The two nemeses were locked together for a moment while River'eah was temporarily stunned. For a moment, he thought Metora had truly finished the creature off.

The two princes struggled. Cryacur cried out as the blade drove right through his body. While Metora was a brave man, however, he was still a man. The Black Ash Prince was not.

Metora's grip was so tight on the blade that, when he was thrown away with such force, the blade came out of the Dark One's chest and landed on the ground, an arm's length away from his motionless body.

Frustrated and furious, Cryacur moved to attack but a massive charge of bolts paralysed him. The Black Ash Prince was so intent on destroying the last Flame Tree that he passed up a perfect chance to eliminate his old enemy. He came forward, ready to do battle once more.

It had taken almost an hour for Metora's troops to fight their way towards the fortress. Kuring-gai, Isla, and Lorian made the return journey in minutes.

The Bond troops who had survived were also pulling back,

joined by their Nunearanor allies.

"We never got close, brother. Bardon's troops got a few charges in and forced open the door, but that's as far as they got!" Nemarluk called to Kuring-gai as they passed him down the hill.

"We're leaving this place right now! Get back to your shuttle!" he called back.

"We'll see you back home," Nemarluk replied before moving away to organise his troops.

The group made their way across the sleet and rock towards the command shuttle, which was hidden behind drifts and a small, rocky outcrop.

Kuring-gai continued to look behind as the shuttle came into view. Oberon's metal form was instantly recognisable making great bounds across the ground.

A black cloud appeared behind him that quickly dived past the flank of the droid and headed towards the shuttle.

Oberon jumped into the cloud which instantly dissipated revealing the Black Ash Prince's neck, held tight by the impossibly strong arms of the Sangrillion.

Kuring-gai was astounded to suddenly see Cryacur lift the huge droid above his head, ready to smash him to pieces. River'eah appeared and turned the ground the creature was standing on into a pool of water, which he then sunk into, allowing Oberon to break free and continue towards the shuttle. River'eah turned the water to ice for good measure before joining the rest.

Soldiers of the Bond hurriedly boarded, bringing their wounded with them. Nepta was at the open door waiting for Lorian Shane. She had stayed managing communication equipment which had recently been destroyed by enemy fighters, leaving her to watch the battle as it unfolded.

"Master Shane, it's good to see you alive."

"Barely, Nepta," he whispered, his first words for some time.

Isla helped him aboard then was in turn helped by Kuring-gai. Startled by a loud crack, he turned to see the Black Ash Prince break free of the ice.

"Quick!" he called to Oberon who was paces away.

"You can't leave him here!" Isla was almost crying.

Kuring-gai turned to face her. "I'll find him. Now get your droid aboard. Oberon will go with you. Go!"

The shuttle was already beginning to lift off as Oberon arrived. He boarded, blaster still firing, with Nepta close behind.

"Nepta!" Lorian reached out to help the droid steady herself while walking up the ramp.

The Black Ash Prince roared into the attack. With what seemed simple ease, Nepta was ripped to pieces before Lorian's eyes.

"No!" Lorian let out an anguished cry.

Kuring-gai was brushed aside, lifted off his feet and thrown onto the ground, his body rolling away from view.

The scent of burnt flesh filled the transport as Cryacur closed in. His eyes were fixed on Lorian until in a flurry of movement he was suddenly gone from the ramp and the shuttle lifted off and away from the surface.

All those pent-up emotions burst forth from Lorian who pounded his fist on the floor of the shuttle. He couldn't help it. He cried as much from the pain of seeing the death of his beloved friends as from the new burden now on his shoulders.

Isla held him close, and she cried too. There was nothing to do but let the tears flow for all the horror and eternal pain this horrible day had brought.

The Black Ash Prince watched the shuttle disappear, his mind already concentrating on how to knock it from the sky. He would pursue it. He must pursue it. But first he would inform his Master that his insights had been correct. A Flame Tree lived.

"Track that ship. Destroy it and anything it lands on," he ordered a Diamalord officer who had appeared with more troops as they cleared up stragglers and wounded from the battle.

In all the confusion of one of biggest fleet actions in years, the shuttle managed to locate and land on the *Tanami*.

They had seen wrecks from both sides, drifting ghost ships abandoned by their crews. Holed, smoking, fire-ravaged, they hung in dead space spilling out their contents. Wreckage was everywhere — smashed fighters, chunks of hulls, and bodies with their final, pain-filled moments forever frozen on their faces.

The flagship was heavily damaged. Only two of the four engines were working, most of the communications systems were gone, and many of the cannons were also damaged or destroyed.

During the journey, there had been little conversation on the shuttle. Everyone kept their thoughts to themselves, exhausted mentally and physically. Most tried to sleep.

The flagship's hanger had been converted into a makeshift medical station. Many crews from other ships had been rescued and ended up here. Many wounded were also coming in.

Medical staff immediately took on all the shuttle's wounded. Isla sat with Lorian. She didn't want to leave him alone, but knew that, actually, he wasn't alone. Oberon stood tall an arm's length away.

"Isla?"

A familiar voice brought made her look up. It was Bree, who sat down next to them and embraced her cousin.

"We thought we lost you."

"Have we made it through?" Isla asked weakly.

"Most of us. We lost twelve ships."

"My family?"

"Alive. Talia was wounded when the bridge was hit but we cleared the moon and are about to meet up with the Bond fleet. What's left of it anyway."

"The whole thing was a disaster," dead-panned Lorian, whose head still remained down.

"But Metora's planning was meticulous, wasn't it?" Bree protested.

"Metora didn't come up with this plan and he's no longer here to defend himself," he added angrily.

Bree's face turned pale. "He's dead?"

Isla nodded. Her stiff, royal persona could no longer hold back her own tears. Her cousin cried too.

"This is a day of death. The name of Wolven Moor will be cursed forever. Talia will want to see you when you're ready."

"Go. I'll be okay," said Lorian.

Isla knew he would. Oberon was here.

She squeezed his hand and then let it go. Arm in arm with

Bree, she left the hanger.

Lorian's legs were aching, so he stood, his eyes still fixed a million miles away.

"Did you know about me, Oberon?"

"No. But I sensed something that was unhuman-like."

Lorian lifted his head to look up at the droid. Its metallic body was scorched and covered in dirt.

"What do you mean — 'unhuman'?"

"I sensed a higher spiritual power, one that is not encompassed by physical or material things. Imagine if you closed your eyes and you could feel heat on your skin. You would not know exactly what it was or see it, but you would know it was there."

"What will we do now? I can't go back to Anueth knowing this, if we get back at all. What the hell am I meant to do? River'eah can't just dump this on me and then disappear, expecting me to . . . to do what?"

"I'm afraid I don't have the answers. Perhaps River'eah will reveal them when it is the right time?"

"We don't have time. I don't want to go back to Anueth. I just want to disappear."

"Then that is what we will do."

BREAKING

Imperial Command's War Council had been watching the events at Wolven Moor unfold from their underground bunker system deep within Redsee.

From the time of the opening attack, there was high hopes and excitement, but that euphoria had been quickly brushed aside when the fleets joined combat.

The officers muttered their frustrations over data boards and map readouts. Though this was all the Bond could muster, the enemy seemed to be able to throw unlimited resources into the fray. How could the Bond survive the Axis' coming offensive?

Many had panicked and left the room to console themselves alone. Those who remained had withdrawn, becoming quiet, miserable people who no longer smiled. There was simply no chance of victory.

Admiral Zuke had grown quiet too. His orders had gone out virtually by the minute and each made the situation more confused for the fleet. By the time the report had been sent, decoded, and put before Admiral Taurus, the situation had changed. Compounding the frustration was the news the *Aquila* was out of action and unable to lead the fleet. Three further large ships with experienced commanders had declared they were unable to carry on with flagship duties as their own ships were under fierce attack or damaged.

Vice-Admiral Dyndarumm had whispered his displeasure at the constantly changing orders. He knew exactly the confusion these orders would cause. He had been ignored, however.

It had now come to the point where the fleets were no longer taking Zuke's orders and there was no one left to take full control to complete the mission and save the Nunearanor and the Bond fleets.

Zuke sat sullen in his chair. This last development had boiled his blood.

"Where is the fleet?" Zuke thundered. "Order them to re-engage communications. How can I command when I am ignored?"

Dyndarumm sighed deeply and closed his eyes. He was champing at the bit to tell the man what was going on, but he feared the wrath of the Admiral. Finally, he found his courage.

"Sir, they are under heavy attack. There is no time for complicated manoeuvres. We must withdraw or else we will lose everything. Every ship, fighter, pilot, crew-member, and soldier will be gone and there will be nothing left to defend the Bond. They're demanding an answer . . ."

"So, he is speaking with us?" Zuke abruptly interrupted, talking over the Vice-Admiral.

Now that Dyndarumm had started, however, his courage increased and he kept on going.

"The last reports showed his casualty list with a footnote that this is only a partial report. A decision needs to be made."

Zuke said nothing. An officer approached Dyndarumm.

"Sir, new information from the *Aquila*."

"Good."

Dyndarumm read the information on his data panel. His eyebrows raised for a moment before he regained his composure.

"Admiral, I have been informed that Captain Journ has re-established command of the *Aquila*."

He did not read out the full message and kept it to himself.

"So, there is a captain who appears to be in control. Why would he need to bother with any of my orders?"

"Because he is trying to save the fleet. You're being ignored because the situation is moving too rapidly! Why can't you see this?"

"How dare you raise your voice to me!"

"Get them out, Zuke." Dyndarumm had calmed his voice.

Zuke finally looked at Dyndarumm. "Let the Elector decide," he said deadpan.

The Vice-Admiral was stunned. "The Elector is a man with basic military skills."

"Is he not the Commander-in-Chief? He can give the order. I won't have blood on my hands."

But you already have. Dyndarumm could hardly disguise his disgust. He took a moment to scan the room. The staff's expressions of shock and repulsion mirrored his own.

"You've wiped your hands of Wolven Moor then?"

Zuke did not reply. He knew fully the state of his cowardice. Its weight pushed him deep into his chair where he sulked, his hand coming across his face to hide his shame.

"Well? What are you waiting for?" Zuke snarled without looking up.

Dyndarumm waved over his own aide. "Take my place, I'm going to see the Elector. Ring ahead. Tell him I'm coming."

Time was now measured in blood. Every second it took to ride the elevator and then the sub-railway to Sentinal Tower gnawed at the Vice-Admiral. He muttered his frustration at the seemingly slow movement, mixed with his disgust at Zuke. The man had to go. He would find further courage and report to the War Council exactly what had happened.

That hurdle would be in the future. Right now, he had to ensure there was something left to command.

Exiting the sub-railway, he reached the elevator that would take him to the crown of Sentinal and the apartments of the Elector.

A message came up on his data pad.

The Elector is asleep and his aide is refusing to wake him.

Now he was even more furious. The guards posted let him through without hindrance. The door opened and he was greeted by Crowcraw's aide, a slippery fellow dressed in black. Dyndarumm knew him from his time on Zuke's staff but had had few dealings with the man.

"I have urgent business with the Elector."

"Of course, General. His Excellency is waiting for your report. Follow Me."

Dyndarumm walked quickly and reached the main door before Quisto, who merely smiled meekly as he entered the code to access the private apartments.

Crowcraw was seated at a table reading reports, fully dressed and seemingly more alert than a man who was supposedly just in bed. He rose to meet the General.

"Vice-Admiral, what is the urgency of this?"

"I need you to order the fleet to withdraw from Wolven Moor."

"Me?"

Dyndarumm could see Crowcraw's immediate confusion and quickly brought him up to speed with the unfolding disaster.

"Zuke has requested that the decision be made by you." Dyndarumm was aware of himself dropping the Admiral's title, but Crowcraw seemed to give no indication he had noticed.

Crowcraw looked to Quisto with an alarmed silence, seeking more information from his aide.

"My order? Why isn't Admiral Zuke in command?"

"He is, my Lord, but we need a decision now. Have you been keeping up with the battle?"

Crowcraw finally seemed to pick up the urgency in Dyndarumm's voice.

"I am unaware of the situation. What would you have me do?"

"Let me, my Lord. I have been studying the hourly reports," Quisto offered. "It seems to me that the fleet should stay and complete its mission. Surely we are close to victory?"

Dyndarumm gave the man an indignant look, "The fleet is suffering massive casualties. The batteries on Wolven Moor have not been eliminated and four Axis fleets have been identified in the area, two of which are ready to encircle ours and eliminate it. We were betrayed, my Lord. Our plans were leaked to the enemy. I'm sure of it."

"Do you have proof of this?" Quisto rapidly responded.

"How else could things have gone so wrong? They were waiting for us, including the Black Ash Prince."

Quisto turned to the Elector. "We have the honour of the fleet to consider, my Lord."

"The fleet will be destroyed within the hour. We can't delay this."

"But we must be close?" Quisto continued to debate the issue.

"No, Quisto," Crowcraw said. "Today we live by the adage, 'better to live today and fight tomorrow'. Order the fleet back Vice-Admiral."

"At once, my Lord."

Dyndarumm didn't wait any longer and left the office. Quisto watched him go. What a day it had been. he was delighted at the state the Bond was in. He had done his best to wrench a few more deaths for the Axis. Now he would see what fate had in store for the Bond's precious fleet.

"This is a horrible day for the Bond, my Lord, but hopefully there will be light in this darkness," Quisto said, his joy veiled by faux concern.

"Yes. I hope it all works out for the best."

Quisto was thinking the same thing.

Dyndarumm had sent the order back to the command centre, prioritised to send to the fleet.

Moments later, it arrived on the bridge of the *Aquila*.

"Another priority message from command." Warrant Officer Rewann was expecting another barrage of orders from Redsee.

On reading it her excitement levels rose instantly.

"Captain, Command orders all forces to disengage and return to Trinity."

Journ quickly read the message himself. The *Aquila* had taken a pounding, even the bridge taking a direct hit. Many terminals were destroyed and their crews killed or injured. There was still lingering smoke that the air conductors were filtering out. There was also the business with Taurus and his son.

A mutiny was the last thing he expected. He was worried about the signal sent to Redsee, which he did not read or authorise, and the problems it would create. He had bigger problems to worry about, however.

It had taken all his skills to try to hold off the Axis, but the fleet was nearing breaking point.

"About bloody time," he muttered. "Get this to all ships, open signal."

The signaller nodded and began sending out the order.

"Let's save what we can!" he called out to his officers, then looked back to the view screen which was alive with Axis ships and wreckage. His heart was heavy. Half his fleet had been lost. Some of the Nunearanor had reached him but there had been no word from any of the strike teams on the moon.

There would be time to mourn, but not now. It would take all their effort to get away and reach safety. There was no way he could keep on beating off the Axis fleets. They were far too strong. There was only one card left to play.

"Send a further message. Scatter fleet. Good luck and see you back home."

It was every ship for itself now.

It seemed the remains of the fleet were waiting for just this moment. They had been pursued by the Axis for hours on end. Fighters and ships had been pushed to their limits. Any craft that broke down was doomed. Ammunition was running out and pilots and gunners alike were exhausted.

The barrels on the capital ships were red hot but they couldn't afford to stop firing. It would mean death. Commanders had few ships left to issues orders to. Some ships had no commanders and were fighting a lone war against a numerically superior enemy.

The Axis could smell blood and sensed their enemy's defeat was close at hand.

On the bridge of the *Warloch*, Master Murlex was suitably pleased at what she saw. She had been placed in charge of the Axis fleet recently after killing her rivals. That's the way you climbed that mountain in the Dark Lord's service. To prove you will kill to achieve a goal was the ultimate proof of loyalty and determination. She was also brilliant at strategy and command. Her devotion to her Master would see his will branded on the galaxy and she would not hesitate to destroy anything that got in her way.

While the remains of the Nunearanor fleet had linked up with the Bond fighters, the assault on Wolven Moor was all but dead and much of the enemy fleet had been broken up.

The Bond ships fought back as best they could. They would link up with other ships and form improvised battlegroups and counterattack Axis ships. The battle had long ago become so entangled that high command's orders were useless. A ship survived on the skill and bravery of her crew as much as from firepower and protection.

The order to disengage was the survivors' saving grace. With their last ounce of fuel, ships that could blasted into lightspeed. They disappeared in all directions, anywhere other than Wolven Moor seemed safer.

The remaining larger ships did their best to allow smaller cruisers to escape by protecting them with blaster fire until the last moment. By concentrating firepower at a weak point in the enemy's defence, it would clear a path for escape.

The instant that Bond ships were going into lightspeed, the Axis commanders knew a withdrawal was underway and they increased their efforts to destroy every Bond ship. Now, as the fleet's pincers closed in, they were hampered by their sheer numbers. Hours before, it had been deadly. Now they were getting in each other's way.

Wreckage around Wolven Moor also inhibited movement. Murlex ordered the *Warloch* and other heavy ships to move forward, deliberately smashing into half-destroyed ships, just so they didn't have to make wide evasive manoeuvres. They smelled blood. Space was filled with it.

The Bond left their dead behind. The last battles were dying down as the Axis ran out of targets. The odd isolated Bond fighter swooped about, trying to make itself invisible among the ruins of friend and foe's ships. If they were lucky, they snuck away. Some were not lucky and remained with their comrades at Wolven Moor.

The snow plains of Wolven Moor were now scorched black from laser or missile strikes. Deep, long grooves and impact craters, tinged with whispers of smoke, showed where fighters had crashed after ending their death plunge.

Then there were the bodies. Both human and droid were found around the ruins of buildings at the base of the cannon complex, as if a giant ship had opened its guts and the bodies had tumbled out, falling in heaps upon the land.

A quiet hung across the battlefield. Veterans call it *the death breath*. At times, there was simply no one left to make any noise. Wounded lay still, afraid to give themselves up for fear of being executed. Broken Striketroopers stumbled about with their arms, legs, or heads shot off. Some were still looking for targets, others for a place to finally die.

Smoke rose from fiercely burning buildings and defensive bunkers, climbing higher than the fortress itself, its blackness framing the ruin of the scene and signally the defeat of the Bond.

Though battered and sore, Kuring-gai had climbed up from the gully where he had been thrown. The heat of Cryacur's hands upon his body had been intense. He was thankful his armour had absorbed most of it.

He was surprised he had kept his wits. Maybe it was because it had happened so quickly and he was nearing the end of his endurance. Somehow, he had landed on a short platform and managed to hold on and prevent his body falling hundreds of metres straight down into the massive chasm.

As he had fallen and landed with a crash of dust and snow, he had seen out of the corner of his eye the shuttle pass over the chasm. *Good, very good.*

Now he had to save himself and find Metora.

He raised his head above the lip of the gully and saw that the way was relatively clear. A few damaged droids moved about, but there was little movement. The fortress garrison had yet to come out and begin the clean-up.

Ignoring the pain in his back and arm, he lifted himself out of the gully and ran to the nearest cover. Looking around, he did a double take as he saw the remains of Nepta scattered about. The droid's head looked straight at him, her once golden eyes now just grey holes.

There was no sign of the Black Ash Prince. His burns seemed to begin aching again at the very thought of the monster. Using the cover of the frozen rock and ice, he made his way back to where he last saw Metora. On the way, he avoided Axis troops that had begun to move about. With one scoop as he ran, he put on a discarded Axis helmet. He grimaced with fury on seeing Striketroopers shooting wounded Bond soldiers. If only he could shoot back, but he had no weapon and it would be certain death.

There was nothing for it but to move on. A little further on, he stole the uniform from a dead Diamalord, knowing full well his dark features and hair would eventually give him away. He was hoping for just a few seconds of advantage. It was certainly better than running about in the uniform of the Khoru.

Time was getting on, the sun was setting, and the temperature was becoming noticeably colder. From his briefing, he knew that sunrise here at the polar circle was short. He made a wide arc to avoid the road he had run along while retreating from Cryacur and went through a small outcrop before coming out at the original battlezone.

Every few steps he had to stop and flatten himself to the snow as Axis troops filed past. Here, the snow had melted and great chunks had been blown from the lower wall of the fortress and the rocky hill it sat on. It had been a fierce and unnerving clash of arms for Kuring-gai. He had not come across parallels in his own history. It was a world beyond him and this one. The spirit war had entered reality. He could still see the great flash of lightning and fire from Cryacur and River'eah and he wondered where the old man had gone. He had simply vanished as abruptly as he had appeared.

Without being detected, he reached the ruins of the guardhouse and looked about. Again, there were broken walls, equipment, and bodies. If Metora had been found, then surely there would be more activity here. He decided to backtrack along the road, one eye out for the enemy, the other looking at the dead he passed.

He came across a small pool of blood and drag marks. A broken sword lay in the slush. It had been snapped in two and its metal scorched. The drag marks then became footprints leading away and back to the chasm Kuring-gai had come from.

After pulling himself out of the chasm, he had probably run straight past him. Kuring-gai carefully made his way back to the chasm. There were blood spots and footprints. He was cautious enough to rub them out as he went. No wandering Axis patrol would be able to follow.

Finally, he came to the chasm. A stiff wind was now blowing up from its depths. There was rock now, and the footprints were harder to follow, but he knew Metora had to be here somewhere.

A few metres down, a ledge wound its way along part of the chasm. He climbed down quickly and began carefully walking along the ledge. Up ahead there was a crag and, as he came closer, a large boulder partially blocking the way. After a few further steps, he saw that it was actually a cloaked figure.

"Metora!" he whispered.

"Kuring-gai?" came a weak response.

Kuring-gai kneeled next to him. "Are you hurt?"

"A bit sore. Did everyone get away? I saw the shuttle leave."

"All but us."

Metora seemed to relax. "Good. I thought he would get them."

"No, it was close. Poor Nepta was destroyed, and I ended up almost at the bottom of this," Kuring-gai said while giving the chasm a long look.

"Poor Nepta. Did Isla and Lorian get away?"

Kuring-gai nodded, "Uninjured, as far as I know."

"Did I really try to jump on him?"

Kuring-gai laughed. "Yes, it was brave, but also stupid."

It was Metora's turn to laugh. "Is he about?"

Kuring-gai shook his head. "I haven't seen him. There are a few troops about, but it's quiet. We've both had a few of these quiet moments."

"I blacked out for a little while, then walked back. After seeing the shuttle take off, I came here. It's peaceful."

"True. No wonder our forebearers hold this as a special place. But I sense sadness here, too."

They both sat looking out at the frozen landscape, lost in their own private thoughts.

"I wish I could enjoy it longer, but we'll freeze to death if we stay."

"We need to get back."

"It would be nice to disappear for a while."

"No, not now. Lorian's life has been marked."

"Why?"

"You're not the enemy's most wanted anymore. It seems our young friend is a Flame Tree, a pure blood child."

Metora's eyes widened despite his exhaustion. "Wow. There have always been rumours of more descendants."

"This is different. He's not you or me. He's not a descendant but a child of the Ethereals, a first born. He'll hunt him across the galaxy."

"Is this true?" Metora was even more shocked at this revelation.

"River'eah says it is so and even Cryacur believes it."

"River'eah?" Metora asked.

Kuring-gai sat down and wrapped his cloak tight around himself.

"I have not heard that name in all my life, only in history, but seeing him take on Cryacur like that was incredible. That was power not of this world. Today, everything changed. The Ethereals have not forsaken us. I believe this."

"What a weight to put on someone's shoulders," said Metora. "Does the enemy know?"

Kuring-gai nodded.

"Then this will be our last chance to sit under a peaceful night."

"He will raise the Sons to counter this," Kuring-gai predicted.

Metora said nothing. He knew of the implications and his family's link to the Dark Lord's most voracious servants.

The two warriors sat there for a little while longer. Their

bodies were tired and resting, making it hard to break away from the sight of such serenity. The light was fading. The stars were now more noticeable in the sky and the wind was picking up. It was a last chance to enjoy a small piece of paradise before the war would drag them back into it.

It was Kuring-gai who broke the quiet.

"We should try and get back now."

Metora knew it too. He rubbed his forehead as his headache rose and fell like a storm raging within his skull.

"Any ideas?" he asked.

"Take this uniform." Kuring-gai was already taking off the Diamalordian jacket.

Most of the Axis forces were busy around the fortress base and were unconcerned with the approach of the two figures. One of the figures fell to the snow, the other a Diamalordian officer walked about seemingly observing the ruins of the area.

Worker droids appeared and began collecting the dead from both sides. Metora wanted to sit down. His head was spinning so much he thought he would vomit. Encouraging words from Kuring-gai who lay pretending to be dead at his feet kept him focused.

The worker droids were putting the dead Bond troops into a small shuttle. Metora thought this was as good a time as any and waved them over.

"Put this one on," he ordered.

They did not respond in voice but immediately two of them picked up Kuring-gai and moved to dump him onto the bodies of dead Bond troops. Metora had to look away.

"Sir, this one is still alive."

Metora shrugged. "Not for long."

The droid did not respond and the limp body of Kuring-gai was dumped onto the pile.

"Where are you taking them?" Metora asked.

"Sector twelve. There are orders for the bodies to be searched before being disposed of in the valley."

He nodded his understanding and climbed onto the shuttle, doing his very best not to look sickened and uncomfortable while doing so.

The shuttle slowly edged away from the battlefield, keeping close to the ground. Metora lined up his blaster at the pilot droid and shot it in the back of the head. The shuttle lost height but Kuring-gai had woken and scrambled to take control before they crashed.

"You know, I should be used to escaping from planets under fire!" Kuring-gai called out. He looked behind him and saw Metora had collapsed against the dead body of a Bond trooper.

Putting aside his concern, he guided the shuttle away from the fortress site. The shuttle was not space-capable, being merely a piece of machinery to move people and equipment about over the surface of a planet.

Despite his attempts, he could not gain full control of the shuttle. Realising it had a pre-programmed flight plan, he kept one eye out for trouble and the other on Metora.

"Metora? Metora?" he called with no response.

He was forced to climb over the gruesome cargo to check his friend. Metora was pale and his skin was cold and clammy.

Kuring-gai saw the shuttle begin to slow and make a wide left turn. Its destination was a small landing field where several fighters and other service craft had parked. Already there were droids going through the dead bodies of Bond troopers.

"Hold on my friend," he said quietly before heading back to the cockpit.

He was acutely aware that his appearance would give him away. There was a discarded helmet which he put on but there was no way of hiding his beard and dark skin.

While intently watching where the shuttle was landing, he scanned the line of fighters. It appeared to be some sort of workshop or repair facility. All the craft stored there bore some type of damage. All except one — a Takeon reconnaissance fighter parked to the far side looked promising.

Kuring-gai needed a plan, and quickly. As the shuttle moved in to land, he returned to the pile of dead, dragged Metora to the cockpit, and waited.

The worker droids were waiting. There were only two Diamalords supervising and thankfully no Striketroopers. But who was in the Takeon?

There was no movement around the ship and it didn't appear damaged.

All he could do was wait. The shuttle landed with a thud and the worker droids went about their work. Each body was lined up next to another while the Diamalords checked them and removed ammunition clips, belts, weapons, and personal equipment. The bodies were then loaded onto another shuttle for burial in the chasm.

The seconds ticked by. Most of the bodies had been removed

and no one had taken any notice of them in the cockpit. Kuring-gai began searching for the override to the auto pilot. Thankfully the machine was of a basic build — *soldier proof* — and it wasn't hard to find the right command.

With a quick burst of power, he lifted the shuttle off and roared over to the Takeon, landing next to it.

Saying a quick prayer to the Ethereals, he took hold of Metora and jumped from the shuttle.

It was then he was noticed by the Diamalords.

"Hey! What are you doing?!" came the challenge.

Kuring-gai ran to the Takeon with Metora over his shoulder. Reaching the steps, he was able to put Metora in before climbing onboard.

Takeons were built for three, a long-range reconnaissance craft built to shadow fleets and spy on planetary defences. Because of that work, they were fast but had few self-defence weapons or shields.

There was no sign of any crew, so Metora was strapped in while Kuring-gai began powering it up. The Diamalord was now running towards the Takeon, blaster in one hand, the other talking into a communicator.

"Great," he mumbled to himself.

A small rumbling signalled the engines powering up. At the same time, a small vehicle approached carrying three figures dressed in flight suits. The mystery of the whereabouts of the crew had been solved. They were just in time to see their Takeon stolen.

Kuring-gai lifted the Takeon off the ground.

"I hope this thing isn't broken."

The Diamalordian began firing, his shots aimed at the cockpit screen where they exploded against the shield. Anything more powerful and they would be in trouble.

The Takeon blasted away and into the Wolven Moor night sky. In moments, it was clear of the atmosphere.

Kuring-gai was planning a quick getaway but the massive wreckage fields he found came as both a shock and a hindrance.

It took all his basic skills as a pilot to dodge the large bits of metal. Though he was a soldier first and a pilot second, he was able to avoid the cracked cruisers and corvettes hanging limp in deep space. There was no avoiding the massive losses the Bond had suffered during the battle.

One corvette took his attention. It appeared intact but was dead in space. The lights along its beam were illusions. At first, he had taken them for artificial light, but now he could see it was a massive fire inside the ship that was consuming everything. Soon the hull would crack and the fire would go out instantly, letting in the coldness of space and killing any crew-member lucky enough to have survived the fireball.

It was like moving through a graveyard with fresh bodies still arriving. It had been a crushing defeat. Could a Flame Tree reverse their fortune? His once cold heart had begun to burn again at the revelation of Lorian's lineage. He couldn't yet imagine what it all meant, but there had to be some good to come out of this. There just had to be or there would be no point in carrying on.

He had no real way of communicating with any surviving Bond ships, not without a communication droid like Nepta. There was nothing left but to pull into clean space and set the coordinates for home before the two Griffen fighters that were shadowing him came closer.

They were close to engagement but Kuring-gai was tired of fighting battles. He finished putting in the coordinates and put the Takeon into lightspeed. Only then did he relax and check on Metora who was still unconscious. Let the man sleep. He will be needed in the next few days.

Lorian wasn't even aware that he had fallen asleep on one of the ammunition carriers parked up against the far hanger wall. The usual bustle of a hanger crew preparing ships for action wasn't here. Most of the wounded had been moved, leaving the place quiet but for the odd trooper pacing about, no doubt wanting to find a quiet, lone place to think and grieve.

It was what he wanted, to think about Trix and Nepta, to wonder what had happened to Imogen and Kahil. He didn't even know what had happened to Kuring-gai and Metora. He could still see Kuring-gai being thrown from the ramp and Nepta being ripped apart. Trix's last words kept repeating over and over. His body wanted to burst into tears, but what were the use of tears? They fixed nothing but made of fool of men and women.

He had been hearing her voice calling his name. In the quiet between his miserable thoughts, she called his name. She was an Ethereal, and his mother. He could feel that, there was no need for anyone to tell him. Strangely, it had begun to make sense. Of course, such a revelation raised more questions than it answered. Did Saturn, the man who had raised him, know? And why him? It might explain why Dez and he were so different. They weren't even true brothers.

What if this River'eah was a liar sent by the Dark Lord to deceive him? History recorded him dying hundreds of years ago. Was this a different man? He could only rub his eyes and temple to try and ease his thoughts.

Lorian had made up his mind that he couldn't go back, and he would leave. A Flame Tree. He knew of them, but they had vanished long ago and held no sway over anything or anyone anymore.

Frustrated, he began to pace about the hanger floor, a habit he had picked up from someone.

Isla had been gone for some time. He should be happier to see her, but it wasn't as it should be. True, he had dreamed about her, but now she was here. Bigger things were on his mind now, however.

Why hadn't anyone told him? He was getting frustrated. His father had kept it secret for a reason. The whole thing confused him. Did he now have special powers? What would it mean to the people to have a Flame Tree around again? Would they even know what one was and what it was meant to do? All he knew was that he would keep it to himself. It obviously meant something to Kaw, enough to have Cryacur try to kill him.

"Damn you, River'eah," he muttered to himself as he sat down on a container, burying his head in his dirty hands.

He wanted to cry again. His mourning for his friends seemed to come in great waves before disappearing, only to return at the slightest thought. Poor Nepta, ripped apart by that creature.

An idea suddenly came to him. Why not return to Wolven Moor and find his friends? No. Madness, pure madness. The moon would be full of Axis forces. It would probably mean his doom too, or capture. Cryacur knew more about Lorian than he himself did. Why does the Dark Lord have such an interest in an ancient line? Why does he fear them? Surely there was some secret that could lead to his demise.

He began pacing again and ended at the mouth of the open hanger. Battered ships stayed close to the safety of the *Tanami*, all grouped for mutual protection. Oberon's shadow fell over him.

"What are your orders, Lorian?" he asked.

Lorian closed his eyes and took a deep breath. After a few breaths he was able to block out the troubles of the universe, focusing on what his next step should be.

"I'm leaving. I can't go back to Anueth. There has to be some answers out there."

"Where will we go?"

Lorian quickly looked up at the droid. The use of *we* had surprised him. Oberon would not leave his side.

"You know this universe better than me, Oberon. Somewhere safe."

"The Dark Lord will be looking for you."

"He'll be looking all over Trinity."

"Then we must leave at once before the fleet docks."

Lorian let out the air in his chest. "I hope Metora and Kuring-gai are okay."

"I do also."

There was nothing else for it but to go. "Can you get a transport?"

"Leave that to me." If the droid was able to smile, it would be wide and mischievous.

While Oberon was gone, Lorian found a place behind the wreckage of fighter. Turning his jacket into a pillow, he tried to sleep, but the noises of the hanger and the shrieking alarms as Axis fighters conducted probing attacks against the fleet all merely kept his eyes closed and his mind open.

It didn't seem long before Oberon returned bringing boxes of emergency food plus the news that he had indeed found a transport. Lorian wasn't surprised that the Sangrillion droid was able to obtain what he had asked for, though how he explained the need for rations remained unsolved.

The transport was in a lower hanger. When Lorian laid eyes on it, the scorch marks over its hull concerned him only for a moment. They had the means now of getting away.

"Any questions from command?" Lorian asked. He couldn't resist knowing if the mission had been made known.

"None."

They boarded and began flight preparations. The transport had been used to shuttle wounded crews from other ships and was full of bandages, used medical supplies, and other equipment that had been left behind.

The shuttle they had arrived in from Wolven Moor was large and more useful for future service. They only needed something small.

Lorian was eager to leave and quickly removed most of the waste, keeping the weapons stored away. Cleaning the blood off the floor and seats had him in deep thought. Using chemicals, he was able to wash most of it off the seats, but the floor took some time. It was impossible not to think about what had occurred on this tiny ship hours before.

"Where are you going?" Isla's voice at the main hatch startled him.

"Isla?"

"Well?" she said as she climbed aboard, her eyes taking in the cleaning process, stored gear, and supplies. Her tone of seeming annoyance made him wary. He saw that she had put a tan-coloured jacket over her torn uniform, but her hair and skin was fresh and clean.

"Oberon and I are leaving."

"Why?" she replied softly and with concern.

"I'm a marked man. Besides I have a new mission."

She shook her pretty head. "You and Metora can be so much alike."

For the first time in what seemed like days, he was able to force a quick chuckle.

She took his hand. "I'm coming with you."

Before he could reply she had let go his hand, disappeared out of the hatch, and returned moments later with a bag and a blaster.

"You don't have to."

"I'm not arguing with you, Lorian. You need the company and I don't have anything else here."

"But you have a family?"

"They'll be alright."

He chose his words carefully. "I don't have anyone else. Your family will need you, as will your people."

Yesterday he would have been glad to have her in his company, but now he was reluctant for her to come as he believed she was giving up too much.

She looked at him with her deep, green eyes and he knew

instantly that this was not an easy decision for her.

"I will miss them every day, but I need to do this. Are you going to throw me out?" she looked to her side where Oberon had appeared at the hatch.

"No," Lorian replied.

"I didn't think so," she smiled mischievously.

Lorian began thinking to himself that this journey was going to be interesting. He was secretly glad for the company — female company. It would mean a whole new set of rules, but Isla seemed able to rough it, as it were. She may well be a princess of Nunearanor, but she was used to hard conditions and fighting.

Oberon had opened the rear ramp and began climbing aboard.

"Don't you start on me either, Oberon."

"As you wish."

Isla leaned close to Lorian. "That's the difference between men and droids. They do as their told and don't argue."

"I'm not going to argue. I just thought you had more important things to do then come with us."

She remained silent as she took her seat in the cockpit, her mind now turned to something Lorian could not fathom and dare not ask. Everyone had their own demons, their own burden to carry.

He powered up the transport and began to manoeuvre it out of the hanger, passing the figure of the Talia who raised her hand in farewell.

Kuring-gai let Metora sleep. The cruiser, *Marla*, had answered his call, but he was aware that he was being watched carefully. An enemy ship declaring itself occupied by friendly forces was the oldest trick in the book. The bulk of the fleets had vanished as they scattered into lightspeed. Every ship would be desperate to get behind the protection of Trinity before any more Axis ships turned up. He punched in further codes, including his own and Metora's, in an effort to ensure the ship's crew knew who they definitely were and didn't open fire.

"Message to craft, activate secret sign," came the voice from the cruiser.

Kuring-gai finished putting in the code and added a message indicating who he and his passenger were.

"Confirmed," came the response.

Kuring-gai moved the Takeon into the small hanger bay. There was a medical party waiting and Kuring-gai wasted no time in lifting the Prince from his seat and taking him to the main hatch. There he was passed into their hands and placed on a gurney.

The captain of the *Marla*, Darci Wun, waited with Kuring-gai after the medical team began moving Metora to a medical ward. Her uniform was torn and scorched from the various fires and damage her ship had taken.

"Good to see you're still alive. How is he?"

"He was wounded by Cryacur. What of the other ships?"

"I don't know. We're headed for Delta 200. There are ships everywhere, a scattered mess. I'd imagine the rest of the ships will be trying to find any dock they can get to."

"What about Oberon?"

Wun shook her head. "I've heard nothing. He could be on board another ship but, like I said, many are heavily damaged and barely able to stay in formation. When we get back to Anueth, we will get a better idea."

Kuring-gai was disappointed. "How close are we to Trinity?"

"Not far."

A warning siren shrilled through the hanger and broke the conversation.

"Enemy fighters inbound," came a voice over the intercom.

"Quickly! Get him to medical!" Wun called out. The medical team began rushing out of the hanger into a corridor while Captain Wun and Kuring-gai walked behind them.

"We've been getting probing attacks for two hours."

"Looks like the Axis will chase us right to that bastard Rahvig," Kuring-gai grumbled.

"Exactly where we're vulnerable."

"Well, they can smell blood. It's what I'd do."

The cruiser was rocked by fire. Its few remaining cannons returned fire and there were flashes outside the hanger bay doors before they closed. An Axis fighter roared past just as the view was blocked.

Then the alarms went silent and quiet returned to the ship.

"Are you injured?" Wun asked Kuring-gai.

"A few scratches."

"What happened out there?"

Kuring-gai could tell that her questions were mixed with concern and intrigue. "Cryacur threw me off a cliff."

"Sounds like the two of you must have a tale to tell."

He merely nodded in acknowledgment. "Do your best to find Lorian Shane and Oberon. It's important. The last Sangrillion droid shouldn't be hard to miss."

"I will." Wun nodded and began heading back to the bridge.

Within the medical bay, there was plenty of work going on. He only now saw that most of the medical team who had taken Metora here wore bloodied and dirty uniforms. All the beds were taken and there were wounded crew sitting on seats, propped up against walls, or on the floor.

"Let's move those that are stable to the crew quarters so we can make some room," a doctor ordered a number of medical personnel. He then moved over to the still unconscious Metora.

"He's got a number of burns on his arms and upper body. Further trauma to the nervous system. Looks like blaster burns," said the doctor as he looked over Metora.

"Like these?"

Kuring-gai removed his armour and jacket to reveal the red rash across his neck and upper body where the Black Ash Prince had placed his hands.

For a moment, the doctor and his staff appeared stunned at seeing wounds made by bare hands. It was the first time they had been so close to the Dark Lord's red right hand.

Kuring-gai was puzzled by such a reaction. How could such a creature create this amount of fear and awe at the same time?

He breathed deeply, exhaustion finally coming over him, as much from the strain of battle as from the relaxing drugs now running through his system.

He sent out messages to Nemarluk and Perreder. They responded quickly. Nemarluk's troops had managed to get away on another shuttle and had docked with the *Aquila*. Finally satisfied, he fell asleep.

While he slept and the medical team treated Metora, the

remains of the fleet reached Trinity. They trailed smoke and hot embers burned within hulls. There were broken ships, ships with only one intact engine, and all were scorched black.

Surgeons and their droids worked franticly to save lives. Horrible burns, limbs shot off, or bodies punctured by shrapnel, they saw it all. The piles of covered dead were testimony to the vicious losses the fleet had taken. Exhausted fighter crews continued to fly cover, ready to drive off enemy fighters.

The coordinated manoeuvres through the defences of the Bond were agonising to the ships' commanders. Some craft were moored together to supply power and communications as engines shut down from damage, fuel shortages, or simple overuse during the battle and retreat. Added to this were the Axis fighters trying to pick off cruisers that had lagged behind. Fresh Bond ships had been sent through Trinity to provide some defence for the exhausted fleet. In everyone's mind was the fear the Axis fleet would appear from lightspeed and wipe out the remaining ships as the Bond fleet was pinned against Trinity. It made moving back to Anueth torturous and dangerous.

One Axis fleet did appear outside one of the main entrances forcing those ships struggling to move through the gate to panic and scatter again. The order to scatter came as a life-saver for many ships as there were plenty of gates and the Axis couldn't cover all of them.

Mahalia sat in the cockpit of her cruiser staring in complete shock and despair at the long lines of smoke trails from the ships that drifted past heading towards the orbital docks, some crashing into the docks themselves. Her thoughts were on her uncle and the allies who had sacrificed so much and seemed to have gained so little.

Ever so slowly, they came in. The working population of Anueth, Mahnarosa, and Taranova who manned the ships' docks were silent in their despair.

Officers began issuing orders for repair crews and medical staff to muster. The well-trained units swung into action as they boarded ships to bring out the wounded.

Very quickly, they were overwhelmed by the casualties. The military hospitals were quickly filled and the overflow placed into civilian hospitals.

Soon word spread of the massive number of wounded and dead. The people of the Bond fell silent. How could their mighty fleet return as a ruin? They lost hope and despair wailed in their words. It was all over. The Dark Lord would come now and there would be nothing left to stop him.

Wolven Moor was silent but for the last of the fires around the old fortress. The Black Ash Prince surveyed the destruction. It was his place. Bodies were being dumped into mass graves and weapons were collected while Axis fighters swarmed over the sky. The surge of victory rushed through his veins. Even though he was amazed at the losses of the Bond, he wanted more. Every ship had to be destroyed. How many had got away he didn't know. What was certain was that the combined Bond fleet was in ruins and would not be able to withstand the final attack. They had done themselves a disservice coming out of their little hole. Fools. For what? To save a few ships and troops from Nunearanor? The pathos of it all made him laugh.

Above all, he had now seen the Flame Tree for himself.

"My Lord, there are no Bond bodies near the south gate," an officer informed him.

"And surrounding areas?"

"None but our own."

"Search everywhere, even out onto the ice fields, the crevasses, and the piles of dead. Metora and his companions were here. I want them found."

The officer bowed and then left.

"My Lord." the commander of Wolven Moor, Augist Kull, coughed, finding the courage to speak to the Black Ash Prince.

"One of our reconnaissance fighters was stolen after the battle. We activated its beacon and it shows it is now close to Bond space."

The Black Ash Prince snarled and slowly looked at Kull who did his best to push out his chest, ready for whatever was going to be thrown at him.

"It only carries three. Also, one of the Bond shuttles that landed the initial troops was able to evade us during the battle. Such a small target would have been missed during the fray . . ."

"Enough of your excuses!" The Black Ash Prince looked deep into the man's eyes. "They always get away, don't they, Commander? Why is it so hard to destroy a simple ship? A single shot would be enough. Of all the targets around this moon, these few ships seemed to slip through. Why is that, Commander?"

"I can't answer that, my Lord."

The Black Ash Prince went to say more but a black cloud seemed to appear suddenly above them, denser than a storm and alien to the white ice and blue crystal sky.

"Leave us. The Dark Lord approaches."

None of the Diamalords wanted to be around when Kaw arrived. They could all be easily dispatched despite their victory. It seemed the private war between the two Princes went on.

"Cryacur," came a deep rumble from the cloud that now exploded in flames and lightning.

The Black Ash Prince went to one knee.

"Yes Master."

"What news of Wolven Moor?"

"The Bond fleet has been destroyed and there is indeed a Flame Tree that walks among us. His body and Metora's have not been found."

"This cannot be."

"They were helped by a creature in the shape of a man. I believe he has been sent as a guardian for the Flame Tree."

Lightning exploded within the blackness of the cloud followed by a rumble of discontented thunder.

"Order your agents to find these things. Who are they? What do they want? Why, Cryacur? Why are they here?"

"I will do as you order."

"Good. Return then to Tere Kaw. The greatest battle of all time is now upon us."

"At once, Master."

The black cloud and its pyrotechnics suddenly vanished, sucked back into the darkness from where it had come, leaving the night sky filled with stars once more.

In orbit was the *Warloch*, waiting for him to return. On the bridge, Master Murlex was satisfied with the ongoing destruction of Bond ships. She was already issuing orders for her fleets to regroup, ready for the final assault. All she needed was the order.

A message arrived from Lord Cryacur, ordering the *Warloch* back to Tere Kaw once he was on board. She breathed in with anticipation. The time had come. Her Master was ready.

THE END AND THE BEGINNING OF THE END

Metora dreamed. Often, he would wake, then fall back, see grey walls, then fall back again into the oceans of dreams. And those dreams were morphing into nightmares.

He saw a face of a human, a young, handsome man who he did not recognise, though his voice was oddly familiar. The figure stood on a barren field looking up at the darkened sky. The remains of a great battle were strewn about the landscape. The figure seemed fearful as it listened to a voice only he could hear. In an instant, the figure burst into flames and was consumed, leaving nothing but a thin vapour of black smoke.

Metora saw no more but suddenly found himself as a child in the palace on Jashir. It was a nightmare that he was familiar with as this one had its basis in reality. He remembered his brother's eyes, white with rage, his face distorted by whatever demon now inherited his body. The roar and rage of the Gorgoth echoed in the palace, windows smashing, blaster fire, and the screams as Jai went about his killing business.

The blaster was heavy in his hands, his heart in rhythm with the fear running through his body. Metora could remember it all. His sights were fixed on those eyes that bore down on him. The single shot he was able let off had no effect. And so, he waited for the pain as Jai grabbed him by his jacket. The burning of his hot skin instantly bore its way through the material leaving scars that Metora had shown few people. With simple ease, Jai threw his younger brother through a glass window with such force that his bleeding body ended up in a small pond. Before he closed his eyes, he had one last image of his brother — grey skin, white eyes, and a maddening look of hunger. It would be the last time he saw Jai.

Metora could remember Jai in the years before when they would help crews repair damaged speeders and learned to use blasters. They would sneak down to the guard quarters and laugh at the solders being yelled at while on parade.

There were always the dark dreams, however. Under the ruins of the palace, deep within its dungeons, dwelt the thirteenth Son of Gorgoth, with fingers broken and blooded from clawing scars into the stone, his fists and head banging against the walls, and crying out as a wounded animal would. Then he would slump to the ground and weep for the things he had done. There, Iminus Kaw cast a spell and placed his gloved hand upon Jai's face, putting him to sleep as the only solution to the madness of the Gorgoth — until woken when the time was right.

Metora was now awake, curled up in a bed, not knowing where he was. He looked about but it took a few moments to recognise that he was in his quarters in Bannade House. His moment of panic stemming from his last memory of being on a shuttle filled with dead soldiers had vanished. He was safe. It gave him the chance to hate his dreams. In frustration, he hit out at the table next to him. He didn't want visions of his brother in his mind. They were occurring too often. He believed in their power. They showed your fears and your wants and there were creatures that could splice their own visions into your mind. They could make you believe lies and, in time, make your mind turn to fantasy and madness. He could only wonder if these dreams were his, his brothers, or some trick of Kaw's.

"Good morning," came the voice of Aunt Dannul through the communicator.

"How long have I been here?"

"Two days. I've been told you've had quite an adventure."

"Two days!" he exclaimed.

What happened to me?

"I'll bring in some lunch for you."

"Thank you."

Metora struggled to get out of bed. Instantly, he saw the red marks on his chest. Now he had a mirror of his old wound. In fact, he had a pair, only needing Kaw's to finish the set. His muscles were tired and his head ached. Cryacur had really hit him hard.

He found himself chuckling as he remembered jumping on Cryacur. How stupid.

"Something funny?" Aunt Dannul asked as she entered the room with a tray of food.

"Ah, just remembering a stupid thing I did." Metora then had another flash of memory. "Where's Lorian Shane? And Kuring-gai and Oberon?"

She placed the tray on a table. "Kuring-gai himself brought you here and then went to Dunmarra. I have no news of Oberon or Lorian Shane."

"And the Nunearanor?" he asked carefully.

"Most of the fleet made it through."

"All of her family arrived safely?"

"Yes, but one of her sisters is missing."

"Sister?" he queried. Queen Zoe had no sisters, as far as he knew.

"Zoe remained behind and passed the crown onto Talia."

"Which one of Talia's sisters?" he asked, though he already knew the answer.

"Princess Isla, I'm afraid."

Metora slumped back on the bed. "And our losses?" he whispered.

"Dreadful. Admiral Zuke has orders for you to be brought to Redsee as soon as you wake."

Metora groaned. "Can't that man give me a moment," he cried out in frustration. "What, am I under arrest? Damn scrum-licker."

"I'm not aware of that, but the guard here has been doubled. If you understand what I mean?"

He did. No one was coming here to take him without a fight. A terrible situation for the Bond to be in but it seemed even Aunt Dannul had had enough of Zuke and did not trust him.

"Kuring-gai also wished to be told when you wake. Shall I inform him?"

"Please."

"Someone has been waiting for you to wake up."

Metora suddenly saw all the handmade cards and drawings over the tables.

Koree had been waiting by the doorway and came running up to her uncle, who embraced her tightly. He was crying and she was too. He kissed her forehead and ran his hand over her hair. She said nothing, knowing she had seen him bandaged and almost in a comatose state.

"Koree has been in here every day, helping the nurse and making you cards. Even a goodnight kiss every night."

He looked at her. She had her mother's eyes.

"Can I stay here?" she asked quietly.

"Of course."

He was still too tired to get up. He lay back and she snuggled up to him. Aunt Dannul left the room, leaving him to gaze out of the window at the grey clouds on the horizon.

Kuring-gai found Metora awake and out in the gardens of Bannade House. It was morning and Metora had the urge to get some fresh air with a mug of good, warm, sive soup. He was dressed lightly, bare foot and no uniform for once. The gardens were bare with the winter, but some flowers were resistant to the cold. Bursts of yellow and red made a good contrast to the white and grey of the trees.

"You're probably wishing you were still asleep?"

Metora turned his head and the distant look that he had previously disappeared with a tight smile.

"Or dead."

They shook hands.

"How is Dunmarra?"

"We've lost a lot of people, everyone has."

"Yeah, and it's my fault. I didn't want to even read any of it, but I forced myself. Have you seen this rubbish Zuke is spruiking? I've been publicly named as failing my mission and I quote," he picked up the tablet. "Prince Metora's failure to destroy the Wolven Moor defences resulted in the fleet being jammed outside the moon system as two Axis fleets converged on to its flanks. Having no room to manoeuvre, they were subsequently ripped to shreds. The action had to be broken off as the mission led by Prince Metora failed to achieve its objective." He then threw the tablet to the ground.

Kuring-gai kneeled and picked it up. "Yes, I've read it."

"Any good news?" Metora asked as he took the tablet back.

"Oberon was seen on the *Tanami* before taking a transport with an unknown pilot and Princess Isla. I assume the pilot was Lorian. The official line is that they are on a mission for the Queen."

Metora remained silent as he thought the news through. Queen Zoe was dead. She had remained behind while her fortress was demolished around her. It would have been Queen Talia doing what Isla had told her to do.

"As long as they are alive. Any rumours of Flame Trees?"

Kuring-gai shook his head, "Only you and I know . . . and Old Father."

"What's his advice?"

"The news would lift people's spirits, but Old Father wants us to be cautious."

"What do you want to do?"

"Tell the galaxy," Kuring-gai immediately replied.

Metora could see the determination in his friend's face. This news had swelled his heart and given him hope.

"But Lorian isn't ready. What a burden to put on his shoulders. Where is this River'eah now? Who and what is he?"

"I don't know, but the spirits do not do things in vain. I believe Oberon has taken them somewhere safe to find out whatever purpose the Ethereals have for him. Why Isla would go too, I don't know."

"Secretly, I'm jealous. This betrayal of my name will ruin me," he looked at Kuring-gai, "I don't think I can do this anymore. The years have taken their toll and the constant criticisms and infighting have . . . have drained me."

"You are not responsible for this disaster. I will defend you, as will the Khoru and the countless soldiers and ordinary citizens who are loyal to you. Even the Gunadar deserters know you. Your time as a rock for many worlds will be repaid. We will be your rock."

Metora was touched by Kuring-gai's passion and loyalty. He knew it wasn't enough, however. That loyalty may save him this time, but there would always be another depressing occasion when he would be further accused with new alleged failings.

"I can't face all those soldiers and families who have suffered death when everyone is looking for someone to blame. I just want to disappear."

"You know you can't do that. It will only give Zuke more ammunition. There are lot of dissidents, my friend. No one expected this defeat to be so complete."

"That doesn't make me feel better. I haven't heard anything

from Joviann."

"I have. I asked her."

"Do they know of the Flame Tree?"

"They do, but not his identity. I have confirmed with them his existence but not his name."

"A good idea. We need to keep this close to our chests. Lorian will need time. I just hope we don't run out of it. He might be our secret weapon."

Kuring-gai laughed. "She said the same thing. The Ethereals will not abandon us. I believe victory is coming. Whether I see it or not, I don't care, as long as my actions and faith make it so."

"You are ready to die then?"

"I lost my faith and believed all was lost, so I prepared, knowing I would not be in Warrawul. Not now, not with a Flame Tree and the Order regrouping. This could mean the emergence of another Sangreal."

Metora breathed in heavily. The possibly of another Sangreal had not crossed his mind for years. After the fall of the Order, it just couldn't happen.

"Do you think the Order have one in hiding?" he asked.

"Possibly. Maybe it's Lorian. A Flame Tree and the Order making contact with us are all clues to something on the horizon. It is wise of them to keep it quiet, but we need them now."

"A strong Sangreal would be a great threat to Kaw." Metora mused over the possibilities.

"Deep in my heart, I'm hoping Oberon has taken the last Flame Tree to meet the next Sangreal and together they will return to us and defeat Kaw."

"All in the nick of time?" Metora teased.

Kuring-gai smiled. "The Order may have studied the laws of the universe, but we are those students. Life lives. It creates what it needs, when it needs. After a fire, new growth appears. A man treated with kindness returns that kindness. Many thought you should be Sangreal."

It was Metora's turn to smile. "In this wreck of a human?"

"It's all speculation of course."

"Of course. This war has now entered a new stage, Kuring-gai. We have done our bit. We can only theorise over what it all means."

"Good always conquers over evil. Now let's get down to the War Council and get this business out of the way."

Metora was slow to move.

"I refused to go."

"Defend yourself Metora. We'll be there. The Chief has also come back to defend you."

He really didn't want to go but Kuring-gai had stood and was waiting.

"Better put some shoes on," he stated.

The War Council was hot with hostility. Men and women argued and threw their voices across the room, some stabbing their fingers at supposed comrades. They cried out at the casualty lists and sought for someone to take the blame. All the while it was the great fear of the Axis move that burned that fury.

Within the crescendo of voices there were some that sat in silence, struck dumb by the defeat. Finding blame would not save them. They thought too about the Dark Lord's attack and had no answer to stop it.

Sitting in his seat, Zuke looked exhausted. His eyes were sunken holes surrounded by worry lines. Word had spread about his seeming abandonment of the attack and his letting it fall to the Elector to make the final decision. To find out who had leaked the news was uppermost in his mind. No doubt it was Dyndarumm. But first he had to find a way to save his position.

Wolfcastle, Chief of the Merenmere, stood and looked directly at Zuke. Slowly the arguments dimmed enough that Wolfcastle was able to call out to the Admiral.

"This is all your doing."

"What am I to do when my officers do not follow my orders. Blame should be squarely on the shoulders of the fleet commander, along with Metora for his failure to shut down Wolven Moor."

Captain Journ sat silently, his face clearly betraying the fact he was restraining to keep his own anger silent.

The War Council had grown silent as the two great ranks began sharpening their tongues. All knew this would be a great clash of men.

"He is not to blame. When the Black Ash Prince arrived, there was little he could do. What would you have done?"

"Completed my mission."

Wolfcastle smiled with derision. "I find that hard to believe. Who can see the Admiral taking on the Black Ash Prince and then destroying a mighty Axis fortress, all without breaking a sweat!" he addressed the Council.

There was snickering and laughter from many people. Zuke remained silent.

"Oh, and don't forget taking on two Axis fleets while managing a rescue mission," he added with glee before sitting down.

Zuke had regained some of his spark and now attempted to take control of the arguments within the Council. "We should be planning our next move."

"Surrender?" Wolfcastle mocked, his hands raised.

"Diplomatic solutions could be an option," an officer from Taranova remarked.

This brought back a return of the storm of arguments.

"We will not be surrendering or offering any terms," Zuke replied.

"A treaty then? Something to keep our way of life," the officer continued.

"Until when? Until Kaw becomes stronger and overwhelms us by trickery? He is a villain and is never to be trusted with any treaty. My people know that all too well," Wolfcastle responded.

"Then our response is?"

"We keep him at bay, like we always have," Zuke said, and that seemed to end the matter.

Wolfcastle wanted to say more but this subject was touchy and he too had no real viable counter solution. It was one thing to want a new strategy. The resources of the Bond weren't up to bold new plans and the defeat at Wolven Moor just seemed to hasten the end.

Within the Council sat a woman. Outwardly, she seemed just as frightened as the others were, but this was merely an act. She had remained silent, preferring the others shout themselves hoarse. She was the Dark Lord's eyes in the enemy's pit. She saw that it was time. The Council was in disarray, its morale destroyed and with no fresh strategy. It was time to strike.

"Council, Prince Metora is here to address us," came the voice of an usher droid.

Metora entered with Kuring-gai close behind. He acknowledged Wolfcastle as he made his way to the speaker's stand.

"Councillors, I am here to address the actions of my battle group and the overall situation on Wolven Moor. We have faced a massive defeat, though we did rescue the Nunearanor. Our plans were well known to the Axis and they prepared accordingly."

"This is all conjecture and yet to be proved," interject a blunt Zuke who seemed to have been waiting for Metora.

"Proved it will be, Admiral. May I go on or should I ask the Elector for a decision?"

There was open laughter within the Council chamber, but certainly not from Zuke.

Metora continued. "The very heart of our forces has been ripped out. We cannot make good these losses, so our remaining forces should be grouped together as a fire brigade to counter the thrusts of the dark armies when they attack."

"When do we hear about why you failed," Zuke replied.

Wolfcastle took to his feet. "Let the Prince speak without interruption."

Zuke remained calm, his eyes shifting to the Chief. "Or what?" He looked back to Metora. "I see you are now championing the strategy that this Council has formed and actioned for past enemy attacks. You berated them as antiquated. You wanted us to attack and we did and were beaten, heavily."

"I did not propose a thrust into deep Axis space knowing full well those plans could be and were passed on to agents!"

"But it is still your strategy. Since you've been in command there has been nothing but mistakes."

"Ophistar was not a mistake, you old bastard."

"Don't *you* talk to me like that!"

"I will speak to *you* like you deserve! You are incompetent, reckless, and worse — vindictive, and more interested in personal spite than winning victory!"

"You are gone! Gone from command, you stupid, well-bred boy!"

There was a great commotion in the room as officers erupted in defence of Metora.

"It's you who should be gone!" Journ yelled out.

The Chief motioned with his hands and the room came to order.

"I don't care what happens to you or me anymore! I proposed a new strategy and was condemned for it."

"You almost brought about a mutiny!" Zuke pointed his finger at Journ who remained silent.

"I retook Ophistar and if you had listened to me in the first place, we might not be mourning our dead!" Metora continued.

"This is a disgrace! You, a prince of Jashir, in meltdown. Go! Go before I order the guards to drag you out!"

Metora remained silent and unmoving. He was furious, so much so that he felt the blood boiling in his head. Never had he been so angry and ready to rip off someone's head.

There was a presence at his side, "It's alright Metora," It was

Wolfcastle. Metora then had the realisation that the Chief's hand was over his right hand which gripped his blaster. Was he that close to shooting the Admiral?

He relaxed his grip and Wolfcastle put his hands on his shoulders. "He will have his day," Wolfcastle whispered.

Metora stepped away from the podium. Desperate to get out he walked head down to the exit.

"You are all frightened souls. Death will be upon us soon," he heard Wolfcastle warn as he left the chamber.

He didn't look back but felt again the presence of someone beside him. This time it was Kuring-gai.

"There is no saving them," he said.

Metora stopped. He was almost on the verge of tears and looked at his friend. "I can't do this anymore. *That* was the last straw."

"What will you do?"

"I can only restore pride in my family's name. The Gorgoth will be unleashed upon this world and I will not have my brother further destroy my name and be involved in such brutality."

Kuring-gai took him by the shoulder. "We need you. Go rest. I believe that peace is coming."

"I just hope we're all alive to see it."

He walked away. Kuring-gai simply watched him go.

On his return to Bannade House he spoke to no one. He packed his clothes, blasters, and supplies, all the while desperately holding back a river of tears. It had been a long time since he cried and he had sworn he wouldn't again. The hurt in his heart from poison words was aggravated by his niece. He loved little else in this world, and it hurt him so to leave her, but he would not let her die in the coming crescendo.

He then headed straight to the hanger. There he selected his personal ship and left Anueth space. He was going home to the world where he was born, believing he would never come back.

"What terrible news," Crowcraw whispered. He was reading the account of the events within the Council chambers. He had preferred to stay away from the deliberations as he knew that there would be great fireworks and he didn't want the stress of being brought into the actions of Admiral Zuke. He felt used and manipulated. If only he could remove the Admiral. But would that create even more problems?

Quisto hurried about with trays of food and reports for the Elector to read. He was in a buzz after watching the fight between the Prince and Zuke. If it had gone on any longer, Metora would have surely assaulted the Admiral but, in the end, the Prince had been dismissed.

"What should I say Quisto?"

"I'm speechless, my Lord. I did not expect such a fiery exchange. These two men despise each other so vehemently."

"Yes, it's true. I should be able to calm these waters but I'm not a Sangreal."

"I'm believing there will never be another Sangreal."

Crowcraw breathed out heavily and closed his eyes.

"Transport has arrived," an officer called.

The Elector's staff began to board, followed slowly by the man himself. Quisto was left alone in the Elector's apartment retrieving the last of the communication discs to be studied.

"Stay behind, Quisto," a female voice said.

He turned about and saw her standing at the door. She was a figure in red armour with a matching helmet that covered her features. She pointed a blaster at him.

"Would it be easier if I stunned you?"

Quisto merely stood up. The voice sounded familiar despite the computerisation. It was Nash Beren.

"The time has come then?"

"The Council will tear itself apart and there is no time left for protracted schemes."

"Do what you will."

A bolt from her blaster hit him in the chest. Before he even fell to the ground, she had gone.

Outside the shuttle began to move off. Crowcraw hadn't realised his aide was not on board. It was his last thought as the ship exploded in flames and fell back to the hanger's platform.

As fire, smoke, and debris filled the platform, the guards and crews ducked for cover. When it was clear, they raced to the remains of the Elector's shuttle, but there was nothing anyone could do. It was now just a heap of flaming wreckage. A fire to toast the final fall of the Bond of Seven Kings.

About the Author

Kristian Becker has returned from the Australian Outback and now resides on the NSW Central Coast, never to have to move again.

Hopefully.

ALSO BY THE AUTHOR

The Book of Gates

The White of Weeping Cove

Age of Anthems: Triumphant Are the True